The Death of Finn

The Death of Finn concerns the sudden death of a brilliant and eccentric young monk, Joe Finn, and the effect that his death has on the people around him, in particular his one time best friend Frank, himself an ex-monk.

Despite Joe's absurd death *The Death of Finn* is essentially a love story, and a story of friendship that endures despite great differences. Joe's death leads Frank to recall how he joined the Order of the Holy Field and met Joe Finn. After a few years, to the jealousy and disapproval of Joe, who like many gifted people is isolated because of his gifts, Frank meets Lisa, with whom he begins an intense relationship. This causes a falling out between them, especially after Frank suspects Joe of reporting him to the authorities. Despite the distance between them, the two friends still care for each other. Joe goes to Los Angeles with a groundbreaking manuscript that the Order attempted to suppress and Frank loses his faith, leaves the Order of the Holy Field to be with Lisa. Then years later Joe is killed crossing the road to get the Sunday papers in Los Angeles. Joe's death forces Frank to look back on the choices he has made, his loss of faith, his years with the Order, the power of institutions over lives, and the legacy of his great friend, the ingenious Joe Finn.

Oran Ryan has been writing full time for 10 years during which time he has completed a number of novels, of which *The Death of Finn* is the first to be published.

Married to Sarah, he is a native of Dublin. He was brought up in Portobello in the City and educated at Synge Street Christian Brothers School, as well as Carlow, Milltown Institute and UCD.

Oran Ryan

23 May 2006

The Death of Finn

By

Oran Ryan

A Seven Towers Publication

The Death of Finn
First published 2006 BY
SEVEN TOWERS
4, ST. Mura's Terrace,
Strangford Road,
East Wall,
Dublin 3.
WWW.SEVENTOWERS.IE

ISBN Case Bound Edition 0-9552757-0-9 (978-0-9552757-0-8)
ISBN Thread Bound Edition 0-9552757-1-7 (978-0-9552757-1-5)
ISBN Perfect Bound Edition 0-9552757-2-5 (978-0-9552757-2-2)

Cover concept: Deirdre Meehan
Cover, book design, typesetting and
Seven Towers logo by Solid Design,
WWW.SOLIDDESIGN.IE
Set in Joanna 11 point on 12 point.
Printed on 80gsm Munken Bookwove Ivory.
Printed by Betaprint, Dublin 12.

Dedicated to the Memory of Liam O'Dea, OFM Cap.

The Death of Finn

BY
Oran Ryan

Prologue:
Joseph Finn, OHF

I hear whispers. Up bright and early. Mind free and clear. Apocalypse deferred. Small mercies. Ready for day. Look in mirror. Beginning to bald a little on front. Beard growing well. Getting short-sighted though. Must go to optician this week. Headaches returning due to eye strain. Sense of someone stirring downstairs. I go down to see who's about before going to choir for meditation. Sitting in the kitchen is Brad. Six foot four ex-football jock looking down the yard at the kitty cat with her three kittens lapping milk. One kitten jumps on the other's tail. The jumped upon kitten turns to jump on her brother, who pushes her away to get at the milk. Mother kitty slaps her two mischievous children. They stop biting and playing and drink their milk. Not enough dried food for the kitties. Brad shambles inside as the bell goes for meditation and prayer and Mass. He runs out with another plate of food. The litter tray is full. We still haven't greeted each other. We go into choir. I feel hungry. Stomach rumbling. Brad looks fed. I was too busy looking at kitty and her kids. Damn. Read from Isaiah. Nothing. Read from John. Nothing. Stomach rumbling. Look over at Casey and Hank. Hank the boxer. We have a lot of sports people in our community. Footballers. Boxers. Might make a sitcom out of that. I'd call it 'Lost in Prayer.' Help me to change things I cannot accept. Like my empty stomach. Look at the monstrance with the Eucharist. The holy hedgehog. Got to stop thinking that. Monstrous. Monstrance. Blasphemous. Look. Now hear this. Blessed are those who. One day at a. Try not to feel too hungry or too sleepy or too thoughtful or too thoughtless and then the Morning Prayer begins. Dammit. I cannot read the text. I realise my reading beforehand has been mostly from memory. Can't read the invitatory antiphons. All can't anyhow. Immanuel is with us. Manage to recite the psalms from memory. Mass begins. I get Brad to do the readings. Pray. Mom and Dad. Frank and Lisa. Pray for departed Brethren and friends.

For all those who have asked for my prayers. Go for breakfast. Brethren in good form. Eat much oatmeal. Bananas. Apples. Check my shoes are tied. Just going across to get the papers. My turn this week. See you soon. Want anything else. Milk? Eggs? Might get a bagel. Dying for another coffee. Okay then. See you in five. Don't drink all the coffee, Brad. I want my second cup with the Times. It's a ritual. And rituals come natural.

I cross road. Get papers and bagel. Then the sound of approaching engines. Sudden impact. Apocalypse? Of course it is.

And then I looked up. Everything looked blurry. Above me I saw people. They were looking down at me. They seemed worried. Then it got so difficult to see them. I really have to see an optician. I couldn't focus. Then it got dark. All I could hear were their voices:
"Everything okay?" I couldn't make out who said that. I'm fine. Couldn't be better.
"Okay? It's… o-okay. Kid? Oh God…"
I wanted to say something. I am not a kid. Can you hear? I want them to hear me. Now look here my good man I am not a child.
"You're going to be fine. Just keep very still. Everything is going to be… Oh, Jesus. Hey! Can you hear me? Oh God! Ambulance! Now!"
"I called. It's coming. It's coming."
"I was just driving down and this guy, well, he was, you know, like, crossing and then this car came round the corner. Must have been doing seventy, I dunno and it hit him. He went right up in the air and landed…jeez…"

So that's that. That was the moment. I can offer no explanation. There is no why. Why it happened. The how is straightforward though. A car hit me. I died. It happens. As I died, which took only a few short moments, I worried about my loved ones – my Brothers in the Order of the Holy Field, my mother Rose and my father, Gerry. At least I gave mother my Giovanni Seipi. That was a good move. I thought too of Frank. I missed him. I thought 'this is going to hurt them all so much.' But in death it's over. One can do nothing. It is all in God's hands.

I was crossing the road. Eight o'clock. Sunday morning. 6TH June. Apt date. I had a fleeting glance of what hit me. I did not per se see it. I saw a blue flash, what I took to be an urban people carrier, perhaps a van. It hit me as I crossed on a 'WALK' light.

Anyway, being something of an infomaniac, I enjoyed getting the papers. Weekdays the papers are delivered. Sundays, not so much. I crossed West 22ND Street to Val's Newsagent. When I go to Val's, sometimes I pick up a bagel, if they have any fresh.

So I went to Val's, got the papers, and came back. I was eating a bagel as I crossed West 22ND Street. The car or van came round the bend and took me with it. As I died, I went to my favourite place. My favourite place is sitting on a carved stone seat looking over a green lily pond with a single white flower blossoming in its centre. Beside the pond runs a hedge and there in the undergrowth I see a white rabbit busily nibbling away. I sit and watch the rabbit and the pond with its single white blossom. In the background I dimly hear people speaking:

"So, where's the driver?"
"Gone, along with the car."
"My God, will you look at that."
"The street cameras got what happened."
"Give him space, people. Stand back."
"God, he is so slight. Light as a feather."
"Don't move him! For God's sake don't touch him!"
"Why not?"
"This is a crime scene."
"What's that he's wearing?"
"It's Joe. Brother Joe. One of the OHF Brothers. He was in my shop, like a minute ago. Don't touch him!"
"Why not?"
"It's – bad luck"
"What?"
"My mother goes to mass there."
Someone else leaned over me.
"Where's the goddam ambulance? Eh? Jesus…We've got someone really fucking injured here!!"
"It's on the way. On the way…"

I read that as one dies the faculty of hearing is the last to go. I can report that to be correct. The voices went. A light seemed to hover. The lily pond with the stone seat dissolved. The rabbit scampered off. I smiled. Everything dissolved. What's next?

Chapter One

Ben

Father Ben Frasier sat alone in his rooms. He poured himself another large whiskey. He usually didn't drink much. So he didn't really pace himself. Already he felt the good whiskey's effects. He looked at the label like a reluctant patient examining his insistent doctor's prescription. Midleton whiskey. With a fresh handkerchief he wiped tears and sweat from his cheeks and face. What he had witnessed earlier today on the street and later in the mortuary had given him so much unexpected grief. Being with the dead and dying was part of his calling. But the body, Joe's body, was so damaged, so smashed. It was the body of a Brother from his own community. Then he recalled talking to Joe this morning. They were talking about kittens. Joe was always rescuing stray animals and taking them to animal shelters.

Earlier in the afternoon he had gone down to identify Joe's body in the morgue. Ben remembered the young mortician advising him, "I must warn you…erm…Reverend…"
"Ben…my name's Ben…"
"Right, Ben, I just want to let you know that this might be upsetting."
Ben nodded.
"I understand…" Ben wanted more than anything to know this person's name.
"Stan…"
"I get it, Stan. Clear as the azure sky."
Stan smiled. Clockwork Orange, he thought. Must be the booze making me think like that. Ben pursed his lips in preparation as the mortician unzipped the body bag. Ben took a long look under the cold light at the young man's corpse, the smashed bones, the damaged head, and the dried blood. He saw.
"It's Joe," Ben said, and then left. He hoped he never had to see anything like that again. Of course he had seen such things before. But never as a priest had he to identify the ruined body of a Brother of the Order of the Holy Field.

He went over to the sink of his room as the memories of identifying Joe came back. He threw water on his face and gently dried himself. He sat back down in his armchair, put his head back and tried to calm himself. People kept knocking at his door. He didn't answer. He thought: 'It will be seven o'clock pm in Ireland. I have to call Ireland. What am I going to say? How will I tell them I let Joe die? I have to call Des. And Joe's family will have to be informed. Des will do that, Deo Gratias.'

Then someone knocked on the door again, and without waiting for Ben to answer, opened his door.

"Father, there are police officers wanting a word with you in the common room. Do you want them brought to your rooms?"

"No, Anthony. Leave them in the common room. Give them coffee and cake and make my apologies. Tell the officers I am presently conducting a telephone conversation with the Superior General of our Order in Ireland and I will be along as quickly as I can. Stay with them and handle the situation."

Anthony understood only to well from the tearstains on his superior's face what he must do.

"Yes Father."

"Thank you, Anthony."

Father Ben closed the door after Anthony, locked it, and then he rang the Monastery of the Seven Towers in Dublin.

"Monastery of the Seven Towers? Good Evening? How may I transfer your call?"

They seem to have employed a receptionist since I last called, Ben mused. It's all too…professional, or something…

"Ah yes. Can I speak to Father Des Murphy, please?"

"That's no problem at all. May I ask who is calling please?"

"Ah yes. This is Father Ben Frasier calling here from Los Angeles, California."

"One moment…Could you please hold, Father Ben? I just need to page him. His room number is not responding."

"Okay, thanks."

Father Des Murphy's soft voice came on the telephone line.

"This is Des."

"Des? It's Ben"

"Hi Ben. Good to hear from you. How are things?"

"Things are not good, I am sorry to say, Father. I have something to tell you."

"I'm listening."

"I have to report a … a terrible accident."

"Oh no, what has happened?"

"Brother Joseph Finn has been knocked down."

"Dear Lord no! Oh my!"

"He was crossing the road not far from our monastery and chapel, bringing the morning papers back. A vehicle broke the lights and hit him. I am sorry to say he was pronounced dead on arrival. There was nothing anyone could do."

"I see. When did this happen, Ben?"

"At about eight o' clock this morning, four o' clock am your time, Joe went out to get the papers. He always liked to get the papers, get a first look at them, I suppose."

"I see."

"It was on the way back the car hit him. A blue Jeep. Hit and run."

"I'm upset you didn't call earlier. Just to let us know."

This shocked Ben. But Des was well known for playing with others' emotions. From somewhere deep within Ben marshalled the strength to deal with Des.

"Des, I think you are being unfair."

"You do?"

"Firstly I have been in the hospital ever since the accident. I had to claim the body, and there is a huge amount of paperwork involved, and they don't understand the culture and tradition of religious life. They don't get Joe was part of the family. They think cult and I try to explain the ancient traditions of our life. Right now I took time out from all of this to call you while I have a grief stricken community and two police officers sitting in the common room chatting to Anthony, wanting to talk to me. Besides all of the above, the doorbell and the telephone keeps ringing, we have enough flowers in the chapel to stock a florist…"

"I'm sorry, Ben. I am as devastated as you…"

Ben felt too angry to respond. He simply changed the subject.

"I was thinking, Father. Perhaps, perhaps it might be better if we sealed the coffin."

"It's that bad, I take it."

"We could also reconstruct. That's another option."

"Perhaps, too. Yes."

"The family will want to see their son, but not as he is. They have some good people here that can do wonderful work. I put it to you."

"What you must do, do quickly. Whatever you do, you have my support."

"I think reconstruction might be the best way. I will organise it. Can you send funds?"

"Send the provincial bursar all the bills. Money is not a problem, within reason."

"Understood."

"Do you have paperwork?"

"Nothing but."

"Can you send me, by fax initially, all the reports, police and otherwise of the accident, Ben?"

"I have them here in the police file. You should have them real soon."

"Real soon?"

"Right."

Ben reached over and began stacking the file pages face down onto the fax machine. Then he took a fax cover sheet, wrote 'For the attention of Father Des Murphy, reports on the accident regarding Brother Joseph Finn, OHF on June 6TH 2—. Time 8 AM, West 22ND Street Los Angeles California Western Province OHF', dialled the number and pressed 'Send.' The fax machine creaked and ground the paper, pressing it through its tiny mill, and on the other side Des saw the paper emerging.

"Are you getting the fax, Des?"

"It's arriving, Brother, it's arriving. In the long run we will probably need the originals for archiving purposes. But that's somewhat down the road. I'll talk to the family, prepare a statement for the Province, speak to the various communities, and we will begin funeral arrangements. We also need to organise to fly the family out and fly the body home. Can you liaise with the various services on your end and I'll get people involved here?"

"Okay, Father. I have started things already."

"Good. If there is anything you need, call me day or night."

"I have to go talk to the police."

"See you soon. I'll probably be coming out with Gerry and Rose Finn."

"By the way, in the unlikely event of Rose or Gerry calling in the next hour or two, tell them I'm on my way out to them."

"Okay Des."

"Bye for now."

Ben hung up and went to the door. There was a note in Anthony's handwriting. The police had gone. They had apprehended someone whom they were going to charge with the vehicular manslaughter of Joseph Finn, OHF. They had it all captured on camera.

Chapter Two

Des and Alex

"So...," Des began. He was trying to think of something to say to his travelling companion. Fr. Alex sat holding a set of worn wooden rosary beads, silently fingering them as he and Des drove out to Rose and Gerry Finn's house.

"So... traffic is pretty bad tonight."

"That it is," Alex sombrely nodded, his long beautifully tended beard shuddering with every head nod.

It was as if the news of Joe's death had sent Alex elsewhere, that he was only physically present there in the car in Dublin with Des at this awful time. Des glanced at his profile, the long thin face only slightly lined, the fine pale skin, healthy despite his age, the tailored black suit, the soft slim hands. 'The poster child for the spiritual life', Des thought, 'what he's wearing doesn't look like a suit. It looks more like a costume.'

Before they drove out Des and he had talked. Alex sat motionless as Des told him what happened. He nodded, darkly acknowledging the details around the death, fingering the sheets of faxed documents sent from Los Angeles by Ben. Then Alex carefully aligned the pages into a neat pile, looked at Des with cavernous eyes and asked,

"How are you going to tell Rose and Gerry?"

"Gently."

"When?"

"Oh, tonight, of course. Lest they get the news from a less desirable source."

"And did you call them?"

"I called them."

"So they are expecting a visit?"

"Within the hour. I told them we are dropping by."

"We?"

"You are his former student master and a respected –..."

"Don't do this, Des. I'll go, naturally. But spare me the nonsense."

Des ignored Alex's obvious irritation, thinking it better to change the subject for a moment.

"The community needs space to grieve. So...we need to organise –"

Once again, Alex was way ahead.

"I was thinking perhaps, a community Mass? Just the Brothers and Priests of the Monastery of the Seven Towers? We could close the church and have one priest on duty at the front office for callers. It would be the usual arrangement, like on feast days or Christmas."

"Excellent. See to it, will you Alex?"

Des enjoyed giving Alex petty tasks like making him instruct heads of communities to organise Masses or insisting he come with him to inform Rose and Gerry. It served to quell, for a time, Alex's personal visions of grandeur. Des treated him so, to remind Alex how the balance of power had shifted in Des' direction.

But there was a problem with this. The problem was that Alex accepted Des' treatment perhaps a little too stoically. 'Maybe he knows something, something I don't', Des worried. 'Maybe he is showing me how to be both obedient and holy for a reason I don't yet know.'

So Alex sat beside him as they drove to Gerry and Rose's place, silently praying his rosary. Alex's prayers kept the conversation to a tense minimum. Des looked at the traffic and the roads and remembered years before this car journey how he and Alex met Joe's parents. It was at a party in the very house they were driving to this evening, that lovely four bedroomed home by Drumcondra Park, with its walks and strange birds and old trees that stretched into one's garden. There they had met Rose and Gerry. Rose, he remembered, smiled and walked up to him and embraced him like a member of the family. It was strange. 'I wasn't Superior General then,' Des thought. 'I was in charge of the Monastery of the Seven Towers. And Alex would not be hugged that evening. One did not hug Alex. He insisted on a handshake. I think his behaviour hurt Rose's feelings. But she shrugged it off. Such a pretty woman. Red hair, good figure. Sexy, without trying too hard. And Rose knew how to throw a party. There were voices and music and people talking everywhere once the door opened.'

"Hello Father," Rose greeted me "You are both so very welcome." I have to admit I was overwhelmed at the opulence. I thought 'How does anyone get this wealthy and stay honest?'

"Hello…" I said. I couldn't remember Rose's name. Here she was inviting Alex and me and I couldn't remember her name.

"Rose, Father. My son is Joseph Finn."

"Ah yes. That's great. I know. Of course. How are you?"

Then I was embarrassed that I couldn't remember who Joe Finn was among the group of three who had taken temporary vows in the Order that day. Why did I come here? I thought. But gossip was rife about the

Brothers who had taken temporary vows. Gossip had it, firstly, that it was unlikely the other two would last long and, secondly, that there was a party at Joe Finn's parents' house. They were rich and had big parties, apparently. That was it, I thought. I came here because I had to. I was in charge of the Monastery of the Seven Towers. I went that night out of obligation, mostly. But I was curious about the lives of the rich and the well heeled. And I liked Rose. She was talkative. Alex was smiling and nodding and listening to her, taking her ideological temperature no doubt.

"My son Joe has just completed his novitiate and is in temporary vows", she beamed.

'Ah,' I thought. 'A Mother's Vocation.'

"Yes. Joe is a fine Brother and I am sure you're proud as punch," I said, looking at the punch bowls. I looked around at all the tables and tables of food and drink. I looked out on the lawn and watched musicians play chamber music. There must have been at least 100 people gathered.

"This is my husband, Gerry. Gerry, this is Fr Des Murphy. Fr Des is in charge of the Monastery of the Seven Towers. Such an interesting name, that. Where does it come from?"

"I'm afraid I don't know."

I turned to Alex, who had remained alongside and silent through all of this. I was anxious to draw him into the conversation. "Alex, do you know?"'

And Des remembered as he approached the Finn's home how Alex smiled all knowingly from behind his tiny glass of orange juice all those years before, how he stared hard into Rose's eyes and said something like "I believe around 1530 when our Order of the Holy Field first moved to Dublin, a Desmond Wenderfeld gave them the land on which the monastery stands. Wenderfeld told Brother Michael Óg O'Ceallachain, our first Irish Superior, that on that very stretch of land there once stood seven towers and that the holy men who lived there withstood many attacks from Vikings and preserved the faith."

"And is it true about the Seven Towers? What one hears?" Gerry asked.

It all sounded like nonsense, but Des remembered Alex looked abysmally downward for a moment, as though allowing the moment's drama to settle on his response, as though trying to fix his mind on something both non-specific, yet deeply significant. It was impossible to tell whether one was in the company of charlatanism or the profoundest integrity. Then Alex gazed at Gerry with near absolute certainty in his eyes.

"Apocryphal, I believe. But Brother Michael was thus inspired to call the place the Monastery of the Seven Towers."

"Which is where Joe is going next week", Rose breezily interjected.

"That's right, Rose," Des recalled saying as he nodded his head anxiously, looking around and suddenly feeling inadequate in the midst of such wealth and sophistication.

And then Gerry stepped away from the circle, "You know something? I've got to go play host, see you Des, Alex. You are very welcome. I hope we see you more often in our home."

"Father Des", Rose corrected.

"No, Des is just fine," Des said, suddenly wanting Gerry to like him and approve of him. Alex did not comment. He had returned to his profound silence, and said little more for the evening.

And that was all Des remembered of the evening, except that he had a headache the following morning. That was how he met the Finns, even though he hardly spoke to Joe that night at all. Weird how one meets people, he thought. Weird how someone like Joe Finn got in at all.

And so Des stayed dreaming of the party, remembering the paintings on the wall, the vases and statuettes and the lovely people he spoke to and laughed with and the string quartet or whatever as the car he was driving pulled into the driveway of the home of Rose and Gerry Finn. Des turned off the engine looking at the house, vaguely remembering the party and looking at Alex, who put away his beads. Des wondered what to do next. They sat together for a moment.

"So, do you want to pray a while, Alex? Before we go in?"

"I don't think we can do that."

"Why not?"

"Because Rose is coming down the driveway right now."

"If Ben has told her over the phone, there is going to be a world of trouble."

"Ben wouldn't do that."

Alex looked solemnly at him and shook his head.

"I know he is one of your protégés, Alex, but he needs a firm hand. He needs to stop drinking too."

"Ben wouldn't do that, Des. I know him. He takes his vow of obedience to heart . He doesn't drink much."

"It doesn't take much to get him pissed as a newt."

Just then, Rose appeared at the window of the car. She opened the car door on Des' side. Des looked at her. Her face was twisted with anguish, wet with tears.

"Tell me, Father Des, what has happened to my son?"

Chapter Three

Frank and Lisa

I had stopped asking myself if I loved my wife. I had stopped wanting to have children. I had stopped seeking promotion, making new friends or wondering what's new. My only friends were Lisa and the quiet anaesthetic of habit. I lived in a nice house and took days off from working as a programmer in Dublin's city centre.

I remember when I woke up that particular Monday I knew I couldn't face another day at the bank. So I called in sick and I drank too much and fell asleep in the sun, with Wagner blaring from the sitting room stereo. Then Lisa came home early. I didn't hear her put the car in the garage, or close the creaky garage door I should have oiled months ago. It was when she drew near my hammock that I instinctively woke up with a start.

"Lisa!"

"I rang your work about an hour ago. They said you were at home."

"I know. I fell asleep."

I didn't want to tell her I called in sick after she left for the clinic that morning. She leaned down and kissed me. I held her and prolonged the kiss. She drew back and looked at me quizzically.

"You know you're sleeping in direct sunlight, right?"

"I know. I drifted off. Too much wine. I have a headache."

"I wonder why. Drinking wine and sleeping in the sunlight will do that, sweetie…"

"You're home early, right? Is everything okay? How are things at the clinic?"

"Fine. If you weren't such a big featherhead you'd remember every Monday they give me time off to study for my exams, and they've agreed to give me more time as my exams get nearer. By the way, you left the music on too loud."

"I forgot about the study time thing. I am a featherhead. You're right."

"The reason why I mentioned the music thing is that the neighbours were complaining."

"I'll turn it down."

"So you haven't told me a thing about why you are at home."

"Worked up enough credits to take the day."

"You don't work up credits."

"What?"

"You write these clever little programs that save time and everyone hates you because you take work from them."

"Don't remind me. We hate it when our colleagues get successful. And if they're self-taught then its worse. I started as a clerk. Then I learned computers. Now I have a nice sideline. Do you know what they call me?"

"What?"

"The 'Clerical Error.'"

Lisa laughed. Then I laughed. I couldn't help myself. It hurt me, being called that. But it was funny.

"That's funny," she said. "That's why they don't fire you."

"Why don't they fire me? If they fired me the mortgage would get paid."

"No it wouldn't."

"Yes it would. Oh, God I have such a headache."

"You started off as post boy. Now you are taking work from others. Anyone else would be gone."

"Again, don't remind me."

"I thought we agreed you would take the money instead. I mean if you had just rung in sick today you would still get paid for the day. You probably forgot that, right?"

I felt really embarrassed now. If I told her the truth I would be shown up a liar. If I lived with my lie I was shown to be improvident and thoughtless, a featherhead.

"I forgot."

"Now I know why you didn't tell me this morning as we lay together in bed and I said to you, Frank, baby, what's on your schedule? And you said not a thing, not a thing…"

"No, Lisa. I…"

Not only was I an improvident person, I was also clearly deceitful person. I hadn't told her I was not going to work. Lisa and I usually plotted our day out neatly. Yet this morning I had omitted something huge. Usually if either of us thought of taking the day off, we would plan doing something together; we would find a way of taking the time off together. Today I needed to be alone, and that made me feel ashamed. I had tied myself up with lies, so I decided to live with my shame. Lisa sensed something amiss with me but seemed too disappointed in me to remain in the same back garden. She turned to back into the house, back towards the sound of my overloud music.

"I have to take a shower. I'm hot."

"I know that. We can study each other, you know. Monday's a tough day for…study…"

"Maybe later, I have to study."

My offer of lovemaking by way of apology meant nothing to her. That hurt me.

"I'm sorry, baby..." I said.

"You should have taken the money. We need the money. The mortgage on this place...Or do something that interests you..."

"I know. I'm sorry. I lied. I rang in sick. I was embarrassed to admit I just got out of bed and rang in sick so I lied."

"I won't get full pay until I get these exams."

"I know, I know. Sorry, Lisa. It's just I hate the bank."

"This isn't all about you. I live here too. We live here together. We're in this together."

"Right."

"Don't lie to me."

"It wasn't a big lie."

My abashed schoolboy look softened her somewhat.

"Turn down that awful...what are you listening to?"

"Wagner."

"Dear God...can't you listen to something... gentler?"

"I need it. I am the most bored systems analyst ever."

"Self absorbed, you might say..."

"That too..."

"You think like a monk."

"You remind me of my mother when you talk like that"

I used the comparison between Lisa and my mother as a weapon of last resort. It always worked, especially when she brought up my time in the OHF.

"I'm sorry," I thought she said. I could read her lips, but couldn't hear.

"What?"

"I said I'm sorry."

I just wanted to end the argument. I changed the subject.

"Do you want a glass of wine?"

"Not on an empty stomach. I have to study. Is that the phone? Frank?"

"I can't hear it."

"Turn the music down."

I went into the house and turned the music down. I checked the machine.

"Okay. You know what? The machine has four messages."

"What?"

I turned down the music once more. I could only hear it as background now. I felt a strange nostalgia for it, as though I were returning from somewhere I found myself once.

"The answering machine has four messages."

"Answer the phone! Frank, for God's sake!"

I picked up, irritated once more by Lisa's bossiness.

"Hello?"

By this time the answering machine had kicked in. "Hello this is Frank and Lisa. Leave a message and we will get back to you. Thanks."

"Hi Frank. This is Bill. I called a few times already. Sorry to keep calling you. I know I should have kept in …"

I switched off the machine.

"Bill! It's been a while…"

I felt a twinge of resentment. I wanted to tell him what I really thought. But I couldn't. I missed him. If I got angry he might go away. I pretended I was okay with his not calling when I felt abandoned.

"Howya Frankie…"

Only my father called me that. I didn't like to be called Frankie.

"I don't know what to say."

"How are you? Eh Frankie?"

"No one calls me that. I'm just Frank. In fact I recall you enjoyed calling me that…"

"Listen, I have something to tell you."

"Okay…"

Suddenly I felt panic. I never remember Bill talking like that.

"Just tell me. What's happening, Bill?"

"There's been an accident."

"Okay…"

"You know Joe went to Los Angeles."

"Joe Finn?"

"We have a monastery out there for-?"

"I know. How's Joe? You know Joe and I got together…"

"Yes, well…"

"- when he was just about to go. It was just before I left the OHF."

"Right, I mean. Look I don't know how to tell you this, Frankie, I mean Frank. I know how close you and Joe were."

"You need to tell me, Bill."

"I know. Joe got hit by a car."

"Oh my God."

"Yesterday, Sunday. He went out to get the papers and he crossed the road on a 'walk' sign, like a 'green man' here, and he got hit by a hit and run driver. I think the driver was caught by a passing squad car and is being charged."

"With what?"

"Vehicular manslaughter. Joe was pronounced dead on arrival in the hospital, God help us"

"Jesus Christ."

Lisa prodded me when she saw the look in my eyes.

"What, what?"

"It's Joe," I said.

"Joe, Joe Finn?"

"Joe Finn. He's dead."

"Jesus Christ! O my God! How? How?"

"Car accident."

"Who is that? Is that Lisa? Say hi to Lisa for me."

"Sorry Bill. Lisa is here. Lisa, Bill says hi. It's a pity you don't call Bill. I miss you. So does Lisa."

Lisa was crying. I felt the overwhelming need to cry. I swallowed the lump in my throat.

Even if I had not been so drunk, I still wouldn't have heard him, heard what he was really saying to me about the death of Finn.

"Maybe a part of you knew?"

"What part? The liver, spleen, kidneys?" I snapped. "Sorry, sorry honey."

Though I had lost all belief, I still felt Joe's presence. It had been a long while since I had heard from him; a while since the phone rang and I heard him talk from Los Angeles. I always imagine it as sunny. I imagine it in the way one sees it in movies. Joe rarely called me. When he did call me, he rarely was one for pleasantries.

"Hi, it's Joe."

"Joe!"

"So how are things?"

"Good. You?"

"Keeping with the program. One day and all of that. I'm happy here."

"I'm glad. Are you coming back to Ireland?"

"For a while. Probably for Christmas…"

"That's great, Joe. We must get together."

"I'd like that Frank."

"So why don't you call when you're in Ireland? Do you disapprove of me so much?"

"I don't disapprove of you Frank."

"You always seemed to…"

"That was my issue, back in another time. It's different now."

"I see…"

"Sorry about that. I was pretty obnoxious."

It was incredible to hear Joe say that. When I knew him he rarely if ever admitted fault on anything.

"You were…a bit," I said. "And you disappeared from our lives. It hurt. I miss…that."

"I'll drop by when I get back to Dublin, my friend. Sorry…"

I felt someone in the OHF had warned Joe away from Lisa and me. All it took was a quiet word to him, mentioned in passing and Joe would interpret such a quiet word as an instruction under obedience. But he never said anything about being warned off Lisa and me. Even then, during that phone conversation, when we were being so honest, I felt he was holding back, perhaps because of a sense of responsibility to the OHF. But it hurt me. The thought of his condemnation hurt me. I changed the subject.

"Are the community treating you well, over in Los Angeles?"

"Very well."

"I sometimes think about the Order of the Holy Field."

"Really? I never realised that."

"Oh, yes. I think about it. It's hard not to. It was such an intense experience."

"Do you miss it?"

"Miss what?"

"Do you miss the Order?"

During the questionable process of acquiring new friends, people sometimes ask me why I gave up being a monk of the Order of the Holy Field. Sometimes, indeed, they straight out ask why I joined. I never have a clear answer. What I do have is a kind of spin on the whole thing of my years as a Religious Brother. I have my rehearsed answer. Mostly I feel embarrassed. I shouldn't. I know I did a good thing. I would say I was searching for a more meaningful life, or that I felt a calling, or I was searching for Jesus. But it's too personal a question even now. The thing is, one is deeply drawn to the contemplative life. One feels a yearning for love and truth not easily satisfied by more conventional lifestyles. I felt after I joined I had found the one real thing in life. Then it dissolved, to my heartbreak. So Joe's question hit a nerve.

"I do at times miss the OHF. I miss the community, the laughs, the sense of togetherness, the sense of purpose. Outside people don't have that so much. Or, maybe I imagine they don't. Maybe it's me. Maybe I was brainwashed for the time I was inside, and it embarrasses me..."

"I don't know. I couldn't carry on..."

"What, Joe?"

"I mean I couldn't carry on without my faith, without prayer and community..."

"It wasn't part of the plan, you know, my leaving like that..."

"I know."

"What happened...?"

"Right, right..."

"Losing the faith. I didn't realise..."

"I know that Frank. It must have been difficult. I should have supported you..."

"I was there...you know forever."

I remember I was trying to explain something to him. Right now when I think of that time on the phone to Joe, I imagine myself dreaming of all the Brethren who had gone to heaven, who were with God, when he reacted suddenly and changed the subject:

"How's Lisa?"

I took his need to control conversations as well as I ever did. I swallowed my annoyance and went with his lead.

"Great. She left the libraries."

Then I was angry at myself for letting him control me. I was embarrassed too I had opened up like that.

"When?"

"Couple of years ago, and started training as a veterinary nurse."

"That's great. A big change."

"She was unhappy in the libraries."

"And she is happy doing the animal thing?"

"What do you mean? You always were an animal lover. You and she are a lot alike. She loves it..."

And that's really all I remember from that conversation. As I recall, he got called away. Something like that. He always had to go. He always had other obligations. Anyway, it was a while back. I imagine it to be about two years ago. He didn't come home for Christmas, or the following Christmas. If he did, he didn't call. Despite the many ways one could keep in touch, despite how small the world had become because of the speed of travel and the speed of cyberspace, Joe rarely communicated with me. I think he had lost faith in words. Maybe it was a sense of disappointment with his writing. But I feel it was more than the physical distance between us. It is probably the workings of wish fulfilment that I still hear his soft well elocuted voice, hear those short punchy sentences, see those jackets and open necked shirts he wore, his sparse truly monk like living spaces, remember his voracious appetite for knowledge and drugs and his tiny appetite for less damaging kinds of sustenance. For years Joe took out his anger and disappointment with the world on himself. Then he went to live in the city of Angels. He cleaned up, gave up his writing ambitions after he produced his masterpiece, and changed. It was as though he found God once more. He re-dedicated himself to the life of a Brother of the Holy Field, seemed fitter, happier, better adjusted. Though my conversations with him went on after he left for the United States, I knew there was no one in the Order that I really knew any more. He had changed. He had become a new man, and the old man in a young body, the one I knew, was missing in action.

That time with Joe is now a series of memories I occasionally revisit in distracted moments, as scenes from another life. And though these memories fade, feelings, I am glad to say, are the last to go. I expect these feelings and these voices will continue. Bill was still talking away. I wasn't interested. He liked to impart gossip. I was less interested in intrigue than before. I changed the subject.
"Do you have the funeral details?"
"Sure, Frank. His body is being flown over this Thursday. The funeral Mass is on Friday at ten o' clock , followed by his burial. The family are flying out to bring the body back."
"Right."
"Sorry to be the bearer of such bad news. This is a shock to us all."
"Yes, Bill."
"He was a fine Brother."
"I could well imagine."
"So, I'll probably see you at the funeral."
"Sure. Bye, Bill."
Lisa went and made coffee. I took a long shower and tried to sober up.

Chapter Four

Father Des

Des stood in the sacristy of the Church of the Seven Towers and looked out through the window in the door of the sacristy that led out to the altar. He could see everything from this beautifully positioned window. Des was tired and irritable, wished he were elsewhere. He felt that empty euphoria that comes from a sleepless night spent nervously waiting. All the hyperactive over-preparations going on all round him began to really grate on his nerves. Too many people were talking. Too much nervous laughter. Soon it would begin. In seven minutes, he, the members of his Central Council, and other priests, twenty-five in all, would walk out to concelebrate Joe Finn's funeral mass. As Regent General, he was automatically chief celebrant at such a high profile event as Joe Finn's funeral mass. The church was decorated with flowers - lilies and roses and ferns - so carefully sensitively reverently placed around the altar. Joe's coffin sat before the altar. It was also covered in flowers. Des noticed how beautifully clean and expensively decorated the altar was, how shining and sunny the church was, how everything seemed perfectly in place and expertly arranged. Des smiled to cover his irritation, a smile that deepened the wrinkles of his reddish browned webbed face, that well worn mask of patient, gentle, self-immolating torment. Then, he drifted from the present moment, lost in thought, lost in prayer, filled with misgivings.

He looked down, trying to focus, trying to find his inner calm. 'O Lord my God be in my mind my heart be on my lips that I may be worthy, to speak your words in my heart O Lord hear my prayer ear my player don't leave me leave me not O Lord.' He surreptitiously checked the room. 'So many people', he thought. Joe Finn had been so well known. Other sundry clergy had arrived. They were not members of the Order. Perhaps they were friends of the Finn family, or old friends of Joe, those local clergy who had heard of or read of the death of Finn, for Joe Finn had made the papers: 'Dublin Religious Brother Killed in Los Angeles. A young Dublin Brother Joseph Finn, OHF tragically died in a road traffic accident on Sunday last...' Reporters had even called looking to interview him. He had declined. Instead he sent Alex, his Student Director, to talk to them, a burden Alex seemed to protest too much before performing too well.

Des Murphy moved to stand before the tall mirror in the sacristy, to check if his vestments were sitting correctly. He had a lump in his throat. He thought of Joe Finn, and then tried to forget. He looked at himself. He looked good. Des fixed his sparse hair and looked at his features, the expression in his eyes. Alex came up to him to whisper something. Alex put his hand on Des' arm. Then he took it away almost as quickly:

"It's going to be fine, Father." Alex smiled. His honeyed voice, polished from years of diplomacy, worked. He visibly calmed Des's rising sense of panic. He saw something, Des thought. He has seen how this has affected me.

"Am I in the midst of friends today?" Des whispered.

"I have no reason to believe otherwise, Father. Would you like me to...?"

"That will not be necessary, Father. Last minute reconciliations make for strange bedfellows."

"I see." Alex smiled. His great Tolstoyan beard hung totem-like in front of his vestments. It intimidated Des. Des knew it intimidated others. People were always imitating Alex's elocuted voice and caricaturing his affected ways. Alex returned to chat to the clergy, quieting their loudness by speaking in a tone of parental softness. Ah, Des thought, that's better.

Des had spent much of the night in reflection in a state of extended shock at Joe's death. He had sat out in the darkness of the great Church of the Seven Towers with only the tiny glimmer of the tabernacle light and Joe Finn's coffined dead body. He had been thinking over this young Brother's life, his contribution to the Order, trying to reflect on the meaning of his death. Besides these thoughts he offered himself in silent contemplation of the eternal mysteries of the loss of yet another innocent life. 'O Lord you are my God, I ask you to help me, help me understand why it is the young, the faithful, and those with love and life and hope to offer that seem to die. You have taken this young man from us, a young man who offered so much promise, so much hope.'

"Father, it's time," Alex whispers to Des. "Des."

But Des is lost in thought: 'I see Gerry and Rose through the sacristy window sitting front and centre. They look, I dunno, hollowed out. They look empty, dead. They were praying, their eyes red, the sleeping volcano of their heartbreak so sombrely visible. Their cheeks pale, both parents beautifully dressed for the end of everything. Gerry is going to read prayers. Rose is going to read the Gospel. Most unorthodox, but God cares little for rubrics. Considering the circumstances I could hardly refuse. Many of the Brothers frowned at such rubrical transgressions. I simply said, "She specifically asked."

She had, and I could not say no. Not to her. Not considering the circumstances.'

Seeing Des' hesitation, feet began to shuffle, throats were cleared.

"Are we good to go?" someone impatiently snapped.

"Okay to go. Ring the bell," Des said coldly, nodding to the chief altar boy, the one with terror in his eyes. The priests walked out onto the altar, two by two, and the martial sound of a thousand pairs of congregational shoes shifting from sitting to standing echoed around the church. The choir began singing the opening hymn of Joe Finn's funeral Mass.

'I go before you always
Come follow me
And I will give you rest.'

And, as it began, and, as the long solemn priestly procession walked out onto the side altar and down to the back of the church, praying aloud the prayers of the dead as the first hymn ended, then turning up the centre aisle, filing past Joe's body, Des felt himself not fully present. He prayed 'Lord help me to be fully present for you at this sacred time. Let not my will but your will be done. Let me not be in the darkened tabernacled church with only this boy's body. I remember the candles. I remember only your light in that night, Lord. Help me.'

And Des continued leading the prayers and the priests filed up to the high altar and the Mass commenced.

Chapter Five

Frank

It was all so beautiful, so solemn, and so heartbreakingly sad. Rose read from the Gospel. It was Joe's favourite piece of Gospel. Blessed are the poor, she read. Blessed the meek. Blessed are those who mourn. Blessed are those who hunger and thirst for righteousness.

She looked out at the faithful as she read, recognising OHF Brothers, members of prayer groups, ex-members of the Order, regulars at Church, some in good suits and funeral hats, others in casual clothes. The smell of funeral is the smell of soap, of frankincense, cologne, and Chanel no. 5.

As she read, Rose Finn looked fearlessly and, with a near macabre joy, out at the people of God, the burning eyes unable to hold back the tears that betrayed her ruined state. With shaking hands she held aloft the Gospel and said:

"This is the Gospel of the Lord."

"Praise to you Lord Jesus Christ," came the answer, then the dull shuffle as hundreds settled themselves for the sermon.

Des walked to the pulpit. He preached without notes. Maybe he had memorised notes, but I saw no notes. It was scary to watch, at least at first. I found myself fearing he might make a mistake, or misspeak, or make some dreadful Freudian slip.

"Good Morning, Everyone…"

Des smiled out at the people.

"Morning, Father…" everyone answered.

Des smiled sadly and once again rubbed his features nervously.

"It's wonderful to see so many here today and I want to welcome each one of you individually to this very sad occasion. Joe is with the Lord, happy forever. And this is our opportunity to say goodbye to someone we loved, a member of the community. I wanted to particularly extend a welcome to Gerry and Rose Finn and to each and every one of you."

"You are all, every one of you, part of the extended family, Luke and Terry, Joe's uncle and aunt, and Joe's cousin, Marie. We may not know you, but we are all connected to each other in ways we cannot imagine or understand. Our love and our condolences go out to you on this sad day. I don't know how many of you here today were close to Brother

Joe Finn. I had the privilege of living with him for a time. He was a fascinating conversationalist, his mind able to cover just about any subject you could mention, while at the same time able to listen, to really listen to what you had to say. He was also a poet and a writer of some merit, and had published a small volume of poetry when still a very young man. I would say, and I am sure many of my Brothers here would agree that we had never met anyone quite like him - his humour, his real affection for people, his compassion, his great humility, and his formidable mind that he never made a fuss about. It is true to say that Joe Finn hated all fuss, and lived a quiet self-deprecating life. There is no doubt either that our Brother Joe was a wonderfully gifted human being who contributed greatly to the life of the Order of the Holy Field. He was greatly loved by the Brothers, and he will be sorely missed by us all."

"I had the great privilege of reading some of his writings. To me, they were simply some of the most engaging and brilliantly written prose I have ever read. I know many of the Brethren here will agree with me. It is with great sadness that we must acknowledge that a great talent and a great future have been cut short at its mercurial beginnings."

"Last night, I spent some time here with Joe in the quiet of the church asking the Lord why he took Joe from us so very young. I spent a long time praying and pondering and, I have to say, I was deeply upset. To be honest, I don't know why the Lord took him, but he did. I can say to you all that it is important to accept God's will, to remember Joe always and to accept that he is with God, the great love of this young Brother's life. But there is still the deep loss that we are left with when we lose someone so unexpectedly. Growing to accept such losses deepens our love of God and our love for each other. To be honest, I think it is the wrong question, a perfectly normal question, but one to which there is no answer."

"In the Gospels, so beautifully and movingly read today by Rose, we heard the Beatitudes, one of Joe's favourite passages, and one he reflected on constantly. The Beatitudes depict a state of perfection, of peace and forgiveness and resignation to the will of God. The Beatitudes can be summarised into another equally famous and beautiful passage of the Gospel. They can be summarised into one simple sentence, one that Joe Finn tried, in all his humanity and humour and warmth and intellect, to live in his short life: Love one another as I have loved you. This is the call of Jesus to us all, to love one another. It is the call to the Order of the Holy Field, one that I extend to anyone here who feels they have a vocation to follow it, not to turn away, not to give up the possibility of this life, which is a great gift from God, a gift Joe Finn embraced whole heartedly and without hesitation."

"We pray for all vocations and we pray for Joe and his family. We pray for love, for forgiveness, that the spirit of the Beatitudes might enter into our heart and that we might answer God's call as Joe did during his life. Amen. Now I think we have prayers of the faithful after a moment's reflection."

Gerry and Rose Finn seemed to be leaning against one other, like two toppling edifices trying not to collapse. I could see her arm around him, and he hugging her and giving her the occasional kiss, then his head falling forward. I could not see their faces from where Lisa and I were sitting. Others were crying, especially after the Gospel reading. I knew Gerry and Rose were crying. I knew too that, if I actually saw Gerry and Rose crying, I would not be able to help myself, and I too would start crying and the worst of it would be I would not know why, except for the pain I felt in my gut, for reason had deserted me. It was easier to sit here and imagine the tears on their faces, as if from a distance, as if as a spectator.

Aside from Lisa, I didn't know anyone seated near me in the pews. I tried to distract myself, tried to swallow the swelling lump in my throat, damn the tears bulging out and dripping from their ducts. O dear God not now, I thought. I looked up at the statue of the virgin at Lourdes; saw her teenage face and heavy maternal body and that snake under her tiny foot that jutted out of her excessively heavy robes as she stood on top of the world. It made me angry. Then I looked at the crucifix, the face of the destroyed God, Jesus twisted in agony, the huge crucifix above the high altar, and I understood for a moment its significance. This face. This body. This is what life does to one. It kills you. I saw the ancient gothic buttresses, the tall, thin, heavenly pointing, ethereal light streaming through the stained glass windows. I wanted to remain solemn, dignified, like a funeral coat, like this church. I wanted the calm serious face of an undertaker, the sensitive but detached voice of the career counsellor. I wanted to be an onlooker. I did not accept how much seeing his coffin was affecting me. I wanted the cold eyes of the analyst; the icy sensitivity of one who understands exactly what is happening, but only wants to know the facts. I would grieve in private afterwards. I gave myself permission to grieve afterwards.

Then my eyes rested again on the Finns. They seemed wrapped up in grief. No success in life, no love of God could compensate for such a loss. They had channelled all they were into their love of Joe. He was their proof of life, the evidence of their love. I imagined they weren't hearing Des' carefully chosen words, words that spoke of Joe's love for God, love for humanity, love for learning, his record of decent Christian behaviour. No one as curious as Joe Finn could walk the path of conventional righteousness as Father Des Murphy recollected. He was, in my idealised world, the Prometheus in their midst, looking for God's fire in a world where the fire had long gone out. But then I had put him there, in that idealised place. He was only human. I looked at Des. He looked tormented as he waxed eloquent. I saw a look of relief as his sermon ended. Then the prayers of the faithful were offered and the Mass moved on to the offertory and the Eucharistic prayer.

Chapter Six

Alex

Just now, I look down the church. So many people. It's so moving, all these people coming here to pray for Joe. I love Des' words. So prayerful. I remember Des as a novice. He had such a presence. He stood out so much from the other novices. He loved the life so much. One saw straight away he had such a future ahead of him. A great future. The only thing he needed to do was apply himself to the life of prayer, the interior life, the 'inferior life', as young Finn once muttered under his breath during one of my seminars. I had to correct him so often. But Des was not like Joe Finn. Des had applied himself. One can only imagine the hours spent thinking and praying over what he might say, and then, no doubt, the abandoning of control over one's words, allowing the Spirit to speak within one, abandoning oneself to God. These people so love Des' sermon. And it's a fine sermon, a fine sermon. And the church is so clean. They have decorated the church beautifully. I like it like this. They don't clean some of the churches nowadays as they should. The floor shines today. Though not too much. I hope no one slips. We have had that problem before. When was it? Was it so far back? So long ago? So terrible. Screams of pain. Old lady cracking her shin. We rushed her to the emergency room. And then, there was the time there was a child running across yelling "Mummy, Mummy." I was giving Communion that Sunday. I remember it well. It was a little girl in a pink flowery dress, looked like an angel. She kept talking loudly with her Daddy. But the Daddy was trying to hush her, hush her and Mummy walks up just there, right beside where Rose and Gerry are sitting. God love them I feel for them, Rose and Gerry. But back on that day, the little girl runs up to Mummy, to whom I was giving communion, and there, just in front of where Joe's coffin lies. The floor was too well polished. She, the little mite, fell forwards, the poor thing and hit her chin against the marble. Broke teeth. Blood everywhere. Rushed to the emergency room. I had to finish Mass before visiting her in hospital. Naturally we paid for everything. Doctors bills. Dental work. We talked it over with the cleaners. We changed the cleaning fluid. We wanted the church clean, clean but safe. And the old lady who fell. I should write a poem about that. The poor old lady who fell. It was the Lord's will that I should embrace this life. I love my verse though. I cannot help it. I cannot help that I love this life and I love to write. It is an impossible bind. Naturally I do not publish my verses. At least not yet. I am tormented by this. My words do not honour God sufficiently. To love and not to love. A man cannot be the servant of two masters. I told Brother Joe that more than once and he said, 'If one does not know one's master how can one serve him?' That answer incensed me. I told him the value of respect and he apologised. But I remember the old lady who fell. We were lucky. She didn't sue. But we paid too. We always pay. Though I shall have to congratulate Des. I love this sermon. It strikes the right note. Congratulations Father. This sermon is superb. I could never understand why Joe joined us, though. I was against it, but one should never be too against anything. God's ways are not ours. Was it his parents? They are beautiful people. So loving. They gave him everything and were so obviously heartbroken that they could not have more children after him. God love them. Des and I shall have to keep up our visitation to them, though I imagine there will come a time when it will become inappropriate too. It will strike the wrong note. And one knows when that moment arrives. A certain measure of over-welcoming on the part of the person or people being visited. An excess of chit chat during the visit. This or this. That is. Tvam tvat asti. That indefinable unease. Soma. It is then one knows one is marginally less welcome than before. But the Finns always seemed to love our visits. They had so much to talk about. They were so comfortable with us. They adored their son. Though I have to say I always had doubts about his vocation. And it was not a question of his gifts. So much of a fuss was always made about his gifts. I think Des hero worshipped him out of a sense of intellectual inferiority. He saw too many great things ahead for the boy. But then Des did have those problems getting his degree, I remember that. We studied together; I never enjoyed him as a study companion. He could never keep quiet and simply read. Always meeting people, making contacts. He was too loud. Though he quietened down a lot after his parents died. And they died so young, too. Poor soul. That was a difficult time for him. A difficult time. He seemed to light up though in recent years. Becoming Regent General. And he is a good Regent General. He loves the Brothers. And then the hope Joe Finn gave him. He kept that secret too. I warned him not to get his hopes up. I told him we are all equal in the eyes of the Lord. All of us. Joe had a bad attitude. He was one that I sought to correct, lovingly I hope. And I have sought counsel and confession many times over my methods in seeking to lovingly correct the Brothers' faults. It was my duty to do so and I told Des as much more than once. I must admit I was hard on one so sensitive. I wanted to strengthen him in the Lord. I wanted to test his calling. Des is finished the sermon. He usually goes on much longer. It must have been quite a challenge for him, out here for so long in the dark. It was a deeply spiritual sermon. And everyone loved it. I think I will go to the theatre tonight. They are running *Hamlet* at the Crypt Theatre. Though I hear that theatre is closing down. Such a tragedy. Though, it's so funny. *Hamlet* at the Crypt. I wonder if they see the humour. *Hamlet* at the Crypt. Gerry looks like a frightened mouse reading the prayers. That suit doesn't quite suit him. Or is it that it doesn't quite fit? Maybe he just bought it and hasn't gotten it adjusted. Maybe he doesn't care. Poor soul. Oh, we're standing, then. That was quick.

Chapter Seven

Frank

I remember when I first moved into the Monastery of the Seven Towers. I was one of two new brothers. We were given our rooms and made welcome by the new community. My other fellow neophyte, Reginald was asked to leave after a week. Already they were calling him Perrin. Apparently, he began to see visions of Jesus in his room, and simply wouldn't come out for prayers and meals. I don't even recall him coming by my room to say goodbye.

But I am ahead of myself. On the day of our arrival, we were showered with greetings. All day the other students, those who were mid-way through or near the end of their studies, knocked on my door, for a chat or to make arrangements for one of the many social gatherings, prayer meetings, study groups, choir practice, pastoral works, all available to a young Brother like myself to join. And Joe Finn, like so many of the others, knocked on my door to pay respects. More properly he knocked on the wood panelling beside my open door. But on that first day so many people were coming to my door to knock and welcome me as I unpacked and fixed my room to my liking that I decided it was easier to leave it open than continually answer it. So Joe stood there, framed at the point of ingress to my room, and grinned. He was dressed in a white shirt, a tweed jacket, runners, and a pair of jeans.

"Yes?" I said.

"That's a lot of books you got there."

"So?" I was a bit amazed at his rudeness.

"Looking for clues?" he said. "Another two boxes and you have already unpacked three? I see a man with faith issues. I sense trouble ahead. You probably get straight A's too. Thoughtful. Serious. Careerist. Eager to please, yet you just can't bring yourself to play by the rules. I like it. You're going to be happy here."

"Have we met?"

"Joe Finn," he said.

"Frank Ryan."

"Welcome."

"Thanks. Come in."

"Can't. Got to be somewhere. Enjoy your stay at Casa Seven Towers. It's not as fortified as you might think. The wine might help."

"Sounds portentous. Stay for a drink, eh? I have six bottles of twine, all gifts."

"You said twine, Frank Ryan."

"Tastes like twine."

"Ah, literary too. So many gifts. Leave them in the common room, the wine not the talents, Frank Twine, at least three bottles anyway. And hide the rest. They'll go missing if you don't."

"I see, well thanks for that, I'll..." But he was gone down the corridor. Then a Brother came to my door to tell me of a table tennis tournament. Then came dinner, then evening recreation, and slowly, as the hours and days and weeks passed, I began to, rather poorly, adjust to my new life, my new position as a Brother in the Order of the Holy Field, my status as a student at University College Dublin sent to study Philosophy and English Literature, my new freedoms and responsibilities, none of which decreased my isolation. I didn't like College and I was a little frightened in the Monastery of the Seven Towers. I had never lived in such a place. The other monasteries were small communities in newer houses. But the Monastery of The Seven Towers was a real monastery. That old building had so many corridors, so seemingly filled with ghosts and histories that I felt constantly on guard, watching the great living building filled with souls and memories. And yet, what was worse was to see its many living Brothers and priests who were all so at home, so completely at ease there. I was uneasy with its carefully observed rituals, nervous of the large congregations who attended Mass, and overwhelmed the monastery's front door, so busy day and night with people always looking for help. How did I get here, I asked myself.

When I look now at the practicalities of my situation back then, I see how prone I was to bond with someone like Joe. But I didn't seek him out. Aside from that brief greeting, I knew of him only by reputation, by his arguing and by the awe and fear that surrounded him. In fact I think I rather disliked him, from a distance.

Then, one night before I went to bed, I made a final trip to the bathroom. As I went back into my room, Joe Finn, who had been coming down the corridor, collapsed in a dead faint not far from my door. As he collapsed, I saw his eyeballs roll upwards so that, as he fell down, his eyes seemed to momentarily lack any pupils. His room wasn't far from mine. I took him there.

I put him on his bed. His eyes lazily opened.

"Call no-one, okay?" he slurred.

"No."

"It would be, embarrassing. Okay?"

"What if you're really ill?"

"I'm not. Intoxication. Anyway I have, as you might imagine, an extensive medical insurance policy. Not only am I obnoxious, I am moneyed despite my veil of poverty."

"But what if you're wrong?"

"Unlikely. Rarely happens."

I looked at his clothing.

"You're dressed like a member of a yacht club."

"How do you know I'm not?"

"How do you know I have faith issues, you arrogant prick?"

"When…when did I say that? O God I'm gonna throw…"

"When we met! When you stood at my door, made some damn rude remarks about my books and my academic scores, and judged my whole life!"

"Tell me you don't, just say it. You're too curious to just accept the gift of faith."

"Fuck you."

"I have a headache," he grinned. "And I am definitely gonna hurl…"

But he didn't. I helped him with his shoes and blue sports jacket and he lay on his bed, holding his head as though it were a Ming Vase about to topple off the mantelpiece. Around him the room was sparsely furnished: a table and chair, an armchair, and of course the bed on which he lay. He had few books. Being a book lover, I looked through them: a history of art I quickly paged through, a bible, a copy of the rule and life of the OHF. Along with the books I saw a shelf of compact discs, mostly classical. On the wall hung a crucifix and an Escher engraving of people endlessly ascending and descending stairs. On his small wooden desk sat what I thought to be a handwritten manuscript of sorts, and a smaller pile of handwritten notes opened where he stopped working on them. Then I saw another book, a small white hard backed book. Along the spine I saw the title 'Flowers for the Day.' It was written by Joe Finn. It was a small book of poems, about thirty or so, mostly devotional. I didn't like them very much.

"Satisfied?" he said to me. I looked over. He still had his eyes closed. I closed the book and put it back where it was.

"Sorry," I said.

"Don't do that."

"Do what?" I asked.

"The guilt thing. Be a sport and moisten my face cloth with cold water and bring it to me." I did as he asked. He draped the wet face cloth over his thin face.

"Ohhh," he said. "Hits the spot. Dear God, Jack Daniels should be imprisoned for conspiracy to cause grievous bodily harm. "

"Don't blame the drug. What are you working on?"

"What?"

"All these handwritten pages."

"Don't touch. I have an interest in the origins of the Order of the Holy Field. Now put down those pages and let me sleep."

I couldn't read his handwriting anyway. Even when he wrote to me in later years I had to spend a very long time trying to decode his spidery scrawl. I left him to languish, closing the door quietly, somewhat offended at being brushed away without being thanked for my trouble. He was extraordinarily arrogant, I decided.

Two days later, a few minutes before evening prayer, a knock came to my door.

"Hello," Joe Finn said.

"Hello," I said. "Come in for a minute. Evening prayer is about to start."

"Right, I won't keep you, then."

"Are you not going?"

"Pressing engagement forbids my attendance. I brought you this. What a lot of books you have. Have you read them all?"

"Some of them. Thanks for the gift. That's the second bell, Joe. I have to go…"

Normally two bells rang for prayers. The first reminded the community that prayers were about to begin. The second was the last call to prayer. Joe rarely attended.

"I hope you like opera. It's Wagner's Ring Cycle. 1990 – 93, Gunther Newhold conducting. I like it. I hope you do."

"What's Wagner's Ring? Jewellery perhaps?"

"It's the ultimate story of power dressing. It's the story of a ring forged from gold from the Rhine that gives its wearer ultimate power only if they renounce love."

"Okay, does the Church have any problems with it?"

He ignored my question. Rather, it was as if I hadn't asked. Had he answered, I might have even listened to it.

"The ring gets cursed by its creator when stolen. It brings death to the wearer."

"Wow." I heard some of the Brothers running down to the choir. Few things were more embarrassing than being late for prayers. Everyone saw you enter the choir and go to your place on a walk of shame. "I have to go," I said. Joe nodded.

"See you later."

And Joe left. It would be more than a decade before I played the music he gave me. And he never asked me if I had. I sat in the choir, fearing I had wrecked something beautiful and new, feeling that supreme thrill one feels when first love comes, a sweeping terror, a sweet rapture, a wonder how someone so obviously brilliant could give me a gift, and if I had spoiled everything by saying the banal 'I have to go.' I had escaped, without knowing it, from isolation, a state in my own ignorance, I did not know I held. Thus the happiness I felt, the thrill, was as confusing to me as it was overwhelming.

Weeks passed and my joy turned to deep hurt and confusion. I saw Joe as one sees any other member of one's community: during recreation times, in the common room, during meals. He hardly acknowledged my existence and yet I was enthralled. As though every unspent feeling I ever had, all the loneliness and disconnection, suddenly found an outlet in this strange contradictory landscape we found ourselves in, both together and alone. Eventually I plucked up enough courage to go ask him to walk with me into town and have a cup of coffee with me. I knocked on his door. It was three o' clock on a Saturday afternoon.

"Come in!"

His room was spotlessly clean. Joe was nervously standing in the middle of the room taking pages and pages of a handwritten manuscript, tearing them up and putting them into a black sack that seemed at least a third full of paper at the time of my entering.

"Frank Ryan. Did you finish your wine?"

"No. I left it in with the community."

"So you're the young poisoner."

"So you do know who I am. I was wondering if you…"

"What is Brother Frank Ryan doing indoors on a day like this?"

"I was wondering. I mean I was wondering if… Joe, what the hell are you doing?"

"This?"

He held up a few torn pages.

"Right, that."

I pointed at the torn pages he held up.

"I am taking pages of notes and text into my hands and tearing them like so, into little pieces and putting them, like so, into this plastic bag. What you want to know is why I am doing this seemingly absurd thing. After all, I must have spent a while writing all those little words onto those now torn pages. Right? Well, it's true, there are hundreds of hours of work gone into these pages. But I have a good memory. And I am under a vow of obedience. You know, they don't take too much notice if you break poverty or chastity, but obedience is a thought crime. I have been ordered to destroy all notes and concentrate on my college course."

"They don't want you to fuck up, I guess…"

"They want me to really fixate on getting a good grade. They want me growing a tumour in some college faculty, earning a fat salary and writing fat mediocre volumes as I mete out tedious lectures to undergraduate and post-graduate alike. Do I look like an academic to you?"

"What does an academic look like?"

"Like you, I think. Thoughtful, serious, interested in pleasing others with bright ideas…Some day you'll believe in God, even."

"Don't ever say that to me again."

"Okay, sorry."

"You wrote a book of poetry. I saw it."

"Lots of people do that."

"Not when they're sixteen."

"I guess."

"You were a big hit."

"No. No I wasn't. It was something instinctual. I wasn't working at being different. I never have."

"Have you written anything else?"

"Nothing published. I like Giovanni Seipi. Yeah. He's the kindest warmest most giving person I've ever known."

"So I see."

Despite the near illegibility of most of the text at first glance, I began to make out bits and pieces, then I found I could make it out by guessing what certain words might be, rather like anticipating a melody in music. I could make out that he had intricately examined all the major texts and many of the minor ones. Some of the manuscript was written in block capitals, thankfully.

"Why can't you just hide the text? This is just a little too forensic to be simply destroyed."

"Because Alex wants the black sack delivered to his room before nightfall."

"That's harsh…"

"Well, an example has to be made. This isn't the first time I have been warned."

"Never heard of him being so tough like that."

"You haven't?"

"No. I like Alex."

"Well then I won't…I mean Father Alex does not like being crossed."

"He's not like the bogey man, Joe. Get a grip…"

"Look, I've been here a while. So trust me. Don't cross Alex. And if you disobey, have some kind of alibi. Have you read his books? Now that you have been made librarian, you have unlimited access to all the gems in his literary crown…"

"You heard about that too? I don't listen to gossip."

"It isn't gossip. It's on the community notice board."

"Oh, sorry. There's a community notice board?"

"You're kidding, right? I'll show you where it is. Important to read the notice board at least once a day."

"I'll bear that in mind."

I had read Fr. Alex's books. I rather liked them. They were thoughtful, carefully written, filled with personal reminiscences, pieced together from the enormous amounts of reading and effort necessary to write works for which there was such a growing market. I didn't want to make Joe any more upset than he was. His eyes were red with tears. He looked at me and I knew from his look that somehow, by some sorcery, some convergence of time and histories, our sympathies were connected. It evoked as much fear as it did doubt and joy. Then, as though he had for a fatal moment exposed himself, he looked away.

"Fancy a coffee?" I asked, by way of an insecure pedestrian distraction from an intense moment. There, we could talk about the little things, I thought. Thank God for the little things.

"Give me ten minutes. I have to take out some trash."

And so he kept shredding. I went back to my room and lay on my bed, waiting for him to finish destroying his work.

I was, as Joe had mentioned, consigned to library work. I loved the library. It had two floors, was at least one hundred and fifty years old, oval shaped, with a domed, stained glass roof, situated on the north wing of the monastery. With each generation it became like all other parts of the monastery, more ghostly and crumbling, twisted with nooks and crannies, more necessary to rebuild, for the building had wet and dry rot. One always saw people working on the building. In the library, though, the Brothers had to act and quickly lest history go to dust. They had to archive old manuscripts because of a fear of decay and damp dissolving the historically significant, the letters from superior to superior, memoirs and letters and photographs and manuscripts and documents that remain to this day irreplaceable. I have seen some of this fascinating material. I quickly appreciated how necessary it was to store what was important and purge much of the accumulated rubbish of the ages. Along with appointing me librarian, they employed archivists, lean young coffee-drinking uniform-wearing intelligent efficient quiet people, friendly and willing and professional. I liked them. They wore white gloves and worked for absurdly large hourly fees. They, the young archivists, had come and gone. I don't know why I caricature them. They, like me, were only doing their job. Except I didn't know my job. Which was why they threatened me. They seemed so focused, so sure of a purpose. They took away dozens of crates of historically useful material for storage and analysis. All that was left were the regular books, some old volumes locked in presses, bits and pieces left here and there, and magazines thrown in a few dozen boxes. I knew I couldn't do this. So I went to see Alex. I didn't make an appointment. One was expected to make an appointment. I suppose I felt so threatened, I wanted to have an advantage. I walked up to his rooms and knocked on the door.

"Father, I'm sorry. I wonder if you had just a moment?"

"Come in, Brother Frank. Long time no see."

Alex smiled mischievously. He looked over me, like a clinician surveying in an instant a specimen he knew if he waited long enough and sought long enough would come to him, and said nothing.

"Father, I know I am supposed to see you every month."

"Frank, Frank, this is your second apology in two sentences. What can I do for you?"

I swore to myself I wouldn't apologise, for anything anymore. Alex was my spiritual director. One went to see one's spiritual director every month. I didn't. I feared someone I admired getting access to the more tormented aspects of my psyche. Instead I fantasised a friendship developing between myself and Alex. It was no wonder I called him 'Father' so often.

"So," he said. "Let's start over... Frank! What can I do for you?" His eyes gazed into mine as he put out his hands to me in a welcoming attitude. His phone rang. He didn't answer. Footfalls approached his door. Then the footfalls walked away. I knew I was in the way. I thought quickly.

"The library…"

"Yes?" he smiled and nodded quickly.

"I mean I can't do it. I don't understand libraries. I don't know the library system and the archivists left such a mess… I mean, there is stuff everywhere. They threw out so much but they left so much too. It's not the amount, Father. Well it is the amount, but what to do with it. In reality we need a person who knows what they're doing, you know…?"

I felt my leg tremble a little as I over compensated with an arrogant swagger. My demeanour amused Alex. He put the tips of his thin fingers to his lips to cover a tiny smile. I felt acute embarrassment. I watched him. His soft, almost fluffy well combed beard, flourished. He looked a picture of perfect thoughtfulness.

"I hear you. And you are perfectly right. You need a professional to teach you the ropes. We will get someone to come in one day a week, two if you're lucky."

"Yes, Father…" I blurted out, interrupting him… "Someone trained in library work, rather than another Brother who would come for a while, and then, then work badly for a few weeks, resent the work and just stop turning up…"

"I see. We need to fix this. Leave it with me for a while. I need to source a few people. Okay then…"

"Thanks Father…"

And then one Saturday I heard Alex in the library. He was speaking in a stage whisper. I seem to remember working alone that Saturday. Joe would happen by for a chat usually on my library Saturdays, mostly to take a book or return a book. Today he hadn't called. I missed him.

"So… Lisa, as you can see, Brother Frank has begun the work of cleaning and tidying the library, but he has come to me asking for someone with professional skills to work with him. Naturally, he has the final say in all matters. But I am sure you will find him more than accommodating. We are thinking in terms of a computerised database with all the books and periodicals and magazines and so on, but you can, if you like, work up a proposal paper, along with a budget…Ah Brother Frank, allow me to introduce Lisa Mc Grath.

"Lisa…"

Like all truly momentous events in my life, I completely missed the significance of meeting Lisa. I was, I suppose, from the first moment, in love with her. But I did not see her. I saw a tall long limbed woman with dark brown hair cut short and well cared for, a attractive woman with a slender body, dressed in a pair of old jeans and a t-shirt, someone who smiled easily and said little, intelligent, sensitive, watchful eyes, a gentle mouth, small hands and feet, someone I felt neither attracted nor indifferent to. I was curious too, wondering what it might be like to work with this person. But aside from the details, I failed to see beyond the superficial.

"Well, I'll leave you two to discuss matters. Don't forget to come to me soon with a proposal. I have a budget meeting next week, okay?"

"Okay…"

"Bye Alex…Thanks"

"Bye. Work hard you two…"

And he left.

"Alex? You call him Alex?"

"Was that wrong?" Lisa looked confused.

"No, I mean. You're not Catholic, are you?"

"Not even a little bit. Why don't you show me around this…very messy place? And we'll work out something…?"

"Sounds like a plan, Lisa."

"Good then. Let's get to it."

Chapter Eight

Gerry

I feel nothing. Or rage. Or just absence. It's pain disguised as nothing. Rose is so quiet. Now we sit. We sit here in front of our beautiful boy's coffin in the midst of all these people. It's like being alone. I remember everything. I remember holding him when he was born. A tiny baby. I said 'this is my life.' I remember his eyes opening, his first words. I remember walks in the park, feeding ducks in Stephens Green, tears over falls from bicycles and long summer evenings and opening Christmas gifts and visits from the relations and every other thing. I remember his sicknesses and his loneliness and I remember watching television and going to the cinema. All I have now are memories of a love gone and yet not gone. Here in this church. People reaching out. All this love. All these hands that reach out. Mouths that say sympathies. They tell us how sorry, how terribly sorry. We smile and take the hands. Nothing matters. Nothing reaches inside, makes a difference. The centre. It's as empty as before. Joe is gone. Everyone you love leaves. Love is not forever. Now all I hope is our friends will help us. I can't go on. I hope I have made a friend in Father Des. He is a good man. But does one really make friends with these people? I wonder. The hurt makes everything suspect. So many come and, so many people, needy like me, who want things from them, from the Brothers, come to them. I am just another punter. If I just dropped by in a year or two, would we still be friends? I wonder. I should trust him. I believe in my heart they want to do the right thing. Maybe I wouldn't be as needy as now. So maybe he wouldn't need me. The Eucharistic prayer is over now. Soon we will be taking Communion. If I did not take Communion, there would be a scene. If we do take Communion everyone will watch us. I wish there were something I could do to change this. I want to be stronger for Rosie. I want her to be okay. I don't tell her these things I feel. I want her to get through this. I just don't know what to do. I don't know what to do.

Chapter Nine

Frank and Joe

I have given up trying to understand the effect Joe Finn had on my life. Overall, he was not an easy friend. He could have been kinder, more compassionate and less judgemental. I forgave him his petty cruelties, and, for the time we were close, I never felt happier or more understood. Then Lisa and I found each other.

I knew little about Joe, really. For instance, I never knew if Joe had many friends. At the time, my lack of knowledge about him didn't hugely worry me. I was naïve in that way, too trusting. Also, I had no social ambitions. Or maybe at that time I wasn't aware of them. I held no interest in widening my circle of acquaintances, or acquiring the kind of friends that might build a future career for me. Perhaps it was those very qualities that made it possible for Joe and me to bond. It was only afterwards, when I acquired other friends who freely introduced me into their circle, that it lamely crossed my mind Joe might have been keeping me for himself, that I was not so fragile or dependent as I thought I was back then, that maybe, just maybe, he had played me. But, back then, as I said, I was naïve and he was my only friend in the Order of the Holy Field. Back then I had lost touch with my outside friends. Back then, Joe and I used go regularly for long walks and coffee in town.

"Twiddles had long hair," Joe said. "He died last month."

"I'm sorry," I said. What a strange name for a cat, I thought. I hate cats.

"He was a great cat."

"I don't remember ever actually seeing a cat with long hair," I said. " I saw lots in movies and in magazines, but not in real life."

"No way. You must have seen at least one long haired cat."

"Don't think so…no."

"Well, Twiddles was one of three kitties born from a cat we called Schrödinger."

"Schrödinger? You name your cats' strange names…"

"Schrödinger was there and not there. She went away into another dimension. Twiddles grew up in our old shed."

"You had…an old shed…?"

Joe nodded. Then, as though bypassing my pointless statement, he went on with his pointed statement.

"Then it got knocked down. Then we found homes for the other two and Schrödinger went away and the shed was renovated into guest quarters. Twiddles was a good cat. Did a lot of lying around and playing with wool and looking pretty sunbathing. You had to brush his fur. Mother used brush his fur with a steel brush. She was so patient about it. Twiddles didn't like it much…"

"Right. You must introduce me to your folks. I'd like to meet them."

"Did you ever have cats?"

"My Dad didn't like cats. Only dogs. We had a few…"

"We had lots of animals."

"I could well imagine…"

Joe talked about his parents, his aunts and uncles, and Twiddles. I was never introduced to anyone, and cannot recall ever being invited home to meet the parents, nor did I ever sleep in those guest quarters he mentioned every so often.

We were sitting at Café Aroma, one of our favourite haunts among the coffee places and bars we frequented, especially on Saturdays. The other places were full or just too noisy to hear oneself think. We were sitting by the window, watching people come and go. Joe wasn't saying much. He usually held forth about something he had heard or read. But today he made a few short remarks and sipped his coffee. The unusual silence brought up my obsessions. I was still obsessing about the destruction of Joe's manuscript. I kept seeing him tear up his work like that. What bothered me most was how little it seemed to affect him.

"I still can't believe you shredded that stuff you'd written."

"I'm sorry?" he looked up, as though finally recalling he came here with another human person, and not some book.

"Your papers, that manuscript. The day we came here to this place for the first time. I came into your room and you were tearing up a manuscript."

Joe frowned and pointed between my eyes with the fork he had been using to eat cheesecake. I felt a twinge of fear. I had angered him, brought up a forbidden topic.

"That was…"

"A long time ago, water under the bridge all things being equal long time ago, I know. And I know I bring it up every now and then, but aren't you upset?"

"I don't believe I am."

"And I don't believe you aren't."

"Okay I was, at the time, you know? But I vowed obedience to God."

"Oh please, don't do that! Don't give me the party line…"

"Well, I believe part of obedience is, well, part of that is taking crap from Alex. He's in charge of students. Now, I know you like him, but I think he is a charlatan. I think he has, like, invented this sanctified, intellectual thing…"

"That's harsh, Joe. I think he's okay."

"You think everyone's okay. Then you embarrass yourself when you see through your own rose-coloured idealisation."

"That's not true. And it's …really cruel…"

"Frank, you're too sensitive…"

"Though I am, like, shocked at what he did to you…"

"Well, there you have it."

"Whatever that means…and by the way you should apologise for the rose-coloured remark. What's the matter with you today? You're being such a prick."

"Sorry."

I couldn't believe I actually heard an apology.

"I didn't know you apologised. I think that's the first time you ever apologised."

"I didn't sleep much last night."

"You told me already you don't sleep well…"

"By the way you look good: That's a really nice pair of jeans, Frank."

"Thanks. Anything else about me you don't approve of?"

"Not your usual fashion victim bargain basement attire."

"Well there you have it. Another bouquet for me. Thanks, Joe. I think…"

"Oh you're welcome. Nice shirt too. Very colourful."

"Thanks. Now fuck off."

"Fact is I've never seen you look so good. Clean fresh clothes. Nice…"

I saw few actual signs of the distress I sensed from him, aside from the thoughtless remarks. Those were nothing unusual.

"Okay. Thank you. Enough already. Come on tell me, what's wrong, Finn?"

"Don't call me Finn. Did you buy them recently?"

"Matter of fact I did…by the way are you writing anything now?"

"I can't say."

"Why not?"

"I don't want to talk about it. So when did you get all this stuff? Did Alex give you the money?"

"You know something?" I said. "I might eat a brownie too with the coffee. Excuse me?"

I raised my hand a little too timidly, a fatal error when hailing a waiter. "Yes sir?" the waiter smiled, turned away from the friend he was talking to and indulgently raised his well plucked eyebrows. "I'd like a brownie too, please…"

"No problem. One minute." And the waiter went on with his conversation with his colleague as though I had never spoken.

"I don't know about that brownie, Frank. Shouldn't you be watching that nice figure of yours?"

"Why?"

"Why not? I think it's important for a Brother to have a good self image, to wear good clothes, to eat well. I like it you took it upon yourself to buy new clothing."

"Why can't you tell me whether or not you are writing something?"

"Because my writing life is like what my sex life might be like if I had a sex life, which I don't, in case you're asking. It's private. But back to that brownie, let me ask you this: who went shopping with you? You don't think I think you had the good taste to buy all this stuff? The shirt and the trousers…"

"Jeans…"

"Jeans, sorry. My guess is you went with Lisa."

"Well you're wrong."

"And she paid for a lot of it."

"I came here to have a cappuccino with you, eat some fattening biscuits and walk around Grafton Street, and so on, do some window shopping, then go home. What the hell is the problem?"

"It's a question of openness and transparency. A friend of mine changes his lifestyle and habits. One minute he looks the self-absorbed academic trying desperately to prove himself to his superiors, someone who wears second-hand, poorly fitting clothes, and the next he blossoms into a walking advertisement for Gap Clothing."

"So I'm your friend…"

"The change is palpable. The energy is upbeat. We have a level of sparkage and all he wants to talk about is whether or not I am writing something. So maybe I am. All that stuff I was trashing was mostly trash anyway. Alex is an idiot, so caught up in his own cleverness but too absorbed in his own spiritual vanity and addiction to power to know what's really going on. I have an idea, but Alex will never let me go through with it. I need to go over his head and I intend to find a way to do that. So you and Lisa, what's going on?"

"Nothing...what if Alex finds out?"

"He won't."

"If you fail another exam he will... I mean you talk about obedience and you can't obey. You are incapable of it..."

"Fuck you. At least I'm still celibate..."

He scowled at me, and then looked embarrassedly at his empty plate and coffee cup.

For a long time I said nothing. Then I said softly "Bastard..."

"Now, now! Not so defensive!"

He put his hand up like a traffic cop during the Indie 500 and smiled into his coffee cup with half closed eyes. "I shouldn't have said that either should I?"

I shook my head again. Then I looked longingly and angrily at the waiter who had finished his anecdotal conversation with his colleague. He had cleverly seen ever vigilant management from the corner of his eye, and had wandered over to pick up some stray empty cups and plates from vacant tables. I wanted my brownie more than life itself. "Joe?"

"What, what's up?"

"Look, you don't connect with anyone, not really, so how can you judge anyone, especially me? You look at me from your smug self-imposed exile and pass sentence. Anyway what are you implying?"

After I said that I was really afraid. I had betrayed myself as we always betray ourselves.

I wish I could remember the exact sequence of events that led me to become involved with Lisa, looks exchanged, smiles, the first touch that made us cross the threshold from friend to intimate, the first kiss or embrace that craved so much for more. I don't remember because I was so emotionally dumbed down, so blinded and numb to the endless crazed beating of my own starved heart, so seduced by my deluded notion of a life of the spirit that starved my soul of intimacy, that I did not realise what was happening to me. We kissed. We made love. We spent time together, secret time, time I could not equate in any manner with the way I spent the rest of my time. There was time with God and the Order of the Holy Field. Then, there was time with Lisa. The schism ran through my mind, my body, my soul. Someone had to see the fissure in me. I knew he knew. My secret was out.

"I think you are in love with Lisa. Don't think I don't see what's happening. I hang around the library. I see what's happening and, if I see it, others will too."

"That's a big assumption, Joe."

"This will cause a scandal. They love a scandal. They love the gossip. "

It had happened one Saturday. One Saturday, Lisa and I kissed. We were talking about something. We were always talking. I think we were debating whether tomatoes were a fruit or a vegetable. Then we kissed. Then we apologised to each other, and then kissed once more for a long time. If one kisses for the first time, self consciously, one measures time too keenly, then timing and performance anxiety can lose the moment. It used happen to me back then. Eventually, I relaxed. Then the following week we made love in a back room on the floor with a coat thrown beneath us and the door blocked with a chair. Afterwards, all I could do was think about her. She took me shopping. That was why I looked dapper.

"You are entitled to your opinion. I think ..."

I felt so angry at him I wanted to punch him in the face.

"Yes?"

The waiter arrived with the brownie. I picked it up and started eating.

"How often?" he asked.

"A few times."

"Be careful."

"I know it's wrong."

Joe looked at me coldly.

"It's a mortal sin, you know? It's breaking your vow. It's separating you from God. It's wrong. That hurts me. I want to understand, you know? But you are better than this..."

"It's wrong. I have to end it."

"Don't delude yourself into thinking you will end this, Frank. This never ends. Once it begins it never ends."

"Very apocalyptic, Joe. Very apocalyptic."

"If you leave her, you will find another, someone else who will not satisfy if things remain unresolved. You are looking to fill a need bigger than merely the glandular. To me, it looks as though you aren't happy, and she is your route out of this life. If you end things with Lisa, you will find another, or you will start drinking, or something else. There is no simple termination point with matters like this."

"So, what can I do?"

"Look inside. See what you want. Get help. Then give yourself the time to decide."

"You know, I think you are pissed. You are, like, very angry with me aren't you, Joe? I mean it feels as though you have found something to beat me up about."

"I'm disappointed, that's all…"

"I have to say you seem a lot more than disappointed, that's all. I feel you are, well, more than that. Look I'm sorry you're disappointed. I didn't plan for this. And I feel really scared and confused, and not a little paranoid. You really have to promise me you won't say anything to anyone."

"Don't you trust me, Frank?"

"Don't ask me that. Satisfy my paranoia. Promise me. Promise me, or does no one make real demands on Joe Finn?"

"You wouldn't feel paranoid about me if you trusted me, would you?"

At this stage I lost my temper. I slapped the table.

"Why are you like this? Friends are supposed to support each other! Are you jealous? Is there something…?"

Joe picked up his book and stood away from the table. His chair scraped the wooden floors of Café Aroma. People discreetly glanced.

"I got to go. I'll see you back in the Monastery of the Seven Towers. I'll see you, Frank. Be careful…"

And he left…

"Joe!"

I shouted. And people, nice, well-dressed, sophisticated, intimidating people, people reading books and newspapers and staring at small hand held technology that made me feel even more worthless and insignificant, turned and looked at me just long enough to take a reading of my emotional state. And that was that.

Chapter Ten

Frank

I would like to believe that from the first my falling in love with Lisa was a good and healthy thing, that I knew it was the right way for me, and that it helped me face up to what I thought was the truth about my life. But in reality, I behaved more like an addict than a lover. I thought about her constantly, felt withdrawal symptoms when not with her, endured agonizing guilt after being with her, and gave up everything to be with her just one more time.

The loneliness, though, was the worst feeling. Being with Lisa isolated me from the other Brothers. It was not that I had any close personal bonds with them individually, but my relationship with her took away my feeling of belonging, my sense of brotherhood with a collective. It psychically cut my ties with the OHF. In despair, I saw my need for her love as a compulsion, a torment, the chasing of something intangible. It was like an addict's desperate, destructive search for a fix. It's not the drug I wanted. It's what the drug does, the calm after the orgasm, the vegetative euphoria of the chemical solution to the problem of time and living and what to do with time. The fix never lasts. The hunger is never satisfied. I was living a lie, a lie I feared deep down I knew I had become. But twice a week, maybe more than that, I found a way to be with her, drink wine, make dinner then love, talk about politics and art and religion, or books or music, listen to her talk about her family, talk about my worries about being a member of a celibate religious order, and what I was going to do…

"You need to lighten up, Frank…"

"How can you say that?"

"I think I just did, honey. I think I just did…I don't think it's all so bad as you say…"

Lisa looked up at the ceiling as we lay on her bed. It was one o' clock in the afternoon. We had made love twice. On the radio, Bach's well-tempered clavier played. Lisa reached over to her bedside locker, stuffed with books and music, and took out a cigarette and smoked it. I looked at it again. It was not so much a cigarette, as a very long thin cigar.

"Want one? My sister got them in Florida. She travels. Do you travel?"

"I don't smoke."

"Neither do I"

"I have a fear of flying. Or falling, I'm not sure."

She smoked slowly and blew the smoke upwards. I imagined incense wafting away like that.

"I don't think you get what's going on."

"Okay, what's going on?"

"I'm in trouble. I'm a member of the OHF. I'm living in sin."

"So, love is sin, is that it? Have you any idea how insulting that is to me?

"No, no!"

"Fuck you, Frank Ryan!"

"I'm in a state of mortal sin, isolated from God, from the Church and from the Brothers! That's what I mean!"

"Oh, well then. That makes all the difference. So long as you're only destroying your own happiness and sullying our love with neurotic guilt, that's okay, then."

"I mean I don't even see too much of Joe."

"Wow, how apocalyptic. Does he know?"

"He might guess something…with his IQ he can probably read our minds."

"That sounds about as exciting as watching an egg boil, or reading some of the propaganda I shelve at your monastery."

"How open minded of you."

"Thanks. What about friends? Does Joe have any friends, besides you I mean?"

"I don't think so."

"So, you're his only friend and you are sleeping with me, don't you think he is naturally going to resent that?"

"Why should he? I trust him."

She smiled paternalistically. I mean how could I be so naïve? That's what her smile said.

"We are not in the business of trust."

"Why shouldn't he come to me if this is really bothering him?"

Lisa turned over on her side and leaning on her elbow rested her head on her closed fist. She held the long thin Florida incense cigar at a distance, trying to cope with her rage at my guilt and self-hatred, trying to accept how I felt. I looked at her. Her skin shimmered in the afternoon light. Her voice softened. I felt calmer as her voice softened.

"I don't think, from what you say, he makes connections easily. I mean, I don't know him. Frankly, I think he hates my guts"

"He likes to make himself difficult to read."

"I guess. And, though he's your friend, you have made a connection with me. I think he might feel betrayed."

"Lisa, you don't understand…" Lisa took my hand and pulled me near her. She balanced the cigarette on the edge of a table. That will leave a nasty burn mark, I thought. She leaned up near me and the power of her aura was intoxicating. I smelt her hair, went to touch it. She flinched. I took back my hand, hurt by her refusal.

"My parents are atheists. Well, not that they don't believe in God, it's like as though we grew up without any religious background."

"Okay, that's not my thing," I said. I pulled away a little more, just to regain my equilibrium.

"I gathered," she said and resumed smoking. I stood up and began walking around the room.

"I grew up in a religious home, very Catholic. And I am in the OHF. I mean before we met things couldn't have been more different. I had a life there."

Saying that really angered her, an anger I recognised had been there for a while, simmering away. She waved her hands at me.

"I don't know about that, really…you live there, and you sacrifice your individuality for a sense of identity. Advertising executives do the same thing. Except they're allowed have sex."

"Jesus, you are so cynical…"

She ran her hand irritably through her hair and interrupted me again… I could never get used to being interrupted so often…

"Listen, Frank… This is nobody's fault. We met. We understood each other. We talked and went out and had drinks and one night, out of the blue we kissed and we ended up making love…"

"Day. It was the day. We kissed and then we had sex, during the day…"

"Whatever."

"What do you mean whatever, Lisa? There was no whatever. This is real."

"And for both of us it was a happy thing, a good thing, a godly thing, if you believe in God. Now you are letting guilt and remorse fuck everything up…"

She was standing right in front of me, wearing only a t-shirt. I was so intimidated.

"I meant to say, before you kept butting in, that before, I had a clearly understood path."

"What the hell does that mean? You thought you had it all worked out? Religion's great lie is in the illusion of having the answers, or even pretending the answer is there is no answer…"

"Is that the answer?"

"Fuck you…" She grinned at me, walked over to the bed and finished dressing. I waved my arms around like a drowning man. I felt dismissed, as though nothing I would ever say would make any sense again.

"I hate lies, Lisa. No lies or no secrets. Now I have secrets and I am lying to my friends and I am breaking my vows and sneaking around and pretending. It's killing me. And last week, in town, some of the parishioners saw me with you. I nearly had a heart attack…"

"So what? You are too sensitive and you let people treat you like crap. So, the nosy parishioners are having afternoon tea and apple pie with some of the Brethren and they see you and me and to their minds we seem more than just good friends. So, they go and mention it in passing to the Brothers and the Brothers tells Des or Alex or whoever and then you are called in for a little chat and you say, yes, that's right, we met in town, and we had coffee, and so fucking what? Who cares?"

"I can get kicked out of the Order for this. They won't take me back. You lose a Saturday job. Big deal."

"Does Joe know about us? I mean for definite?"

I nodded. Though I wasn't sure how definite. I wasn't sure if I still had credible deniability.

"He will confess to his superiors."

"He would never betray me."

"You can't spend the rest of your life suspended between two worlds."

"I know. And I'm tired of having this out with you."

Lisa looked wearily around her messed up apartment and quickly put on her shoes. Despite the speed and distracted nature of her dressing, she looked great.

"I gotta go to work"

"Do you think they know? About us?"

"Come off it, Frank. They have to know. They've probably seen the change in you."

"So how long are you on until? At work I mean?"

"I'm on from two o' clock till ten o' clock tonight and for the rest of the week. Do you want to meet up Thursday or Friday? Maybe go for a drink?"

"I don't know."

"What do you mean you don't know?"

"I don't know how my week is. I mean I'd love to. But I don't know.

Maybe if I call you. I'll leave a message."

"That's kind of pathetic. If you don't want to see me, just say it!"

"Jesus Lisa! It's the best I can do until I know what my schedule is. I don't control my time!"

"Okay, okay! Fuck this!"

We left her apartment. She pulled the door closed and put her key away. As we walked down the flights of stairs I felt people recognised me. They seemed to smile. I wasn't sure if they really did or not. Lisa was talking about moving apartment. Then she mentioned something about my phoning her at work during the day. Then she said something about my not listening to a word she was saying.

"Frank!"

"What?"

"What's the matter? Frank?"

"Some of these people. They know who I am."

"So?"

"Look, I know this is bad. I didn't expect this."

She nodded, as though I wasn't telling her anything she didn't know.

"We need time to sort ourselves out, Frank. You need to decide."

We kissed goodbye at the foot of the stairs, people passing and smiling as people do when the see other people kiss in public. Who cares if they recognise me, I thought? Then I thought of trying to explain the kiss to Des or Alex. Then I gently ended the kiss and smiled and hid my fears for a little while as we went our separate ways.

So she went to work and I wandered into my afternoon class. Though my lecturers touched more than once on the subject of exams, I had little interest. I drifted away, praying and worrying, caught in a state of fear and shame and wishing for the security of knowing what to do next.

After class I went to a phone booth and rang Joe up.

"Hullo?"

"Hi there, how are things?"

"Okay."

"I didn't see you in college today."

"I slept in. I was tired. My stomach was at me."

"I didn't know you slept. Mostly you tell me about pacing and listening to Wagner and going to the toilet every twenty minutes."

He didn't answer.

"Joe, you are going to have to help me out here…"

"Oh yeah?"

"I mean what is happening?"

"Nothing, nothing's happening…"

"So why are you like this?"

"Like what?"

"Angry, withholding, passive, cold, judgemental, irritable, hurtful."

"Quite the shopping list of complaints."

"I think the clinical term is being a complete prick to your friend. Joe? Can you hear this? Joe? Are you going to talk to me? Joe?"

He didn't answer.

"Look, I didn't plan for it or want it. All I'm asking is for you to be patient with me and…"

"All right. I'll talk to you later on. I have to go."

"Joe. Don't do this Joe. Eh, Joe? Please. Joe?"

He hung up.

Then the days dissolved into a tasteless fare of loneliness and guilt and abandonment, until, a few days after, I walked into the Common Room in the Monastery of the Seven Towers, and saw him sitting there. This was the post dinner chat, a time encouraged by the powers that be, during homilies and retreats, for Brothers to talk to each other, a time, so we were told, community life was built and sustained by Brother communicating to Brother. I listened to the rustle of habit, the Brothers leaning back a little too freely to be really at ease, talking with heads back leaning towards each other, nodding, smiling knowingly as each conversational group watched the other, or studiously avoided the impression of having to work hard at casual conversation.

"Fancy a coffee, Frank?"

"Sure, thanks."

One of the Brothers poured me a cup, and then he handed it to me. It was Kevin. Kevin looked after the sacristy.

"Busy isn't it? Eh Frank?"

"It is…Kevin. Very…Thanks." I poured warm milk into the coffee because the coffee looked very strong. Then, I put two spoons of sugar into the coffee.

"Don't see you in here too much, Frank."

"No, how come you're doing coffee today?"

"I do coffee most days. You just don't see me do coffee. I like it. You get to chat to everyone who takes a cup."

"Okay. Thanks"

"After all, communication is the lifeblood of every community," Kevin grinned.

"How true."

"It'll be fine, Frank."

"Thanks, Kevin. I would really like to believe that."

The news channels quietly transmitted their infotainment in the background as Fathers and Brothers mingled, coffee cups in hand, some solemnly watching and listening, others laughing out loud, as visitors came and went looking for specific people they found or could not find. Joe was doing a crossword. I sat down beside him.

"Hey, Joe…"

"Ah, there you are…"

"So what happened while I was talking to you on the phone?"

"What do you mean?"

"We were in the middle of a conversation."

"No. I don't think so. I think you thought you were. You weren't…"

"Yes, we were. And you hung up."

"As I recall, we'd finished talking. One usually hangs up…"

"I talked, Joe. You said nothing."

"You had finished, as far as I remember. You spoke your mind, told me what a withholding sonofabitch I was, then you tried to provoke me into some kind of an outburst. I don't like bullies. I don't like being caricatured or painted into a corner. I think that's kinda unkind. I said I had to go and I went because I had an appointment and as far as I recall that was that."

"Fuck you. Fuck you for this force field you have erected. Fuck you for the defensive nonsense you are carefully protecting yourself with. What fucking appointment?"

"I can't say…"

"You didn't have an appointment."

"Yes I did. Don't tell me what I had and didn't have…."

Joe looked coldly calmly at me. He really wasn't afraid. He had me handled. He knew it.

"Anyway, Joe…It isn't your usual style to cut me off like that."

"As I said, I wasn't cutting you off."

"Are you sure? I think you were."

"Well, there you have it then. You think I cut you off. I don't."

"There was this definite sense of being cut off, excluded, shut out, if you will…"

"Why are you being like this with me?"

"I'll tell you why. Just say I was wrong and I am being touchy because

I'm in a bad space and my life isn't working for me right now. Just say you really thought our conversation was over and you hung up innocently. Okay. Usually we go to the gallery on a Saturday or we catch a movie. I called for you several Saturdays in a row and no answer from your room. I see from the Community chart on the main corridor you have absented yourself for those days, and you never mentioned it."

"I see you are keeping tabs on me. Have you hired a private dick too?"

"Joe, don't do this. You have been warned off me."

"What?"

"I know. You've been warned off me…"

"There has been no warning, Frank. This is paranoia, pure and simple. And I am sick of this shit!"

"I call occasionally to your door, and, though I can distinctly hear music turned down low, and, in spite of the fact there is a small light playing under your door, you don't answer my knock."

"I'm sorry about that. That's all I can say."

"You are sorry?"

"Sure."

"Don't tell me you don't know who it is or that you didn't hear the knock. I knocked at least twice - once on Tuesday and once on Wednesday. What is going on, Joe?"

"Nothing."

"Please tell me."

"I have to say this Lisa business puts me in an awkward position. The Brethren are beginning to talk."

"No shit, Sherlock."

"If I am seen in your company, they will know that I know. It will be obvious. You were seen in town last week. Some of the parishioners told some of the Brethren and then word has gone up the chain of command. Expect a knock on your door sometime soon."

"How very Gestapo. And you were going to tell me this exactly when?"

"I am telling you this now. I wanted to tell you."

"Don't lie to me Joe Finn."

"I am not lying to you! How dare you!"

"How dare I nothing! This is about you needing the establishment more than me."

"Oh, please."

"No, no. Don't sneer. This is about your fear of losing the respect of the authorities."

"Nonsense. Jesus!"

"If anything they're using you to get to me."

Joe stood up and stormed off. His swift departure knocked against my coffee cup and saucer. It tumbled away from my hands as he strode away, his heavy shoes thumping the carpet. As my cup spilt whatever dregs were left on the recently replaced carpet, some heads turned and smiled good naturedly at me.

"Ah Brother, a cleanup job for you," Brother Alex smiled.

"Yes Brother, I feel privileged to be able to engage in yet another Christ-like activity on this day of days. I wash the ground the feet of the Brethren trod upon. It's so virtuous. You should feel jealous," I smiled in return.

"Oh, I do, Brother. I really do. It's good to see you able to clean something up, for once," Alex replied. I looked at Alex. He looked so calm, so happy in his world. He was smiling down at me, as I knelt, rubbing the newly laid carpet with a disintegrating tissue, and I knew I felt hatred in my heart and it hurt me. I went and got the cleaning fluid and there, in the midst of the chatting Brethren, cleaned up Joe Finn's mess.

Then I left the common room, noticing Kevin had gone as I left. Where the hell was Kevin? Who will wash up? Me? Not likely. I went up to Joe's room. I knocked on his door. No answer. Once again, the silence continued. Fuck him, I thought. I hate him. I hate him and I wish he was dead. I'll beat him to death with a two by four. I will strangle him with a bootlace. I wanted blood, and, though my blood came to a slow boil, I didn't see him for days. I think he went home to Mom and Dad. Then he came back, and, when he came back, we talked again. Joe came to my room and apologised for walking away like that in public and embarrassing me. He said he hadn't been sleeping again. He was a lifelong insomniac. When he did sleep, it was mostly in bouts, catnapping and waking, pacing and reading, then falling asleep. Lately, though, he said it had gotten particularly bad. As a result he had withdrawn into that hazy twilight of neither waking nor sleeping.

"I thought you had been sleeping."

"I had. Then I stopped sleeping for no good reason. I took pills for it. No use."

"You take too many pills."

"I guess I am anxious. It's just I am having a hard time dealing with all of this."

"With what?"

"I'm unsure."

"Eventually you are going to have to tell the truth, Joe. The truth will get you, if I don't."

"I think you maintain a little too much confidence in the power of truth, Frank. It comes from reading that awful Freud. No joy there, I fear."

"Fuck off, Joe. I'm serious."

At night, I would sometimes see him sitting alone in the choir hours after we had prayed the divine office. The bell would ring for vespers and we would troop in and recite the office and I felt so close, so close to these men, so much a part of this beautiful world of prayer and faith and hope and then I would remember Lisa and feel guilt, unworthy of being a member of this ancient and venerable institution. And after prayer we would go to the refectory for the evening meal, everyone chatting away amiably and I would act my way through the affair. Joe, if he turned up for food, rarely sat beside me after the common room carpet incident, despite our quasi-reconciliation. I would see him talking to other Brothers, people he had little regard for but whose company he suddenly preferred for their uncomplicated relations. I guess it was more important for him to feel secure within the OHF than not be lonely and be with me. After all, my status had shifted. I was a part and not a part of the Brotherhood. He would rather feel friendless than return to the tangled web of our personal history. Weirdly in the midst of our drifting apart, we started to talk again. We would sit and chat, or go for drinks, or sit in company watching television, or even once or twice attend College. Joe was supposedly attending University College Dublin, just like me. But we no longer said important things to each other. He was drifting in a lot of ways, looking for a lonely place from where he could act, making endless notes, reading endless books and drifting.

But I knew I was alone. It was a pain filled freedom, a clear cold certainty that felt all too familiar. I knew these external signs of friendship meant little. I had a clear sense of an irrevocable loss of a shared understanding that I knew, with heartbreaking certainty, I would not recover. Though Joe did not share himself, we had had a sympathy that usually comes from family membership or a similar powerful shared experience. I knew Joe somehow knew what it was like to come from my family, and I from his. I knew what it was like to grow up feeling different to other children, yet wanting and failing to belong. I knew what it was like to desperately look for love and truth and meaning in all the wrong places. I knew all these things because I saw my own biography in the person and dispositions of Joe Finn, and he in mine. Our friendship, and its failure, was an act of faith in the possibility of some kind of mutual understanding and, because of it, we began to grow, each in our own way. There was no group encounter, no therapy, no soul sharing, that cult of salvation espoused in relationships. We were too sceptical for that. Maybe if we were braver, we might have survived it all with a lot less hurt. But losing Joe Finn around then made me value memories more than anything. I began to write things down. I began to see how memory defined all I know and could know about anything, which was precious little.

One final clear memory of Joe at this time was catching sight of him late in the evening, when he would be reading by a single light in the choir. Another was seeing him alone in the huge church, after the big oak doors had been locked and the security systems put on. He would be alone there in perfect stillness, as though absent from his body, hunched over whatever text he was contemplating. I knew he would be furious if I disturbed him. I knew he was furious with me anyway. Somehow, I had broken a vow between us. I had been unfaithful to him. I sensed it. No, I knew it. By now, I was too guilty and too confused to talk to him. I went on, or rather drifted on, not knowing where I was going.

Then, I knew what Joe had done to me when Alex approached me one Friday afternoon. He waited until I was just about to go into my room and appeared on the corridor, raised his hand, smiled and put the hand he had raised in messiah-like fashion back beneath the comfortable folds of his perfectly tailored habit. I had never met Jesus, but I always thought he took spiritual advice from Brother Alex.

"Brother Frank, I'm sorry to trouble you, but would you happen to be free this afternoon?"

I had to make myself free at any time for Alex O' Brien.

"Yes Father."

It was Bill who really warned me about Alex. I generally trusted Joe's ideas more than his judgement of people, which really means I admired more than emulated him. As he didn't get personally involved with people much, it seemed to me he didn't have good emotional intelligence. But Bill did. Bill had been in other Orders. Bill had an emotional IQ of 180 in my book. Bill had seen this all before.

Bill was the one other friend I made in the Monastery of the Seven Towers. Bill was someone I trusted almost as I trusted Joe. Bill liked to drag you into his room after lights out, feed you whiskey and talk into the small hours. It had happened a few times, and, though I enjoyed the experience and gleaned much information, I hated the hangovers and the resultant sleep deprivation. It was like an intensive course in an ancient and increasingly popular subculture that one paid for with a slight psychosis and many dead brain cells.

"There are those who have become one with the Alex Continuum," he said "And there are those who do not."

"So," I slurred, "what's the Alex Continuum?"

The night Bill told me about Alex, he had just returned from giving a retreat. He was flush with money. "The nuns love to tip hugely," he would say. We had gone to somewhere really expensive for dinner and now it was extended nightcap time. Bill's full face was shiny with oily sweat, his hair uncharacteristically disordered. He suppressed the effects of the alcohol and looked at me with the smile of the detective who has finally unmasked her quarry. His voice no longer sounded drunk. He wanted me to hear this, but, equally, didn't want me to know how concerned he really was.

"The Alex Continuum is a group. But it is more than that. It is a nameless sphere of influence."

"Wow, very secret cult."

"Indeed. It is a group of Brothers who cling to Alex for support, advice and advancement in the Order. They are well known, but not normally referred to in public. Mentioning the Alex Continuum in public or as a negative can lead to censure and getting the worst postings to the most awful monasteries in the Province. Actually, quite a few of those who join the Alex Continuum leave the Order, or are encouraged to do so."

"I'd heard that somewhere. Someone said that once."

"Those who don't leave are groomed for positions of power in the Order. Quite a few of the top people on the Council are members of the Alex Continuum. I have heard rumour he has his own bank accounts – strictly against our vows of poverty – property, credit cards. One thing he shares with your friend Joe is a love of opera."

"Look Bill, whatever you might say about Joe, he loathes Alex. I know you and Joe don't get along, but Joe really loathes Alex."

"Good, glad to hear it. Frank, pass the whiskey bottle."

"Sure. More ice?"

"No. I have enough," he rattled his glass. Then, having poured himself a finger, he glanced at his watch. "Must be getting to bed. I'm on the early Mass tomorrow."

"Okay, one more question. Then I'm going Bill…"

"Sure, go on…"

"What happens to all those who go?"

"Go? Go where?"

"When Alex gives them the bullet? I mean, there must be real competition for places on the Alex team. So why leave the Order just because he says so?"

"He is in charge of the students, so he can fire whoever he chooses. The Council rubber stamps his dismissals, but it's whatever he says. He will be working to get rid of you and Joe if you don't join his team."

"Did you?"

"I'm a lawyer. I don't need to."

"And he didn't kick you out?"

"I'm a lawyer. What can I say?"

"I heard stories about this, Bill. Not about Alex. But stories like this. Old Brothers' tales to scare the young into obedience. And those who stay get the top jobs?"

"They get the top jobs. Des, Vincent, Fionn, Paddy, Ray, all of them were made king or queen by Alex…"

"I have to get some sleep, Bill. I'm wasted. Good talking to you. Thanks for dinner. Never had lobster before. Embarrassing food to-"

"No bother" Bill grinned. He was a model of refinement, well cultured opera loving country gentleman, just like his nemesis Alex. His kind sharp twinkling eyes smiled their omniscient smile.

"You have to know your place."

"I know."

"You don't, not really. There is Des. Des is Regent General followed by his Vice Regent and Director of Students, Alex. Alex is a combination of two unofficial sources of power in our Order. Alex is the kingmaker. He amasses the votes and political will necessary to get a particular Brother or Brothers into power. He's also what we called, well still call, a sage, a source of spiritual insight in the Province. There are other lesser sages in the Province, just like there were other lesser kingmakers in the Province, but none like Alex. Alex has also made the Order a lot of money. Naturally, that gives him more power and of course credibility, and, with those publications to his name and his well attended directed retreats to select clients…"

"This is all a bit cynical, don't you think?"

"It's how it is. Below Alex the Vice Regent are the five members of the Central Council.

"I know…"

"There's the Regent, Fr. Des and Vice Regent, Fr. Alex and Council have responsibility for the well being of the Brethren, missions to new territories, Fr. Peter, current and capital expenditure Fr. Gerard, Vocations and other sundry responsibilities Fr. Luke."

Bill was speechifying, something he only did when too drunk to hold a conversation.

"I know the Council, Bill. I'm going to bed."

"All I'm saying is, be careful."

"Goodnight. Thanks for dinner…"

"No bother. You need to be really careful, you hear? Finn is a pawn."

I ignored him. Bill had taken me to dinner to show his solidarity. He knew about Lisa.

I was thinking about Bill's words as Alex surveyed me from the calm lofty heights of his palatial intellect. To my naïve perceptions he seemed safe within his intimidating holiness, connected to the great and the good, portentously intelligent, unconstrained by the need for promotion or recognition, and very scary.

"Two o' clock, then? After lunch? You are sure I am not taking you away from anything?"

"Yes Father. No Father."

"I understand. Nothing important. It seems it has been some time since we got together. Only for an hour, you see. Are you okay with that?"

I nodded and smiled in nerve racked reflection of his kindly smile. Not that I had a choice in the matter. When the Director of Students asks to see you, you have to be okay with that.

"See you then, Brother."

"Yes, Father."

'Nothing unimportant', I thought.

"Brother."

"Sorry Father?"

"Though I am an ordained priest, we are Brothers. Call me Brother, please. We are all Brothers here, Brother Frank. Though some of us are ordained, we are all Brothers here. All equal in the eyes of God."

"Sorry, Brother."

That little homily marked the terminal point of my tolerance. There was simply no way I could face Alex. The little 'Brother' homily aroused only a deep irritation in me. I knew I wouldn't be there at two o' clock. Instead, I went looking for Joe. And Joe, as usual, was nowhere to be found.

Chapter Eleven

Joseph Finn

One hears so many things. One hears that one's earliest memories are suspect. I think that's true. But how much of what we know can we test? I remember being two years old. I remember sucking on a bottle. Or was it a breast? I remember feeling abandoned at night and crying for Mommy and Daddy. I remember standing up in my blue wooden cot, crying. I cried and called. Mommy. Daddy. Mommy, Daddy. But they were out. Perhaps they were praying. The room was dark. I could see the crack of light under the door. Then, things got better. I remember walking. I remember my first reader. Happy Venture Reader. Dick and Jane. I remember the first words. Here is Jane and here is Dick. I remember the picture of Mommy calling the children. Dick and Jane were out playing in the garden with a kite. Mommy was calling. They were playing and Mommy says 'Come in, your dinner's poured out.' The dog Rex was chasing the kite. Rex was a small Scottie dog. The kite was red like Jane's dress. Nicely co-ordinated. Mommy was standing at the door. She had a lot of make-up on and her figure was as perfect as her hair. Time for hot chocolate. They must have gone indoors. I remember a lot. I don't know why. I remember I was five years old on my first day of school. That day they gave me Happy Venture Reader Book Two and then Book Three where Dick and Jane move to another neighbourhood after Mommy was caught dealing drugs and Daddy came out as gay. Actually, I'm joking. I remember school. I remember the first moment on the first day of the void, for that was how it was. I remember I stood at the foot of the stairs and, having waited, walked with Mother to the car. We drove to Mater Misericordiae School for Gifted Children, a mere five miles on a clear day heavy traffic no bothers. My first schoolroom was room fourteen. I remember my first schoolroom, those clear sense memories of chalk boards and the smell of orange juice from plastic cups and tiny glass bottles of milk and Irish lessons and lots of paint and Lego and beautifully carved wooden bricks. I remember room fourteen was a good distance away. It was up three flights, a hard slog on the first day with my new shoes and my white shirt and my tie and my jacket, an outfit that made me stand out a mile from the other children, Mother encouraging, not seeing how she had dressed her son to look like a refugee from Tom Brown's Schooldays. You are such a good boy. Then, after Mother disappeared, there was teacher smiling and welcoming, Miss Mitchell. Miss Mitchell was a nice lady. She ate Tuc Biscuits with a little piece of carefully cut cheese on top during lunch time. I can still feel the sexual frustration in each careful excising of one piece of cheese from the next. One two three. We were God's children. All the smart kids were good children, so Miss Mitchell said. I looked into Miss Mitchell's eyes and I was happy. I didn't need her. God was with me. Though my parents had abandoned me to this place, though I was expected to learn and excel, it was not important. I did not need my mind. I had God. God was calling me. That was all that mattered. It was from there on I loved God. I was five. I have, I suppose, always felt this way. One comes from God and will return in the end to God. The feeling never goes away. It is the meaning of everything. It was this real knowledge I longed more than anything to pursue. This was the central miracle of my life - looking at five years old on a frustrated middle aged teacher, and knowing that I was not alone. I joined the OHF at nineteen years of age. I joined because of that moment when I was five. I also joined because of Alex. I was taken in by him at first. When I was twelve, Alex came to Mater Misericordiae School. He gave a talk. "Now children," (he called us children) "God calls us to do many different things in life. He calls us to work as doctors or nurses or scientists. I know how many of you here are destined for great things, but the calling to the religious life is God's greatest gift to us..."

Grainne, she put her hands up. I loved her. I loved her fringed hair and her pleated skirts and white blouses and her small perfect face and white smile and her tiny gold rimmed spectacles. She was a goddess, a diva, a muse. I think she became a psychiatrist afterwards. Though I haven't seen her in a decade, I remember her. I remember her question.

"But, Father Alex, what about Jane Austen and Marie Curie and Doctor Hans Christian Bernard? Surely these people gave us wonderful things, and helped us all?"

"Yes indeed, my child, these people greatly contributed to humanity. But who are the real heroes? Or, more properly, do we know all the truly heroic acts that go on all around us? Of course not. What religious life offers is a very special way to do important things, not things which one sees or hears about on the news or in books, but a secret calling in his heart to find God along an ancient and mystical tradition going back to the time of the apostles. In fact, there has been a mystical and monastic tradition going back thousands of years. Every culture has it. Ours is within the Catholic faith and we in the Order of the Holy Field are especially proud of our holy tradition of saints and missionaries that go back to the time of our holy founder Giovanni Seipi."

As he spoke Alex's eyes wandered like a searchlight around the class. And then he saw me. He smiled a little and continued speaking...

"We have a great many scholars in our Order, writers, artists, poets. We feel that all gifts come from God and give honour and glory to God. That is what our Giovanni Seipi wrote and this is our ancient tradition..."

Paul put up his hand. I didn't like him. He smelt. Once I found a card belonging to him. It had the name of his therapist on it. He was embarrassed when I gave it back to him.

"So you don't get married. Are you gay?"

"No. I am not gay. We don't marry because God asks us not to."

Miss Parker stood in the corner watching Alex talk and smile and gesticulate and respond to the questions. This was a younger Alex, more vibrant and playful, beardless and handsome. The Alex I knew when I joined seemed more troubled. His political pursuits had perhaps weighed him down and dampened his spiritual ambitions. Parker watched him like a hawk and didn't smile once while she spoke. She smiled at some of the questions and listened intently for any comments that might trouble the children unduly. At two thirty, exactly forty minutes after Alex entered our class, she stopped proceedings.

"Well, ah, Alex, I'm afraid we are out of time. We have to go down to Greg for our art classes. People I want to thank Father Alex O'Brien of the Order of the Holy Field for coming in today and talking to us about his way of life. It shows us all there are so many different lifestyles out there and we should think about them all because, even if we agree or don't agree with what another person thinks, we should at least...."

Miss Parker put her hand up to her ear in her most patronising pose. The class like good little Pavlovian puppies responded:

"Listen and learn," and eyes rolled in boredom.

At this point her voice dropped. I was nearby. I caught most of what was said, and lip read a little.

"Thank you, ah, Alex. They had you on the ropes there once or twice. How'd you like being asked if you were gay?"

"Excellent question..."

"Paul is very sensitive. I believe in time and with the right support, he will be a fine artist..."

"I have to say, Sheila, I've rarely spoken to a more intelligent group. Average IQ, one forty eight? Incredible..."

"Who told you that?" Miss Sheila Parker looked angrily at Father Alex, who seemed to know too much about the class profile he had just spoken to.

"I asked your head teacher, Mr Farrell."

"I see. That's nice."

"He very kindly invited me here. He comes to our Church. I believe there are some scores higher than that number."

He has probably even seen their individual files, she thought. What a bastard Farrell can be.

"We don't discuss such things as a matter of policy, Alex."

"Sure, Sheila."

"And we don't encourage that kind of competitiveness. It does more harm than good."

"Absolutely, Sheila...," Alex caught my eye at that point. He smiled and nodded and as he walked out of the classroom he pointed to Shelia's desk. He had left a card, a leaflet and a number. I picked it up and put it in my mála mór. I wondered if the class had seen or even cared what had happened. As he and Miss Parker left, uproar ensued. But at that stage they had gone out of the room. I read the card. On it there was a picture of the Monastery of the Seven Towers. Underneath the picture of the monastery was a quote. It read: 'This is the rule and life of the Order of the Holy Field.' It said: 'To observe the holy Gospel of our Lord Jesus Christ and to follow him to the end.' It all somehow seemed right and fitting. I felt happy. I took the leaflet and the card and kept it.

School taught me little. I remember commenting to a teaching nun once upon a time how I always thought school largely a waste of time. She looked solemnly at me and said, "Joe, that's arrogance. You ought to watch that." Typical teaching nun, I thought. But I really thought so. I could read and write before I went to school. I simply read a lot more while I was there. I didn't like it much, but took a degree after as I didn't know what to do after I left school. Then, a few weeks after finishing my degree, I went down to the Monastery of the Seven Towers, and asked to see Alex. I was very obviously afraid.

"The first thing I want to say to you, Joe, is you need to relax. I can see how nervous you are and you should take it easy."

"Yes Father."

I was really nervous, because I wanted to join. I felt God wanted me to join. I saw nothing else in my life but this.

"I see from your school Leaving Certificate results that you received eight grade A's. That's an exceptional score. It seems you are well on your way to fulfilling your potential."

"Thank you, Father."

"I see also you have published a small book of poetry 'Flowers for the Day'

"Yes Father. Did you read it?"

"No as a matter of fact I haven't. But I really think that's great. I write myself. Are you working on something, at the moment?"

"No Father."

"Nothing at all since 'Flowers for the Day?"

"No Father."

"Would you like to talk about why?"

"I lost faith in writing, really. I think it is largely a waste of time, time better spent helping people."

"I see. Those were fine poems, Joe."

"I don't think so, Father, but thanks."

"What have you been doing the last few years?"

"Working, Father…"

"Not in college? Again Joe, I think you shouldn't run away from your abilities, if that's what you're doing."

"N-No, Father."

"Working at what?"

"Hospitals, charities, homeless shelters…"

"I see, Joe. You seem like a nice young man of course, and that's good, and I see you come from a respectable family, and I am glad to meet you. But the real question you need to ask yourself is why you want to join the OHF. People join for all kinds of reasons, not all of them good. Some do it to escape life; some do it to escape dysfunctional family situations. We even had one who wanted to deny to himself he was gay. You are not gay, are you Joe?"

"No Father Alex."

"I see. You come to the Order of the Holy Field to find yourself, not to escape yourself."

"Yes Father Alex."

"Brother. Joe the first thing you must come to understand that we are all Brothers here in the order. You may call me Brother. I think we might consider you for our postulancy programme next September. It lasts a year, and you will be in Cork City for that time. I suggest you find yourself a job and we will ask you to see a psychiatrist for some testing, just to see if you are up to the rigours of the life, for it is a difficult life and not for everyone, you see. I see you attended Mater Misericordiae School?"

"I did, Father."

"Extraordinary place. The Order of the Holy Field is truly a place the gifted might find a home. An old friend of mine is headmaster there, Alfie Farrell. I haven't seen him in a while, is he still head man there?"

"No Father. Sheila Parker took over two years ago. Alfie got fired."

"I see. Well, we'll leave it at that for now, Joe. I will be in touch. You have given me all your details here, have you?"

"On my card, Father. Thank you for your valuable time."

"You too, Joe. By the way I would like to make a small gift of this…"

He handed me a two hundred and fifty page hardback book called 'The life and Times of Giovanni Seipi' by Father Alex O Brien, OHF. "It's a little something I wrote last year, by way of introduction to one of the great people of history. Our founder Giovanni Seipi."

"Thank you, Father. I will certainly read it."

So, I took it home and read it, and many others. And thus began my obsession with Giovanni Seipi. Alex was furious because it interfered with my studies. To be honest, I had no interest in my studies. I was fascinated by Giovanni Seipi. "Brother Joe, I have on many occasions told you to leave this business with Seipi behind. It is interfering with your studies. After you have completed your degree, you can perhaps return to studying his life, and perhaps produce something worthwhile on him. This obsession is not good for you. It is premature and destructive. You need to go through the formation process, complete your studies and then decide, along with the agreement of your superiors, on a course of action. We have talked about this before, haven't we?"

"Yes, Brother."

"Someone with your abilities should be doing far better than this. If I don't see a marked improvement in your examination results, something in line with your Leaving Certificate results, I am going to have to take…"

And he paused for a suitably furious word –

"Action?" I suggested. I had the faintest impression of more than the professional disapproval of the Master of Students for a poorly performing student.

"Yes," he said. "Action."

And he did. He took action. "Bring your notes to me," he said, "shredded."

"Yes Brother." I took him the notes. I wanted to give him the satisfaction so he would leave me alone. I had to improve my scores, give the impression I cared about college. I was sick of academia. I wanted to pursue my own interests.

So, as I said, I brought him the notes. Frank was as appalled as my parents by what Alex did. Mother said "It's such an injustice." Dad turned white with rage. But I wasn't worried. I had lots more notes where they came from. I was planning to write something myself. I had to find a working space, though. The problem was I had to get away, away from the Monastery of the Seven Towers, away from Frank and his problems. Yes, I needed space to work. I was unhappy.

Chapter Twelve

Frank

I didn't show up for my meeting with Alex. So Alex went looking for me. He left a note pinned to my door. The note was in an envelope. The envelope was sealed. The writing on the envelope was in block capitals, typed. So, while preserving the veneer of confidentiality, everyone would know who left the note.

Dear Brother,
We were due to meet this afternoon at two o' clock.
Please contact me at your earliest convenience. Alex

It read like a couplet from a sonnet, or the first part of a limerick. I tried to finish it: how would it go?
We were due to meet this afternoon at two o' clock.
Two o clock two o clock rock clock fuck defrocked convenience in convent in lenience serious no grievous. So, I read the second line again.
'Please contact me at your earliest convenience.'
And then I had my quatrain:

We were due to meet this afternoon at two o' clock.
Please contact me at your earliest convenience.
For this absence I could have you defrocked
Your trespasses are bordering on the grievous.

I mused and smiled and knew whatever levity I made of my fears, the threat inherent in the copper plated script was unmistakable. It worked. I felt gripped by this overwhelming urgent, guilt-ridden need to go see Alex. He drew me to him with an irresistible force.

On the fifth floor of the Monastery of the Seven Towers lay the Central Council Offices. One went through tall carved oaken double doors that hung beneath a carved stone crucifix to enter that area of the monastery. I had rarely had occasion to go through these doors. I had once delivered messages, like any good novice, enthusiastically delivered messages. On one other occasion, before I had taken vows, Alex had wanted to discuss my future in the Order. He had plans for me. I only guessed a long time afterwards that he probably had some plan to assimilate me into his sphere of influence, as Bill put it. I learned he usually did this by suggesting a career course for one of his prospective people. I liken it now to being asked to spy for your country. If you refuse you are branded as not one of us, unpatriotic. You find life doesn't go your way and your career falls into terminal decline. Alex would see it differently. He saw what was best for the Order, what kind of skills the Order needed at any given time. What a particular individual wanted was less important.

I listened to Alex that day without comment. He suggested I take further studies in either Canon Law or Theology and consider an academic career. Naturally, I agreed. It was what God wanted. What God wants, she gets. It was what my superiors wanted. Resistance was futile.

Then, there was the day he had left me the aforementioned note that summoned me to these rooms, his rooms in the Central Council Offices. Just being called there was statement enough in itself, thrilling and scary all at once. I was not long out of temporary vows. I was finishing my degree that year. Then I would be sent to study Theology and Canon Law, I didn't know where. If he found out about Lisa, my career in the OHF was over. Alex had sent for me and I was terrified of him.

Alex was in his room when I went to his door. He was on the phone, lingering like a real estate magnate over an extended business call. I had no idea who he was talking to but it all sounded intimidatingly significant, at least until I was within actual earshot. When I was close enough to make out words, the conversation was terminated.

"Come in, Brother, come in. I am sorry to have delayed you like that. Sometimes it's hard to end conversations with those kinds of people who are unused to getting anything other than undivided attention."

For this trespass, I thought, he could have me defrocked. But, as I am not a priest, that can't happen. For my trespass he could have me shot. It's over, I told myself. Wake up, Frank. The Alex Continuum has you.

"Father I, I wanted to say I-"

"Well, do sit down." He indicated the comfortable leather chair before his desk with an imperious finger.

"Thanks, you, Father, Brother, I mean, thank you."

"Make yourself comfortable. Please relax. I am sorry if my behaviour makes you in any way uncomfortable. Perhaps you would like to tell me what happened this afternoon, no?"

"I'm sorry, I—"

"Well, I have to say you were noticed around the monastery. Pretty gutless not turning up like that. You were, as they say, a no show. I am angry, you know. Angry, yes. How do you feel about me? What is your real opinion of me, Frank Ryan?"

He fixed me in a look that wanted answers.

"I am really sorry," I offered by way of oblation.

Alex waved his arms in rhetorical wonderment. I was terrified. Perhaps he was calling down fire from heaven or something.

"Where were you? Where's Frank? I asked around and what do you know? You hadn't left the building! You were looking for Brother Joseph! Joseph! Why? Why would any of us look for Brother Joe? Does he have the answers? Does the smartest man we have ever known have the answers? No!" Alex shook his head. "You, like so many of us, mistake intelligence for wisdom. Smart people often make the worst choices because they don't listen to their hearts... Brother Joe has his own issues. Perhaps, I thought, Brother Frank is looking for answers. You might think I'm too tough on him. I love Brother Joe. Let me save you a futile life of searching, Brother Frank. The answers are in there!"

He was pointing at my heart. His voice softened suddenly. I was riding the roller coaster of his shifting moods. He must have had experience interrogating prisoners, I thought. He had me in his thrall. Then he went on:

"You know, you must be really hungry by this stage, not having had dinner and not going near the kitchen all day. It's five o' clock. That's what, eight hours since you have eaten? Maybe you have eaten elsewhere? No? Not good, Brother. I mentioned to Brother Gerard and Kevin and a few others that I missed you, without in any way wanting to provoke controversy. And Kevin said he hadn't seen you. But the others, they said to me they had seen you knocking on Brother Joe's door. I know you and he spend a good deal of time together. I also know that you seem to be having a good deal of difficulty this weather. I know it because of the expression on your face, the look in your eyes. Even the most passing of glances can tell so much to one who knows how to see. And I see a good deal of anguish in your face, Brother. A good deal of suffering. You need to know how to suffer well. You need to listen to yourself. You cover it up well. You can get along. Do your job. Attend class and produce the necessary work. You have a very good mind and I like to see the Brothers use their gifts to the fullest possible extent. Our holy founder, Giovanni Seipi, founded the Order with the intention that all the Brothers who came to the Order might be all they could be, whether they are thinkers or artists or carers or ministers. And I think, if you want, you can go far in the Order of the Holy Field. Another thing I like about you, Brother Frank, is that you are organised. I like that. You know how to plan your life and you can juggle complex arrangements to suit yourself. But what you have goes deeper. You think deeply over things. I believe that is why you and Brother Joe are such close friends. In many ways, you remind me of each other. You are, of course, very different. But I see too you are troubled, Brother Frank. I see that you are troubled in a way that Brother Joe is not. Joe has his own particular troubles, things about himself he hasn't faced. We both know what I am talking about…"

I started to say something. Alex stopped me.

"Please, let me finish. I know you might imagine otherwise, but you are not on trial here. You need to make a choice. This is the kind of suffering that does not go away by escaping, either into the world, or away into the arms of a lovely lady, and she is a lovely lady. No, don't protest, I am not judging you, and I am not going to say anything to the other Brothers. I know. But neither my immediate superiors, nor the governing Council know. And I am not going to use this against you either now or in the future."

"How do I know? You have something of a…reputation."

Alex tugged on his long beard, and then pointed at my chest. He was leaning forward, his demeanour far from the gifted manipulator I imagined him to be in these circumstances.

"I know you do not like me, Brother. I guess you know me, or think you do. We really don't know each other. If we did, we would be more forgiving than we are. Maybe I have too many faults to ever be liked by someone as honest as you. But I am not here to make you like me. Neither am I here to make allies or to control your fate. Such control lies in the hands of God. I do not want that kind of responsibility. But I do believe this - and I have spent a considerable time with the Lord on this one - I do believe you have a calling to this life. And I do believe that, if you decide to pursue this calling, you will do much good. There, I have said it. You have a month or so. Then, I have little doubt the rumour mill will begin to grind out fresh food for consumption. Remember this too, Brother, it is unfortunate that a place such as this has pairs of eyes everywhere. But it does. The Brothers do not deliberately spy on one another. We are here to love each other, believe it or not, in as much as our human frailty allows. The fact that we go on is something of a miracle, I often think. But you simply cannot be too careful. No really, I mean it. You have to be more careful. For instance, all I did was ask in passing, in passing I tell you, had anyone seen you, and there you had it. Three of the Brothers gave me the same sightings of you…three…"

He held up three slim whitish pink, perfectly manicured digits. These were hands that had never done anything other than pray, hold a pen, or reluctantly touch another hand in friendship. And, at that point, Brother Alex's phone started ringing again. I was reeling from the impact of what had been said.

"I think that will be all, Brother. Take your time. Let the Lord guide you. And come back to me if you need anything. And, if you are not going to keep an appointment, leave me a message. I am very busy."

"Yes Brother, I mean Father."

He picked up the phone.

"Brother Frank?"

"Yes Father?"

"Fix this problem. Somewhere there is a clock ticking on it. Oh, you should get something to eat. And take the evening off. You don't look well."

"Yes Father."

Chapter Thirteen

Lisa

Until Frank resolved things, I knew I had to be discreet, no matter how much I hated the charade. Like anyone who didn't really understand life, I hankered after honesty and truth, at first. Then, because of all the grief and pain, I wised up. Until I wised up, I hated deceit, especially when it came to love. Now, I know love and deceit are inseparable.

I grew up in a happy, comfortable, stable home, where Mother and Dad stayed together and loved each other and were discreet about their affairs. They were so discreet I was twenty three years old before I realised Dad had girlfriends, or maybe one girlfriend. Perhaps I should have felt angry and hurt. Or I should have felt betrayed. I don't know for sure. He had a heart attack two days before his fifty- third birthday. I was coming into visit him in hospital after a late shift in the library and, as I turned down the corridor where his room was, I saw a slim woman in jeans and grey hair leave his room. She seemed in a hurry. I ran after her. I don't know why I did it. I had this desperate need to know her. I stopped her just as she was about to get into the lift. As I stopped her and held her, I remembered all the security cameras, and having stopped this slim attractive woman, I had technically committed an assault.
"Sorry," I said. "I'm sorry to trouble you."
She had the bluest eyes. I think I loved her once I saw those eyes. I remember her eyes because I recognised them again when I saw Frank's eyes. Frank had her eyes. Blue as an azure sky. Blue as lapis lazuli. I knew immediately Frank and I were meant to be together when I saw his eyes, so unconventionally magnetic.
When I saw his eyes, I remembered hers. She had the aura of a bohemian professor of a Midwestern university who had narrowly missed winning a Pulitzer in her younger more radical, literary days - that kind of breezy assertiveness only the gifted and disappointed bring to their dealings with life. I looked at her and felt myself smiling. I was so attracted to her, irresistibly drawn. From her combed back hair, her full lips, her fair skin, her slim body, from that sensual, intelligent, happy world, she smiled. And I smiled too.
"So you're Lisa."
"And you are?"
"Kathy. I am a friend of your father. From work. I hear he is going to be

fine. That's great news, don't you think?"

"Of course," I said.

As if I had a choice to do anything other than agree with her. No, I thought, I would really prefer Dad would die there in his hospital bed five days after his heart attack, two days after his fifty-third birthday. I made my excuses and left Kathy. In Dad's room, Jeanette was sitting talking to him. She had flown over from England that day. Being a doctor, she was filled with doctorly concern and tears. She had spent much time talking over his charts with other doctors, and was now distributing sage advice to a man she never really got on with. In the far corner sat my other sister, Philippa. She was even less prepared for this than I was. Suddenly, the strongest among us was the weakest. Philippa, the corporate lawyer, sat crushed with fear and grief. She looked at me with tear stained eyes and smiled weakly.

"Mother will be along soon."

"Okay. How are you doing?"

"Badly. Is he going to be okay?"

"I think so. I heard he will. This will pass, so they say,"

"Did you meet Kathy? She works with Dad."

"I met her just at the lift door. Nice lady."

"I didn't like her at all." Philippa stood up and went to the door.

"Do you want a hot chocolate or a sandwich?" Jeanette asked indiscriminately. I nodded, having forgotten how hungry I was. Dad was sleeping and we knew Mother would ask to spend time alone with him.

"I'd love one."

"I'm going to dinner after this. Fancy a bite? My treat, I insist."

"Sure. That would be great, Philippa. I love the jacket, by the way…"

"What about Mother?"

"I asked her. She said she had already eaten."

I sat down beside Dad. He looked so weak. His face looked ashen. I held his hand and started to cry like the others. I understood. I knew, somehow, from the impact of meeting Kathy, that I am too like my father to ever really judge him. I never mentioned my suspicions to either of my sisters. It was unthinkable to them that he would ever be unfaithful to Mother. It was unthinkable to mention it, or to imagine Mother would be unfaithful to him.

So, when I think about inviting Frank over for dinner now, I know the kind of evening that would ensue. On the surface everything would go splendidly. Dinner is dinner in my parent's home. They serve the good stuff. Mother is the cook. She would ring me up in work and ask me what Frank normally eats. Dad is the wash-up person. The food is good food well cooked. Talk? Dad's got a repertoire of excellent table talk. Mother tells long stories rather well. They always involve members of the family other than me. I shelve books. And the evening would pass off flawlessly. And then they would ask, in their kind warm inquiring way, the inevitable question:

'What is it that you do, Frank? Eh, Frank? What are you about?' Implying – 'if our daughter is to date you, you have to pay. You need a position. We need your co-ordinates on the socio-economic scale. We need a flow chart, some projections as to where you see yourself going career-wise. After all we have her vital statistics. We know her future is, shall we say, somewhat limited. Not like her sisters. They made something of their lives. Lisa has issues. And how far is someone going to go on a librarian's salary?'

Having established my mediocrity, my failure in every imaginable aspect of life, they would await Frank's answer. I imagine the answer Frank would give.

'I am a monk,' he would say. 'And a career in God lasts an eternity. God takes care of his own. He sends cheques and sage financial advice. God looks after every part of creation. He will take care of Lisa and me.'

But Frank is not a monk. He is a member of a religious order. That is not the same thing. He would say he explains his position in the world as a monk to make things simpler. People don't understand the culture. And then, the silence at the dinner table. Good God, who is our daughter having sex with? Mother would be tucking into her pasta. Dad would be dawdling over his potatoes and eyeing the wine bottle, because he would want another glass, to Mother's disapproval, because of his heart condition and bypass surgery, and I would be looking across at Frank, and Mother and Dad would be looking at the glances being exchanged between Frank and me and the hypocrisy of it all. But Frank would be game for it, if I suggested. Needless to remark, like a good member of the family, I have kept the secret of Frank's identity. I am the Lois Lane to his Clark Kent. And I have never suggested dinner with Mother and Dad.

I know the relentless desire to change people is a symptom of one's own problems. But looking here at this church, this service, these praying people, this dead friend of Frank, there are so many things I want to change. People should listen. We tried to tell Joe important things. That we were in love. That it was something that happened, despite all the obstacles in our way. I think of Joe who wouldn't listen and it reminds me of my parents. Frank had Joe as a parent. Mother and Dad have each other. I have them. We are all tied up. It's like bondage. People like to torture each other. A little torture releases anger and frustration and disappointment, keeps the critical mass of hate at bay. Dad nurtured his delusions of grandeur, thinking himself unappreciated by his bosses, walking out of jobs until he found one where he was a small fish in a smaller pond. Dad should have done so much better. He had so many degrees and qualifications. There was always another qualification he needed to feel worthwhile. There was always another lover to take so he might feel good, feel he counted. But nothing satisfied. No increase in salary, no knowledge, no hope. So, after his heart attack, he took a less stressful job. He downsized again to fit in, to survive. Perhaps his sense of inadequacy drove Mother into other people's arms. Mother and Dad forgave each other. I don't know if their children did. Perhaps Kathy understood how unappreciated he felt. Though Mother was always covering for him in company, she resented his lack of real success beyond the merely monetary. Mother maintained the family and stewed in her own frustration.

Thinking about Joe makes me worry about Frank and me. Maybe, I think, he will always be in love with Joe, the love young men have for one another before wives and lovers come along, the love of brother for brother, filled with passion and anger and rivalry, the unrequited love of a gay man for the unattainable other, that first terrible love that rarely passes muster. Maybe I will always come a close second, especially now Joe is gone and soon to be sanctified in Frank's memory. All the bad parts of Joe's personality will be forgotten, how he abandoned Frank and judged him, how cold hearted he could sometimes be, how loveless. I suppose, despite all that, I loved Joe too, in a way. Joe is the reason we stayed together. I wanted Joe to leave and become part of our family, our circle of loved ones. Then, I worried Joe would become the other person in our family, like Kathy was with Mother and Dad. I worried I was suppressing myself to protect Frank, that I was intimidated by his intellect and personality, frightened by Frank's temper. I worried I was attracted to him because he reminded me of my father. I fear his Catholic past just as I fear my own godless past. I fear the differences between us might destroy us.

Now we are left alone in our new house and our life. Mother and Dad hardly ever call. They disapprove of my marriage, always a good sign I think. So, in the end, no summit conference ever occurred. Frank never came to dinner. And, because we were left alone, Frank and I stayed together and my sisters' marriages have not been successful. Perhaps their need to succeed does not translate well into their love lives. One needs to give up all hope to love well. I have never succeeded in anything except with Frank, thanks, in part, to Joe. Now, at Joe's funeral, we look at Joe and looking at his coffin and the prayers and the church and this so very beautiful place, I look at my clothes and see I should have taken in the collar of this black suit. And we look at each other and I see Frank is crying and we see what might have happened to us. We might never have made it this far, if not for Joe.

Chapter Fourteen

Frank

A few weeks after his disappearance, I found out from Bill, who had friends at central command, where Joe had gone.

"Wicklow, boyo, Wicklow"

"I hate when you say boyo. It's so-"

"Accurate?" Bill grinned.

"Condescending, actually."

"My, aren't we in a good mood? Drink your coffee, and, when you've stopped feeling sorry for yourself, I'll tell you the news." Bill looked at me with an indulgence tempered with the parental disapproval of one older and more experienced member of this ancient and venerable institution.

"Wicklow? Why? Wicklow. What's in Wicklow?" I asked.

"Real estate."

"Oh. That makes sense, I suppose. Why wasn't I told about this?"

"Everyone knows. You should gossip more. It's a way to survive in the jungle of our social life."

"I don't—"

Bill interrupted me.

"We have a house down there, boyo. Some old friend of the Order - a millionairess who sold antique furniture. She left property and land down there to the Order. We never sold it. The Order keeps it for people who need to get away quickly. It's a safe house."

"Safe from what or who?"

"I believe Des drove your friend down there himself, Frank."

"That's a bit intimate, isn't it? Des usually doesn't bother with ferrying students who want to get away." I watched Bill move his toast around the sideplate as he stared absently at the table, thinking of an answer.

"I know. Word is Joe has a book he wanted to work on."

"I should have guessed. Are you going to eat that toast?"

"Feel free. It's a tad chilly, though. I'm running late as it is."

"Doesn't matter. Hot or cold. Thanks Bill." I munched on the toast.

"Alex has a problem with that, you know. Joe writing stuff…"

"Just because Alex couldn't do it at Joe's age." I said. Bill shook his head.

"I wonder if that's it, Frank."

"Why?"

I was surprised at Bill. He was rarely in the habit of defending either

Joe or Alex. When he did, it was usually to demean them just a tad. With that prejudice in mind, I wanted to see Bill's perspective for myself. Bill went on:

"I mean, it's not that Alex has anything against intellectual pursuits. Alex wants him to finish his Masters degree, get a Doctorate and spend some time in Rome, doing advanced research, I don't know."

"He wants me to do that too."

"You must be so proud. Almost an equal to Joe. Anyhow, after all that, Joe is to come home to Ireland and teach or write books. But there's no legislating for genius. Those guys do their own thing."

"Sarcasm doesn't become you, Bill. Joe isn't a genius. That's all nonsense. We have loads of Brethren far smarter and better qualified than him. If Joe isn't intimidated by the intellectual firepower in the OHF, he is an idiot. "

"Then you don't know your friend, boyo. I could tell at ten yards he was something special."

"Something special. What does that mean? I mean he hasn't done anything. Reputations, as you above all people know, are dangerous things."

"He tries too hard to fit in, for one thing. Wasting his energy."

"I don't know if I agree with that, you know," I mumbled as I nibbled the last crumbs of toast. Bill nodded and went on with his musings on Joe Finn.

"- and he is acutely aware he is not one of us. Don't you ever feel like you are more like his pet than anything?"

"You say the nicest things, Bill. For fucks sake! A pet!" I got up and put another piece of bread to toast. I was intimidated by Joe enough without Bill needling me on that sensitive issue.

"Sorry."

"I never tried to compete with Joe and I never became his friend for the kudos value. In fact, there is no kudos value. He is a complete outsider. No one really knows what the hell he is doing in the OHF in the first place."

"Perhaps he has a vocation, Frank?"

I hoped desperately none of those statements were true. But because of general paranoia and guilt over Lisa, I saw enemies where none existed. Bill looked chastened. I had never seen him like that. I always felt he was the powerful one. I felt that about most people.

"Frank, I'm sorry. Really."

"Forget it. I'm in a bad mood. Maybe I am too close. Too close to see what's going on between us. Maybe I am his pet."

"No, you're not."

I buttered my toast and poured more coffee, increasingly worried that the monks who came and went might overhear this increasingly intimate discussion. Bill looked anxious to leave, but equally wanted to continue talking. Brethren came and went. A few sat at table with us. Bill lowered his voice as I went on eating.

"No, you're not, his pet I mean. Though, Frank, maybe I wish you weren't as close to him as you are, maybe that's all I want. Maybe I don't think you two are particularly good for each other. I think he suffocates you somewhat, doesn't give you room to bloom. But what can you say to two people bound together like some couple that are poison to one another? Maybe my seeing what seems to be an unequal friendship makes me fear for you, Frank."

"What do you mean unequal friendship?"

Bill put his hand on my shoulder and looked at me with great compassion. I saw how handsome he was, what a decent man he was.

"I think you are in love with the guy, fascinated and enthralled. He has got all the brains and all the money. That's hard to compete with. "

"Look Bill. We are not, Joe and I, you know, intimate or anything, I mean, ever. It's not like that."

"Whatever. I am not concerned at this point."

"But Bill."

"But this thing you two have going, this love, is blinding you to how selfish he is. Joe only cares about his own obsessions. He has no friends. You know that, except you, of course."

"So he is a little selfish, Frank. We're all a bit like that."

"The Order is even more selfish. The Order wants Joe. They want his brains. They won't let you have him. Why do you think they indulge him like they do? Any of the rest of us, who argues like he does, refuses to study and generally makes a nuisance of themselves would be chopped up for dinner."

"Oh, that's just Joe. He's an asshole."

"And Des wants to keep Joe at all costs, like his own personal sacred monster, his saviour, something like that."

"Maybe he wants Joe, eh?"

Bill chuckled at my suggestion.

"Well, He is protecting him, Frank."

"Right, that he is," I muttered. Bill interrupted me.

"Nurturing him. It's creating a lot of resentment among the ranks, especially among the other students. The Central Council were up in arms too. Des was a goose step away from a revolution in the Council. A coup d'etat. Apparently there was blood on the carpet over Joe getting the house in Wicklow for a month or however longer he wants. Stick to beat him with, Des - you see. Crazy. Big fight. I think it's crazy, personally. It's privileged access only. Only the top brass get the house, you see. Des is trying to keep it all a secret, but word is Joe won't play ball on this one. Des wants Joe to lead some kind of revolution."

"That would kill Joe. Joe won't lead anything."

"It would kill us all, Frank. Joe doesn't care about a career. He doesn't want a degree. He has all the contempt of the genius for knowledge, you know."

"I could have told them that," I said. Bill nodded and fondled his coffee cup.

"Apparently Des knows Joe has his own agenda," he said. "Joe did some kind of deal with Des."

"What about exams?"

"He'll be taking them in September."

"Next they'll be sending him to one of their approved therapists. Try and break him down a bit."

"That's a bit...apocalyptic, isn't it, eh Frank?"

I paused for a minute and looked out the window. Then I said: "I imagine so. It's just Joe doesn't trust therapists."

"A lot has happened since Freud."

"So? What the hell does that mean?"

"So if you're right, and that's what he thinks of therapy, imagine what he thinks of religion? This is all one big game, a deception. I don't even know if Joe is a true believer."

"I think he is, Bill, really. A lot more than I am."

"It doesn't matter anyway, if Joe comes up with the goods, everyone is happy."

"Come up with what goods? What do they want with Joe?"

I felt angry at myself, angry that I hadn't figured this out before, angry that my own blindness and trust in the brethren that politics were afoot.

"You see, Frank, clever people are ten a penny. People like me are ten a penny. I always did well in exams, always got along. Clever people, they go to school and they go to college and they are respected and they get a good job, a career in professionaldom, like me for instance, or whatever. That will never happen with Joe Finn. He is too gifted, too troubled. He will never have a nice safe career. He will always upset the applecart. Des sees that. Alex sees it and resents it. He wants to shut Finn down. So Des has his chance to use Joe."

"There are no gurus. Don't you listen to Van Morrison?"

Bill grinned.

"Neither Des nor Alex would agree with Van the Man. Joe, well. He has real imagination. He can combine fact with accurate vision. You know that."

"Joe doesn't want that. He just wants to find God. He doesn't like himself much."

"Joe is a guaranteed win-win situation for the Order, so long as he stays healthy and productive."

"I didn't know," I said.

"Didn't know what?"

"What they wanted from Joe. That he was their meat puppet."

"He isn't, Frank. I don't think they intended any of this. From what I can gather this is between Des and Alex. Des is going through some kind of crisis, a breakdown of sorts. He has wanted to set up a separate powerbase from Alex for years now. But he hasn't been able to find the right ideology to do it. I think Joe is part of that agenda. Alex has all his books and nurtures all the young intellectuals. If Joe writes something new, then Des can bring this new literary gem to the Council and say 'Look what I have done!'"

"It's a total fantasy on Des' part, Bill. Don't you think?"

"It's Desmond's own personal act of political suicide. On the other hand, Joe might, you know. He just might do it."

"If he does, it won't be what they want to hear."

"Do we ever really want the truth? Des is weary of the political savagery."

"Aren't we all?"

"Each side has their own people. No one is sure of anything. I'm not sure of anything." Bill looked at his watch. "Good heavens, man! I have to say Mass down at the convent."

"But, Bill, you have just eaten."

"So what?"

"What about the hour's fast before receiving the Eucharist?"

"So, I'll give an especially long sermon."

Bill left the table. Then he turned and looked me in the eye.

"By the way, what's this gossip I hear about you?"

"You know it's true, Bill." I looked at him for a long time. His default friendly smile faded. He looked troubled.

"I see. If you need."

"I know where your rooms are, Bill. Go and give your long sermon. God has a stopwatch you know."

Bill grinned and rushed out. I munched my toast and looked around the busy kitchen. Some of my fellow students sat down and we talked for a while.

I had, by that stage, unknown to myself, withdrawn emotionally from life in the Monastery of the Seven Towers. I had my own life, one that intersected at various points with my religious life. It was rather like a relationship one knows is beginning to fail but one goes on until one has the strength to make the break. I listened to my fellow students and thought about Joe. In time, one picks up the details. In time, I learned Joe brought few, if any, supplies with him to the house in Wicklow. It was all laid on, and, according to Bill's elaborate, resentful description of the place, it was beautiful and richly furnished with genuine Victorian fixtures and fittings, situated near the sea, along a coast road, away from everything that might prove a distraction. Des and Joe did shopping along the way and the fridge and freezer had been filled. Joe was urged to eat at least one full meal in the day. Joe ate little at the best of times, and slept less. I imagined him trying to sleep in the master bedroom and hating the opulence. He hated the opulence in his parents' house as his father's wealth grew and his mother's resentment of it grew in equal measure as she retreated into religion. I imagined Joe working and drinking into the small hours, surrounded by books and articles and pages and pages of notes, or maybe working in his bed with a Proust-like self enclosed hiding space, trying to write something, only to be endlessly disappointed by what he produced. He told me later he attended daily Mass at six in the morning in the local church, remained afterwards to say daily office, returned to the house, made breakfast, then sat down to write approximately three thousand words per day. I didn't believe a word of it. He was too haphazard a worker for such Wagnerian disciplined productiveness - no pre-manuscript outline, followed by a pre-draft, followed by a finished sequence, followed by countless copied corrected manuscripts, until the final perfect piece of art emerged from his emaciated depths. But still, he produced something. At the end of his stay he had the guts of a slim volume. As he never showed me the manuscript, I have no idea what it was about. Some rumoured it was so controversial that it denied the divinity of

Christ. Others say it was a study of comparative religions, something which found particular mosaic roots in ancient Egyptian religions. Finally, I have heard it was none of the above, but a book of prayer, a devotional work that Joe had been working on for some time, but never finished.

I never really forgave him for not taking me into his confidence and allowing me share in his creative endeavour. I denied my resentment over this and portrayed myself to myself as the frustrated friend, the supportive, understanding companion, who understood from a distance, the vagaries of the creative process. I did this partly out of guilt over my affair with Lisa, partly because I wanted to find some way of reconciling the irreconcilable, heaven and earth, Lisa and my life as a monk, Joe's enmeshment in the matrix of the Order's troubled political life. I wanted to find some way of deciding on the right thing to do. And, all the while, life went on around me. While my friends continued with their lives, I desperately wanted things the way they were before. I knew that was impossible, but I oscillated wildly between hope and despair.

Joe came back on a dead Sunday afternoon, twelve weeks after he initially disappeared. For me and some of my fellow Brothers, he had just gone and disappeared. To the powers that be, he had taken a long break for the sake of his health. That Sunday I was scheduled to answer the door and the phone as part of my duties. I was to have the evening off and had decided to see a movie later on. I was sitting in the front office listening to the radio when, through the smoky glass partition, I saw the front door open. In came Joe in a pair of jeans and a t-shirt that had the words 'Hardcore Pawn' written on it. I came out of the office, walked over to him and hugged him. He looked ill, underfed, and his blond hair was too long. I also noticed the beginnings of a beard on his face that added to his overall post-imprisonment demeanour, and, for the first time, I saw tiny lines around his eyes and at the edge of his lips. Seeing those tiny signals of decay on his face disturbed me. This face should be perfect. Flawless. Not thin and angular with thin lips. His eyes should be clear, untroubled. Not as though he had seen something terrible, eyes like some shell shocked trooper. I had idolised him, and there, on his face and in his eyes I saw the first refusals of my friendship, the first signatures of the end. He had gone away and told me nothing. He had written something, probably something difficult and significant, and had told me nothing about it. Moreover, he wasn't able to understand that I had fallen in love with Lisa. But I knew I had fallen in love with him too, but with him it was different. I imagined that for Joe, so long as I loved only him, I was accepted. So long as I depended on him, I was accepted. But then I knew I was hiding my culpability, my sin, my betrayal of the ideals of the Church and the Order, by blaming him for being arrogant and narcissistic and cripplingly needy. I imagined I could argue that it was not only I who had changed, not only I who had started thinking outside the Order's credos, not only I who sought escape. I debated all these arguments obsessively, but when I came to Joe it was not a question of winning arguments. It was a question of keeping friends by any means necessary. I was as anyone who is in love. I was afraid of rejection. I was afraid of being left alone and adrift in the universe, cut off from him, from Lisa, from Mother Church.

Chapter Fifteen

Joe

I went down to Wicklow, to this palatial so called cottage bequeathed by the unfortunately named Mrs Barnabas Jones, art collector, spiritual zealot, and onetime husband of Barnabas Jones of Jones and Wilkinson and Associates, corporate lawyers for steel magnates, before he tragically died on a golf course ten years before Mrs Jones succumbed to cancer. She bequeathed the house, through Alex, to the Order of the Holy Field. That's how I got to go there for three months in obscene self-indulgence while I wrote about Giovanni Seipi, who lived a life of exemplary abstemious self-sacrifice for the love of Jesus Christ. I drank a lot of champagne and worked. In the evenings I wandered the beautiful ghostly woods surrounding lakeside cottage. There I watched the squirrels and the foxes and thought over the life of Giovanni Seipi. My imbibing of the house supply of champagne annoyed Des when he found out.

"It's expensive stuff. Only for special occasions."

"Sorry about that. Champagne is a weakness of mine."

"I don't give a damn! Stay away from the champagne stash!"

Obviously the stash belonged to Des. I drank most of it anyway. I reasoned in the way all alcoholics reason that I was involved in some very thirsty work. And I was. One cannot think normally and proceed with the insanity that I was immersed in. My Giovanni Seipi believed it was the freaks who shall inherit the earth, not the meek. The Gospels prophesy love for the unloved, riches in heaven for the poor, justice for the abused. The dead live and the lost are brought back from the living hell of separation from God. I look for these things on this planet. I looked for these things inside me and in others. I saw little of it. No love filled longing. No tears and prayers and eternal contemplative seclusion will change what I have failed to witness. Rather, I see a new world order, a world where the planet will be unified under one ruling body that will transcend state and creed and ethnic origin. And, in preparation for it all, farseeing right living responsible parents send their children to school and to college and the children become part of the machine of state-sponsored, acquisitive, militaristic capitalism. Giovanni Seipi was once such a good son. Then, he gave up his life and found God. He rejected the life of good citizenry, a stable loving home, and became his own person without meaning to and became what he called a child of God. But Church and State have twisted his message and turned him into a good little child of Church and State. His life is a clarion call to give up and find ourselves once again. Only those mad enough to think differently, the slackers and the dropouts and the travellers, those who loathe this cold competitive empty western life, really have a chance of surviving. Hence my champagne and my seclusion. It is not the meek who shall inherit this earth. It is the freak, the deviant, the lost that the Christ - the real anointed one - "no Godhead but all too human", will go seeking. The freak shall inherit the earth. Only the freaks will be left after we destroy ourselves. And I know I am not one of them. It kills me to admit such a thing. No pun intended. I am part of the establishment. It can't be helped. They have me. The matrix of the establishment has me. The establishment will only let me live if I sustain it, begin the renaissance in the Order, produce something that will bring us back to the truths of our founders, effect a reformation. And I cannot do it. All I have is my beloved Giovanni Seipi. Not that I haven't tried to serve them, do what they want. I have done the heavy lifting. I have searched and researched and I can't give them the answer I know they want. And yet I have vowed obedience. I take such vows seriously. But I find little of value in what the founders of the Order of the Holy Field have written or what my superiors want. They want change on their terms, which is really no change at all. There is much of value in what Giovanni Seipi did in his life, mostly because of his phobias and psychoses. Once he began to abandon any rational thought and behaviour, his life finally came together in one great incoherent whole. Most of what he did has since been washed of any real significance by subsequent writers, enveloping him into the fairy land world of Christian right thinking, mummified by scholarship, dulled by cliché, poisoned by idolatry. It has been turned into propaganda about following the teachings of the Gospels, about charity to our brothers and sisters in Christ, resisting temptation, about poverty, chastity and obedience, but little of substance, and so very little about solving the problems of life. And this is how we live in the Church. Reality is for lesser mortals. We have the truth, after all - something bigger than measurable, logical, perceptible reality. The Church has survived much in the same way the Order has survived. It has turned its saints into public relations exercises. The Church has survived not because it has dedicated itself to the perfection of its members. It has achieved limited success in that endeavour, a monumental understatement, I think. The Church and the Order have survived not because it has necessarily behaved honourably in its dealings with people. It has committed horrific atrocities. It has damaged its members at times irrevocably. The Church has survived through the millennia because of its power and influence. It has survived by remaining identified with the ultimate good, no matter what questionable deeds it perpetrated. The Church is at one with God, thus anything is permitted. Thus, if one believes in God, then one believes in the Church. If one identifies with Christ, one identifies with the Church. One will do anything to protect the one thing of value: the ultimate good. Humanity, with all its failure and corruption, is therefore a secondary consideration, and remains dedicated to the one true good: the perpetuation of the Church. The same is true of the Order of the Holy Field as the Church in microcosm. Despite its failings it remains the Church in miniature, working in the field of the Lord, serving the poor and seeking life eternal, despite the shortcomings of its members.

To escape this one needs to leave the world of church or state or religion. One needs to leave normality as one knows it and embrace eccentricity as the one true faith, as Giovanni Seipi, the freak who inherited the earth, did. By this, I mean a radical turning away from the demands and expectations of society and the world, of religion and politics, and embracing one's true identity before God, following the example of Giovanni Seipi, assuming God only really knows us. But the Church killed him. They took him away from his freedom. They killed him by the walls they built around him. They wrote sanitised biographies of him. I know what that is like. In this matter, I have failed. In this matter, it is Frank, not I, who has the true advantage. It is Frank who is the true freak. I see him jettisoning this craven acquisitive spiritual life. I see him leaving everything behind, God, the Church, and friendships. And, knowing him as I do, I know there is nothing to quite match the exquisite loneliness of those who are different, those who know that there is little they can do to explain how, by what pattern of events, they have become so much the other that they have become the object of derision or fear or anger by others. I could trace these events in my own life, a dubious autobiography, as all autobiographies are dubious activities, written by those who fear the erasure of death, the abyss of being forgotten. I am so different I cling to belonging. It is not without significance that Wagner conceived his own autobiography at a time in his life when he was uncreative, penniless, and felt himself abandoned by his friends, which, in Wagner's case, probably meant that only a few kings and queens were answering his letters. Biographers are the skilled propagandists of the literary community. They interpret the lives of past luminaries according to current tastes and political predispositions. Critics are the gatekeepers. They decide who remains fashionable, and who is rejected for the new modern time. And we are the sheep who follow these blinkered shepherds. It is no wonder we are lost.

I came back from Wicklow ill, bitter, and with a biography of the founder of the Order of the Holy Field for the most part written. I was hard done by to keep a civil tongue in my head when I saw Frank acting as doorkeeper. I had gone away to avoid him. And there he was, waiting for me. Despite myself, I had thought often of him.

I had spent night after night in that Wicklow house, in that big four poster bed in various states of drunkenness and stonedness trying to get to sleep. I kept hearing noises. I kept getting flashbacks. Moments from my past rising up like ghosts, making me toss and turn no matter how much I drank. Then I would spend hours enraged, angry at tiny moments of feeling ignored or slighted by the Brethren, angry at my parents, angry at my little petty ordered world. Things that had never been such an object of hatred before now hurt like a tumour. I was looking for things outside to objectify my suddenly uncontrollable frustrations. I focused my frustrations into my biography of Giovanni Seipi, our Order's founder. There was, after all, so much to focus on. He became my father and I sought to kill him, as all artists kill their father. The prospect of returning to that repressive place, that world of intrigue of the Monastery of the Seven Towers, was too much for me. But I had to go back. I was too tired to work any more. I only had a little mechanical writing left. In my exhausted state, I needed a quiet regular life once more. Then, Frank hugged me as I stood in the hall of the Monastery of the Seven Towers and I managed an anaemic smile, remembering how angry I still was with him. Usually I made an effort when he hugged me. That Sunday I didn't. He embraced me and felt the cold I felt inside and stepped back with a hurt confused look in his eyes.
"Welcome back."
"Thanks."
Then suddenly he was embarrassed. "Sorry," he said.
I told him I was very tired, that I had forgotten my sleeping pills that I was going upstairs to take one and sleep for the night. I would be better in the morning. But I hadn't forgotten any pills. I brought them all with me. I knew I would not feel better in the morning. I would

only feel rested. The manuscript would not solve the problem. It would only serve to make matters worse. I knew that. I had gone away to free myself, to give the Order a peace offering, a reason to let me work in an atmosphere of creative freedom. Instead, I had typically committed creative suicide by killing off Giovanni Seipi. With Giovanni Seipi, myth and history have largely become indistinguishable. Myth has become history. History has become dogma. Dogma has become edict. But I disliked not him, but what they, the writers and hagiographers, had done to him. His sainthood has become a license to annihilate our humanity. I disliked his pride disguised as humility, his indifference masked as compassion, his self-love masked as altruism. He was a lost soul looking for nirvana, and, down through the centuries, countless other orphans, lost souls, have found a similar home working in the field of the Lord. He gathered together a group of wandering mendicant penitents he called his Order of the Field of the Lord, eventually starving himself to death because the Brethren began to live in houses paid for by a local bishop. It became impractical for five hundred men and women to live in fields and ditches. They were getting ill and dying young, something too romantic for words, something even the holy founder must have found deeply upsetting. The numerous miracles attributed to Giovanni Seipi, eventually leading to his canonisation, remain unsubstantiated. Having read accounts of his life, to me the miracle was that he survived his childhood. His writings are dubiously sourced. Basically anyone in or around him, could have written them. It is not clear he was literate. All in all, I painted an unclear slightly twisted portrait of the founder of the Holy Field, the twisted image reflected by the sources around him. I embarked on the exercise to try to love him, to try to find a focus for my life. I did find love for him, but not the Giovanni Seipi everyone else knew and loved. I knew when I had finished the manuscript there would be trouble when they read it. They will want something they can give to the Council, something they can publish. And I don't know if they would want this published. Their reach rarely exceeds their grasp. I don't know if I want it published. I don't know what to do anymore. The distance between what I think I know and a clear course of action shaped the greatest chasm.

Chapter Sixteen

Lisa and Frank

I broke up with Frank because he couldn't decide between me and the Order of the Holy Field. I broke up with him because I couldn't take the lies and the hiding and the endless tension we lived under. I broke up with him because the heartbreak was killing me. I broke up with him because I wanted us to be like any other couple I knew of. I wanted him to be someone who would go with me to dinner at a friend's house and talk like anyone else. I broke up because being with him while he was a member of the OHF was the loneliest place in the world for me. I had him as a lover and yet I never really had him. For months we had argued about this. For months I felt I couldn't take it any more. Finally I knew I couldn't. The slightest thing started the same argument. It was always there, always latent in every thought, word and deed that passed between us. When I was fired by Alex from working in the library, it was by letter and no explicit reason was given. But Frank and I knew it was because of our relationship.

"So what do you think?"

"I'm sorry they fired you. You can sue."

"You have got to be kidding. I wasn't hired to have sex with you. I was hired to get the OHF library in order."

"No, I'm not kidding. You should sue them. Then they have to prove they know about us. And they can't fire you for having sex with me."

"You will have to lie."

"My, how will I ever manage to lie?"

"Don't. Jesus Frank."

After all I have so little practice lying. So, I'll lie-"

"Don't do this Frank."

"My entire life is a lie. Every time I open my mouth-"

"Which is a sin. It's a sin to lie."

"I know."

"So you'll lie under oath for me."

"Why is this such a big deal? Lisa? It'll never come to that."

"Why?"

"Because they will settle. They are swamped with scandals. It's all kept underneath. They don't want any more negative publicity. They will pay you the balance of what they owe and that will be that. You get to pay off your debts in one fell swoop."

"How did they find out? Was it Joe?"

"I have an idea who told them. Joe is away now. Rumour has it he is writing a book."

"About time he did something with that brain of his. Whenever I see him now he's either drunk or stoned. Or both. He reminds me of my sister when she was an intern. Why don't they do an intervention or something?"

"They like the dysfunctional genius. God knows he might do something dangerous if he was functional. Brains are overrated. It leads to misery and isolation and misunderstanding and-"

"Do I detect a hint of self pity, Brother Frank?"

"I was taken aside by Alex. He gave me one of his friendly warnings. That guy knows how to terrorise."

"Maybe you're scared of him and he played you."

"No, it was like psychological warfare. And he was so polite about it."

"I don't care about that. He is right. You need to decide. Frank, I can't go on like this. Why are you here? It's two in the morning. You come here and you stay with me. Once we made love, now we fuck and you complain about the Church and go back to your life of servitude and obedience. It's insane. You are a slave. They have you! I hate this. I hate to see you like this, so arrogant, so sure of your independence, of how right you are, when all the while they own you. This is not a life. I feel more lonely after you leave than I ever thought imaginable. I feel more empty since we got together then I ever did. I feel empty because I know I am in love and we are not lovers, not any more."

"I don't want to argue about this."

"Why not?

"I can't."

"You are actually going to have to make an effort to answer."

"I have exams."

"Fuck you. Exams. They aren't even finals. Your finals are two years away."

"I know."

"Frank, we have to talk. We have to talk! We have to! We have to!"

"I don't want to get into the verbal ping pong. I hate it. It's torture. Nothing comes of it."

"Nothing comes of it because you won't do the right thing. You don't have the balls!"

"Fuck you. It takes a lot to come here, be with you, and steal away so no one knows."

"Frank, I don't want to be the other woman. I won't be the other woman. I won't be like my Mother. I can't."

"Please stop. You are not your Mother, and I am not your Father. I'm not betraying you by being in the OHF."

"My Mother was the other woman."

"I know. You told me about your parents' affairs. I'm sorry."

"Frank I can't go on. This is wrong. This is a lie."

"It's unavoidable."

"Of course it's avoidable."

"Yes, well you are not your Mother, are you?"

"My Dad was married to someone and in love with someone else. I don't want to end up like my Mother."

"I know! Okay? You don't need to drill this information into my head! This is torture, absolute torture. Jesus!"

We looked away from each other, nervous of the anger and the hurt and the frustration welling to the surface. We were both a little drunk. I was drunker then he.

"This I do know about you, Frank Ryan – there is no talking to you. There are some things you cannot hear. Are you going to tell me to stop shouting? Worried someone might hear?"

I had him by the shoulders. He shook me off.

"I think you need to give me time. Please it's late. I have exams coming up."

"No! We are always on your schedule! This ends now. Now!"

"You are the one telling me to keep it down." He said, a tiny smile narrowing his lips. He pointed to the wall. "As you said, they will start banging on the wall. Your apartment walls are thin."

"Fuck the walls! Fuck the neighbours! Fuck you. Fuck everything. Fuck this sick fucked up life you live. It's a lie and it's making a lie of you. It's not a life! It's a disease! You are a smug bastard. Now I know why you stay in the OHF. It's not because you think God is calling you, it's because it gives your ego such a boost. That's why you can't commit. It's too cosy not to!"

"I'm going. I can't take this! See you around. Bitch!"

I grabbed him by the arm.

"If you loved me you would choose. You would make some kind of choice. If you loved God you would choose. Don't make me the villain of your life. You always were free…"

"Nobody is free. We all have our chains. I have my chains. The OHF. I chose them first and I have to be given time. I'm sorry."

It was then I knew it was the end. It felt as if all the air in the room drained away. We have just lost cabin pressure. Oxygenate. I looked Frank in the eyes, and yet knew this was not the Frank I knew. This must be what he is like with his Brothers: distant, cold, cynical, disconnected, and yet superficially friendly. This was not the sensitive vulnerable man boy I had gotten to know. I thought, 'I knew this would happen, but not so soon. I always do this. I always choose unavailable men. God I hate myself for being so stupid.'

"It's all about you, isn't it Frank?"

"No it fucking isn't just about me! It's just more complicated than what you're making it out to be."

"You won't come over during the day. According to you everyone's talking about us. We don't go to shows. We don't go for dinner. We don't go out. I'm like a whore."

"No, not you're not!"

"Someone you fuck and talk with for a while and then leave behind some salmon and a bottle of champagne. Your time is up, Frank. Time for you to make up your mind. I'm sorry."

"You need to stop pushing. You have to! I, you always exaggerate! You always over dramatise everything. You are always picking fights. Causing friction! You get off on it!"

"Frank, please. Please Frank. Please baby. Please. This is destroying me, not just me, both of us. I need clarity. You won't listen."

"I'm sorry."

"It won't work for us any more. I can't live like this. I can't fight God."

"Fight God? Who said anything about fighting God?"

"I did Frankie, I did."

"Lisa, I don't know what I believe any more. And don't Frankie me! Fuck Frankie!"

"I think belief is a choice."

"That's garbage. I've so many doubts about everything. I'm too confused to decide."

"Do you love me?"

"I love you. Do I choose to love you? Is it a choice?"

"Look at me. Frank?"

"I love you."

As he said this Frank looked away, just for a second, and then looked back. We had been holding hands as we sat together on my sofa. I saw he looked away. I started to cry.

"What? What?" He looked alarmed because of my tears.

I stood up and walked around my apartment waving my arms like a lunatic. Then I stopped, folded my arms and stared hard into his eyes and said

"You couldn't love me and treat me this way. I won't be that woman"

"What woman, what?"

I was about to answer. Then I stopped. I had all the answers ready for him. I had thought it all out. About how love was a choice and if he loved me then he would make a choice. That living between two worlds was destroying him and me. That something had to give, that our healths were suffering. But I didn't. I was too tired. I was too sick at heart and hurt and lonely and angry and frustrated from repeating myself. I had told him so many times how I felt and he hadn't heard me. Then Frank, worn out from study and the overwhelming sense of having lost control of his life, exploded in rage at me.

"Jesus! Jesus! I'm tired of arguing. All we do is argue! All you do is tell me how you can't go on like this. You can't imagine what it's like for me."

"You can't imagine what it's like for me. I never expected to get trapped inside some fucking family cliché."

"I'm sorry, Lisa. It's guilt. And it's shame. The guilt and shame and the fear that at any moment they might see us."

"I hate you. I wish I was dead."

"I had this life and although it might be ridiculous to you."

"You are ridiculous. You are a castrated man. You have no balls."

"It was a life I loved, a good life to lead. I helped people. I worked in hospitals and clinics and I helped people with addictions and all kinds of problems and I did it for a long time before you and I met."

"You don't need God to help people. Just basic decency."

"This was something I wanted to do. I had chosen it freely."

"Chosen freely. Love of God. Good for the team. What am I, your fucking cheerleader?"

"And I had no doubts but that I was doing the right thing. No I didn't."

"Yes you did. You're Catholic. You know how to fool yourself."

"And now I don't know anymore. I don't know what to do. I don't know the difference between the good I do and the good anyone else does…"

"Good is good."

"I know. We were told differently, that what we did was special."

"I don't know about that. Sounds like the party line. I think you should think about that."

"All we do is argue."

"Wow, you noticed, eh?"

"Lisa I think we-" Frank tried to calm himself. "I want us to resolve this," he said, "I want things to be back to the way things were."

"You're dreaming, man. Wake up! This can't be fixed with talk. We talk in circles. And every circle is a downward spiral. It was never like this before. Not like this! It was never this bad. It never hurt like this. I never felt this bad, this sad, this fucking dead! Sad. I've had it."

"I'm sorry."

"It's so easy for you to say sorry. You like your guilt..."

"Don't. Please Lisa, please don't-"

"I think you should go. Please go."

"I don't want to go."

"I, I think you should. Now!"

"I love you."

"I love you too."

"Please stop crying. Lisa, Lisa, I'm sorry."

"Okay, okay. Just go. Get out! Out!"

"I'm sorry. I'm sorry."

"I don't think we should."

"Okay."

"I can't take this anymore. Go Frank."

This heartbreak, I thought. 'I won't have this argument anymore. No more sleepless nights. No more wondering if you'll call or not. No I can't do it.' Frank took me in his arms as though holding me might repair this disintegrating fraying connection, this dark terrifying realization of what had already been lost. He looked into my eyes with a desperate seriousness.

"I love you and I want to fix this thing first."

"I don't feel well. I feel sick. I want you to go. Please go, Frank. I'll call you..."

I wasn't going to.

"I'm sorry."

"Just go Frank. Please go. Call me in a week. Please think about what I said."

"Okay." Frank took his coat and went to the door.

"I'll see you."

"Okay, then...I..."

"Call me."

"Bye."
"Bye…bye."
The door closed with a soft well oiled click.

Chapter Seventeen

Frank

Being a selfish man, I took great comfort in my misery. Though final exams for my Bachelor degree approached, and, though mountains of carefully written notes awaited review and reflection, I lay on my bed day after day, wept, drank vodka, and listened to music. I thought, 'everyone I know leaves in the end.' It did not cross my mind that I was instrumental in keeping them from getting closer. Knocks came and drifted from my door. Notes were left for me, even one from Alex that I ignored. Not one to be ignored, he came up to me one day in the refectory after I actually managed to eat a little dinner. He smiled. I looked at his skin. For a man of his years, he looked the picture of health. Perfect clear eyes and skin. No body fat. I am developing a paunch, I thought. I hate that. I'm drinking too much.

"Are you all right, Frank?"

"Yes Father."

"You don't look okay to me."

I didn't respond to him. Things had been said, discussions about my well being, well, discussed. But I wasn't going to talk. I looked at him. He had a kindly smile. I managed a smile. Then I just walked away from him. I didn't want to talk. I wanted to go to my room and just lie there till this feeling of death left me like all the rest. But Alex caught up with me. He said,

"I'm sorry to see you in pain. Look, Frank, I don't want to pry."

"Don't, please..." I didn't give a damn what he thought.

"If you need anything call me, okay? This will pass. I know."

He put his hand on my shoulder. He had never touched me before. I looked at his hand. Then I looked him in the eye. He took his hand away.

I said,

"Thanks, Father."

He shook his head sadly, smiled and walked away. Then I went to my room. I poured myself a drink and looked at the ceiling. I shouldn't be drinking alone. I wasn't sleeping. I was lying awake at night, crying, and thinking about Lisa. She had changed her number. When I tried writing her, she returned my letters unopened. So I stopped trying to communicate. I lay there and drank and waited for the feeling of rage and hate and acedia and desolation to lift. I hated her. Then I missed her. Then I wanted to die. Then I wanted to pray. I wondered who had told the authorities. I suspected Joe. Joe had abandoned me too, away writing whatever it was he was writing. I was alone. I wondered if friendship and love are illusions. I wondered if we are all really alone. Perhaps this connection we feel with others is another construct of the mind. I took comfort in the notion that everyone else is delusional and waited for this feeling to pass.

Two months later, I had stopped drinking. I had begun to sleep and prepare for my exams. Then, Joe Finn walked into the main hall of the Monastery of the Seven Towers, in jeans and a t-shirt, with his bag of books and his clothes in a rucksack, and his standard issue bad attitude. I was glad. For those first seconds it was good to see him. I forgot all my anger.

"Frank. Good to see you."

"Where were you? You went missing. There were rumours."

"I had to do a job for the Central Council."

"What kind of job?"

"I can't talk about it. Not now. I have a headache. I have to rest."

"You don't look so good."

"An extended period of intense concentration. I need to sleep. I'll talk to you soon."

I went to embrace him. He pulled away from me.

"Whats going on? Joe?"

"Nothing."

"Give me a hug, then."

"No."

I looked at him. He had always been reticent about contact. Noli me tangere. But I ached. I missed Joe. I needed a hug from him, a sense that everything was all right between us, that we could at least work it out. But he wouldn't go there with me. I was angry, still very raw from my recent rejection.

"Fuck you," I said.

"What?" Joe looked shocked.

"Fuck you!" I pushed him hard. He fell back a few steps. He straightened up and went to push past me. I stopped him. He seemed confused.

"Frank, leave me alone! Okay?"

"No, it's not okay. Where have you been? Why have you cut me off? And who the fuck do you think you are thinking you can treat me like some pet. I am your friend, your equal."

"Pet. What the hell are you talking about?

"You can't just dismiss me like a butler when I do something you don't like. Fuck you!"

"I'm tired. I don't want to hug like some charismatic brainwash love bombing session. I am mentally shattered. I have a blinding headache and I am going to sleep."

"Fuck you Joe Finn! You can't do this - give me this tiredness speech crap! What the hell is going on?!"

"My, we need our anger management techniques. Keep your voice down. We are in the front hall. There are people, members of the public, right beside us in these rooms, you know, getting confession or counselling."

"Fuck you for not contacting me for three months!" I hissed through my teeth. I had never given myself permission to be this angry. It felt good.

"I was …. I'm sorry about that."

"You can't do this and expect me to sit idly by!"

"Then don't sit idly by. Go talk to Lisa. She knows all about breaking things up. Now get out of my way!"

I grabbed Joe by his shirt and shook him, right there in the middle of the hall, with all those members of the public pretending not to see.

"Lisa and I broke up."

Joe smiled.

"Ah, now I get it. Look, Frank, I'm sorry, really sorry…but maybe it's for the best…I know it is."

I let go. He stepped back, picked up his rucksack and strode out of the front hall. I shouted after him,

"Have you betrayed me? Eh?"

He didn't answer.

"Have you told them of my sins? Have you?" I went on after him leaving all the money and the phone ringing and came after him, desperately, obsessively looking for some kind of answer, an answer I couldn't give myself.

"They got to you, Joe. Eh Joe? Stop! Stop!"

I caught him. He looked terrified, as though I was going to hit him.

"Tell me, Joe. I'm sorry, sorry about before. I was upset. Please tell me!"

"Listen to me, you lunatic. No one or nothing can fill the void, okay? Whatever childhood trauma you are working out, go find some one else to blame. I'm not your patsy…"

He had shaken me off again and had been walking away all this time, trying to brush me off. We had left the main hallway and turned down the enclosure and had walked to the foot of the stairwell to the common rooms, the guest rooms and the Brethren's rooms. He put down his bags and baggage and turned around and looked at me with an expression of cold savage rage.

"You are being completely paranoid. You know that? I didn't break you and Lisa up."

"You did if you informed the authorities. And you hurt me. Badly. I have been shut out of your life with no explanation."

"You have no idea of the kinds of pressure I am under."

"That's not my fault. Did you tell Alex? Joe? The truth…"

"No. No I didn't."

"Look me in the eye and tell me you didn't sell me out."

My hands were shaking. I was so afraid and angry. I had fantasised about this moment, about confronting Joe. I had imagined what I might say. I had long tried to construct some kind of obsessive compulsive script. Suddenly, my outrage at everyone knowing about my sleeping with Lisa was his fault.

"You did this to me. You fucked everything up. You left without saying a word. To me that spells guilt. You couldn't look me in the eye and tell me you were leaving."

"You talk as though we were engaged or something. I don't owe you anything."

"So it seems, Joe. So it seems."

Some of the Brethren passed. The phone rang in the distance. They greeted Joe.

"Welcome back, Brother Joe."

"Thank you," Joe said. Others passed.

"Luke."

"Joe," Luke nodded.

"Brendan."

Brendan nodded. They passed down the hallway and out the front door, nodding to me. They must have heard me, I thought. I grabbed Joe and pushed him up against the wall, his thinness verging on the insubstantial.

"All I can say is, I hope the book was worth it."

"I said nothing to anyone. Possibly someone saw you. Everyone watches everyone here. That's why we live in groups. It's a corrective measure. If God isn't watching, someone else is."

"That's all one ever gets from you, Joe. Ideas. Nothing useful. You don't make friends. You have alliances against your own isolation. I don't believe you, Joe. I think you told Alex. Then you went off to the house of pain in Wicklow to do a little mental masturbation. I could beat the living crap out of you, you-"

I waved my fist, angrier than I have ever felt in my life. I wanted to kill him. Joe looked coolly at me. This time he didn't flinch.

"I'm going to bed. You're out of your mind, Frank. You need help. The reason why you and Lisa got together is because you never found God and you clung to her and she, because of her needs, found you. It's a relationship of convenience, as most relationships are. I'm sorry others know. It wasn't me. Jesus, I always knew you were-"

"I hope the book was worth it Joe. It cost you a friend. You have no... no heart. You don't let love in so all your ideas have no root in the real. I hope the book is good, Joe. I hope it is, because you'll be paying for it for the rest of your life!"

"Brother! This is outrageous!"

Des appeared on the stairs. I looked at him defiantly. Then, I turned my back on Joe and Des. I stalked away and went back into the office. Des didn't follow, which I thought strange. I expected some type of verbal thrashing for my unwarranted outburst. But he stayed in the outer hallways at the foot of the stairs and entered into some kind of low key discussion with Joe. Then, some of the other Brothers appeared on the stairs. I imagined afterwards that Joe stomped off upstairs to his room. The phone had stopped ringing. Then it rang again. I watched it ring and ring. Eventually it had to stop. I thought it had to end. This has to. Eventually, it has to stop. Maybe it doesn't, but one can always picture things the way they should be. For a while it helps. But only for a while. Then, it starts all over again. Yes, that's it.

Chapter Eighteen

Gerard, Alex, Des, Luke and Peter

With appropriate gravity, the Central Council sat in silence for about thirty seconds. This was the second morning of their week long gathering. It was a gathering that occurred every six months to discuss matters of national importance for the Order of the Holy Field. A copy of Joe Finn's manuscript, For the Love of God the Father – Giovanni Seipi at Home, the next item on the agenda, sat before each of them. Three of the five Brethren had small smiles playing on their lips. No one knew what to say. Alex started the ball rolling.

"I hated it." Everyone looked shocked. Alex grinned. "Only joking. Brother Gerard, what do you think of the text?"

Gerard was Provincial Secretary and Provincial Bursar. He had published several books of mostly devotional poetry in his early thirties. Since then he had worked on editing books for many of the Brothers. Equally, his election to the Council came as a shock to many of the Brothers, mostly due to his enormously timid character and tendency to disappear on drinking binges every year or so.

"I liked it."

His deeply lined face terminated in an extravagantly manicured goatee beard. He lit a forbidden cigarette and smiled to himself. The no smoking ban was generally ignored during Council meetings.

"I liked the manuscript," he said. "It is raw, written by someone showing talent, but needing time and encouragement to develop the style necessary to express his thoughts. I can't say I agree with his findings though…still this is something that will raise the level of debate in the Province. This is something new, fresh…"

Des nodded and was about to say something as Alex chimed in.

"While reading it, "Alex said, "I imagined it had been written from an attitude of genuine honesty, despite its obvious flaws, especially the last two chapters, which were turgid in style and badly researched."

Gerard drew on his cigarette and waved the smouldering butt in the air flamboyantly, joining in with Alex's reserved admiration with less poisonous words. He said:

"I haven't completely made up my mind about it, except to say it would never pass the censor. I think Joe shows, ah well, real promise. I think we need to encourage his, well, his talent and his insights, for all our sakes. Its been a long time since we had someone showing real courage. I think he has made a good attempt to strip away the centuries of re-interpretation of Giovanni Seipi. He has made many mistakes and the style is, well, awful in places. But he has tried to get at what it might have been like to really know Seipi. I think he has done something extremely brave, well, if he were to work on the text a bit. I think, well, we might consider…"

"Brother Gerard is one of our most gifted writers," Alex interrupted.

"That's not true, I have failed as a writer," Gerard smiled embarrassedly. The brethren looked at each other, amazed. Alex continued, ignoring Gerard's discomfort. Alex put his slim hand on the manuscript, and continued speaking.

"And, furthermore, I agree with Gerard. I think an enormous amount of work needs to be done on this manuscript to make it work. No one can doubt Brother Joe's talent, or indeed his intellect. Anyone here who has had the misfortune to argue with him will attest to his intellect. Overall, though, I found the last chapter and a half almost unreadable. It was so densely packed with information and so poorly formed in terms of stylistic direction. This being said, the real problem lies in the conclusion reached by Joe-"

Once more, seeing Alex was trying to destroy any chance of allowing the text through, Gerard interrupted Alex.

"I agree, but, if you kill this text off, you might do irreparable damage to the author. This needs to be handled gently. One doesn't take an axe to this sapling. I think we do that too often."

Gerard raised his hands in a gesture of despair, aware that a decision had long been taken on the fate of the book before them.

A smattering of monastic heads nodded in tacit agreement with both Alex's and Gerard's weighty opinions.

Peter, like Alex, knew Des was behind the text. Gerard didn't care. He didn't want the Joe Finn ruined, though he didn't know Joe, or hadn't spoken to him. The manuscript had done that. For Peter, the manuscript's controversial nature was a stick to beat Des with. Des, after all, had nurtured and protected Joe up to this point. But more than the controversy, the manuscript's immaturity was an even deadlier weapon, one Peter found irresistible.

"Even if we were to agree to its publication with certain changes and emendations, I doubt if it would help the cause of Giovanni Seipi scholarship. Not as it is-" Peter said.

"Hold on Peter. So what if it's wrong? It might be partially right, and mostly wrong. We can put a disclaimer on it, saying we don't agree with its views, or we don't necessarily share the book's views. We need this kind of scholarship. We need to explore new horizons. This is the way forward. If we don't embrace what Joe Finn brings to the order, I fear for our future."

Gerard angrily slapped the table, and then scratched his beard. Some of the brethren jumped. Then they calmed down, and smiled at Gerard's unexpected missionary zeal. Des had watched Gerard and Peter go at each other. Gerard, usually passive, had been greatly exercised by what he read, Des thought. I'm keeping out of this.

Alex, on the other hand, ignored Gerard's comments, not wanting to seem so crass and obvious by openly opposing him, unlike Peter, who was usually brutally frank. Des watched, and still had said nothing. Alex turned to the other Brothers of the Council. They scratched their eyebrows and looked at the text. They hadn't bothered to read it.

"Does anyone else have any opinions on this?"

Gerard turned the pages of the text. No one else seemed too interested. The manuscript had been loosely discussed over coffee before the meeting. It had been the subject of much derision.

"A rather giant ego trip. That boy has an ego the size of Long Island" Luke said. "I didn't get through most of it. Boring. Overwritten. Highly polemic. Frankly I don't see what all the fuss is about."

Peter smiled at Luke, then said: "One hears the word 'genius' spoken too often these days about Joe. I find it distasteful, and somewhat inaccurate."

Gerard said: "I think this text shows what young Finn is capable of realizing. He should have waited a year, maybe two, sat with his thesis and worked it out. What if we tell him we think it needs changes, but we want to go ahead?" he suggested "That, if he agrees to work on the text, we will reconsider?"

Gerard glanced over at Des. He saw how nervous Des seemed. He knew Des knew he had made a terrible mistake. He knew that if Des backed Joe Finn, it would split the province right down the centre and he would lose the election. Such a little thing as this manuscript could have such a great political price. He knew Des couldn't or wouldn't back this manuscript. It was a suicide note for all political heavy lifters. As Gerard waited and futilely hoped for support for his moderate stance, Peter weighed in once more, this time behind Alex.

"Imagine," Peter began, as he paged through the text for dramatic effect, "trying to sell this in any of our bookshops, or even at the bottom of our churches. It couldn't happen! Worse still, imagine if our Brothers in other Provinces were to pick up translations of this book as it stands now. Imagine what it would do for our reputation."

Des looked deeply perturbed. He is trying to kill me, he thought, with this damn book. I have misjudged the mood of the province. Peter is making his bid for power. And Joe has written this fucking suicide note. And it's only a draft. A draft! Why didn't he work on it for another year? Next year it would be better. What am I thinking? Of course it wouldn't. Next year it would be better written and probably completely unpalatable. How am I going to handle this? I have to step in, assert dominance. And I'll let Alex deliver the message that we are killing the text to Joe. I will let Alex tell him the worst. Then, I will give him a way around Alex, with the condition that the most controversial views be removed. One way or the other, it will have to be rewritten. Then Des smiled and held up his hand for silence. He said:

"Though I agree to a limited extent with Gerard and Peter, perhaps if we try a different tack. Perhaps if we got him to work with one of our scholars. An expert on Saint Giovanni, perhaps?"

"Okay, but I don't want to discourage any of our young Brothers of ability." Peter said. Everyone nodded. Gerard smirked wryly at Peter's hypocrisy.

Des was worried. He worried he was over reacting to a negative reaction to an angry young man's first attempt at serious writing. He was worried moreover he was misreading the room. He heard that along the corridors of OHF houses through the Province it was whispered how support for him was waning, that he was seen as too weak a leader, too conciliatory to the various factions warring for ideological supremacy within the Province.

"But," Des said, continuing his thought, "our wunderkind does not play well with others. And, if he fights, either publicly or privately, with one of our big scholars, it might not go down well."

"Yes," Alex said, smiling sadly. "This is a far cry from 'Flowers for the Day', a book I enjoyed, even if it was written by a teenager. I agree this is a significant step, but not in the right direction, not for us. We want Joe to continue to work and produce, but we also want him to complete his studies. And we don't want him to leave the Order or anything. We have to encourage him as well as guiding him."

"We could order him," Peter answered. "Does anyone actually order him? He is under vows like the rest of us, you know." Everyone laughed. Des laughed loudest.

"I don't know, Peter. I think you are exactly right." Des' voice changed from light hearted amiability at the beginning of the sentence to a tone of deadly seriousness at the end of it as he fixed Peter in a fearless gaze. He needed to take back all he had nearly lost. Discussing Joe's manuscript was an innocuous item on the minutes of their meeting. It must remain as such. Then he said,

"I think you are right when you suggest we need to straighten Joe Finn out. I think we need his gifts and that those gifts need to be nurtured. Though we have many gifts in our Order, I feel we have allowed ourselves to slip, if you will, be too intimidated by a kind of authoritarian terrorism. We haven't truly embraced the creative side of the Order before, and the Brothers and our Order has suffered because of it. We are frightened of our intellectual and artistic natures. We fear disobeying the authority of the Church, when for millennia the Church encouraged artists, writers and people of all creative dints. Within the confines of the faith, of course."

"Of course," Peter said fixing his face in a smile that hid his rage and hate. Des smiled in return, as did Gerard. Then Des went on:

"Before now, we used a very authoritarian line when Brethren displayed artistic gifts. Joe Finn displays both academic and artistic talents. Now, we have given him every opportunity, and, if any of the Brethren who haven't spoken have no objections, Alex and I will speak to him on the matter of the book he has written for our comment. Obviously there is no way we can allow this to be published as it stands. Rome would come looking for our heads if we did. I think Brother Joe has to rewrite a lot of the manuscript and reconsider many of his views. He has included detailed critiques of many of the major sources, but, if he won't work closely with any of our scholars, he will at least have to live with the manuscript closely critiqued by some of the Giovanni Seipi scholars within the Order and within the academic community. Otherwise we will be in a world of pain. Agreed?"

The Brethren nodded. Des looked at each of them, calmly watching for any kind of active defiance. He was satisfied.

"Okay then. Let's move on. We have a lot to get through before lunch and I'm hungry."

Everyone laughed as the meeting moved on to more pressing matters.

Chapter Nineteen

Frank

So, I did the one thing I swore I never would do. I went to confession. Perhaps it was the relic of St Valentine, that allegedly found its home in the Carmelite Church, Whitefriar Street, that led me there to make my first confession after ending my affair with Lisa. Maybe it was that memory of making my first confession in that very Church. I remember myself as a little boy, in cut off trousers and purple cap. 'Come along, Frankie,' Mommy said. I wore a white shirt and a blue and white tie. I had polished shoes, but then, as a little boy, I always had polished shoes because I had been shown by Daddy how to polish my shoes and it was important that Daddy saw my shoes all shiny, like his little boy. It's hard to imagine feeling so small and afraid walking into the power architecture, the stained glass, the flying buttresses, images of Jesus Dying, the statue of the Black Madonna, all the kneeling multitudes. God is love. We are all sinners. I prayed 'O my God I am heartedly sorry for all my hard to remember misdeeds sins wrongdoings.' I remember a vague smell of Brylcreem hair oil wafting in the air as I knelt in the confessional and the priest sitting opposite the grille, sitting in waiting on my sins, a vague impression of his tired smiling face through the matrix of black steel grid. 'Make it up, boy. Devise the script. Need forgiveness. Give me the Sacrament, Father. Forgive me.' "Don't be afraid, Frankie," Mommy had said. Mommy was sitting outside as I ventured into the box, encouraging me to go in. I hated it. I was so afraid. I knelt in terror to confess fabrications. It didn't matter that I didn't know what it meant to commit sin. It didn't matter that I didn't know what God wanted from me. What I wanted, even then as a little boy, was forgiveness. I needed that sense that I was in right relationship with the universe.

"Well, My Child" the kindly priest said. "Well, well, well. Tell me, what do you have to confess to God? Go ahead. It's all right. You are a good boy."

"Well Father. Father, I, I, I was bold."

"That's all right. Go on. Good boy."

"I hit my sister."

"Yes."

"I told a lie."

"I see."

"I didn't say my prayers. I didn't do what Mommy and Daddy told me.

I was a bad boy. A bad bad naughty boy."

"God understands and forgives you, and he loves you very much," the priest said. "And don't worry too much about coming to confession. You have nothing to be afraid of."

I had this sense of wrongdoing. And the priest gave me penance. "I absolve you from all your sins," waving his hands in a sign of the cross using two fingers to trace the invisible through the carbon hydrogen oxygen helium methane argon carbon dioxide ozone atmosphere, leaving in the air some mystical energy that penetrated into my essence and effected, even then, in a seven year old child Frankie boy, some intangible but ontological change after absolution.

Afterwards I was a holy boy. Holy boy, I would think to myself. I felt lighter than air, impossibly happy. High on the love of God. God, like coffee or chocolate or sex or cocaine, was a fix. I needed God. I began to crave such intimacy. I needed that drug. Nothing quite matched the love of God. I began to pray, to seek such highs, highs that would dissipate in time, as I felt rage, frustration, hate, boredom, lust, the second death that comes with just being alive. I needed to get back to the source. I needed intimacy with God. Everything else was a kind of desert. I wanted holiness. Rebirth. Like Saint Dominic Savio, special favourite of Saint Don Bosco. I remember looking for books on the subject. I imagined being on Mastermind, being asked by Magnus Magnusson the quizmaster and polymath: "And what is your specialised subject, Frank?" And I would answer, "Well, Magnus, that would be the lives of the saints, especially Saint Dominic Savio, the special favourite of Saint Don Bosco. Dominic died young and in a special state of divine grace and went straight to heaven." And Magnus Magnusson would smile. He didn't mind questioning a seven year old expert on the lives of the saints. I looked the part, in cut off trousers, polished black shoes, white shirt, blue tie, school cap, and a ready smile.

"Yes sir, thank you, Mr. Magnusson."

And Magnus would begin to question me on my specialised subject, and I would score brilliantly, and God would be pleased with my truly virtuous performance and take me up to heaven in a state of divine grace, with the bonus points of knowing something about this very intimate pure chaste loving special friend of God.

Today though, so many years later, my specialised subject would not be the lives of saints. It would be life with Lisa. And Magnus would not be happy. Magnus dissolves into a priest, Herbert O'Flaherty, stooped to the point of scoliosis with a whisperingly intimate voice.

"Now what can I do for you?" he smiles.

"I would like to make my confession."

"May the Lord be in your heart and in your mind that you might make a truly good confession."

I had always hated kneeling. Instead, I chose to sit. So I sat there, trying to remain completely anonymous, feeling an overwhelming sense of guilt and loneliness, torment and inner rage for offending God, the God of love, for this overwhelming act of selfishness, this desecration, and this act of personal ruination. I said nothing and, after a minute had passed, Father Herbert O'Flaherty, Order of the Calced Carmelites, shod rather than the slipshod, looked at me with an impatient eye.

"Go ahead" he said.

'Say something,' I thought. Tell him. 'Spit it out.' I struggled to speak.

"I am a religious Brother."

"I know," he said. I felt so exposed, embarrassed. I think he knew me.

"I don't see a lot of men your age in here."

"I see. I am in the Order of the Holy Field."

"Go ahead" he said. He really does know me. When did I meet him? I couldn't remember.

"I am a religious Brother, and I have been involved with a woman for some time now."

"Is she married?"

"No"

"Pregnant?"

"I don't think so."

"Are you sure?"

"No."

"How long have you been intimate with this person?"

"A few months. About six or so."

Lie number one, I thought.

"Okay. Assuming this is the main issue troubling you, what do you want to tell me? I needn't remind you that all of this is under the seal of confession."

I had heard stories about the seal of confession, how seals could become unsealed under the right circumstances. Then I thought, 'he can't say anything. He is bound to silence.' If I tell Herbert I killed my Mother under the seal of confession, Father Herbert O'Flaherty, under pain of grievous sin, could not to tell anyone. A priest could be banned from hearing confessions for life if he broke the seal of confession. I looked at this priest through the grille and I liked him. I knew he would never talk. I knew he wanted to help.

"I really don't know what to say. I am in love with her."

"It rarely works out, you know. I have known many like you, young, searching, intelligent, falling in love. It's natural. We live an unnatural life. God makes it possible to do the impossible."

"I have problems with celibacy…"

Herbert grinned mischievously at me.

"No kidding? You know, you had me fooled there for a minute."

"What I mean is…"

"Listen to me, young Brother. You seem like a clever young man, with a good heart. I have seen this literally dozens of times before. And with few, if any, exceptions this is how it might go down: If you leave your Order for her, nine times out of ten it doesn't work out. And, even if you stay together for years and years, and marry even, nine time out of ten it's a troubled arrangement. As I say, I have seen it before, many times. Save yourself a lot of money on therapy. It will only make you crazier. If you remain in the Order and continue seeing her, there is the danger of scandal. If the scandal doesn't come, which it will, I assure you, Brother, it will, there's trouble. Big trouble. There's always the career-relationship divide. You are a religious and she is not. If you get promoted within the Order and people get to hear about your relationship, there's trouble. If you remain with her and she accepts you as a religious Brother, what if she wants a child and you say no? Staying in the Order and with her is a completely insane arrangement, anyway. Of course, some leave for love of a woman, but then there is always the doubt you left for the wrong reasons and a part of you stays with the Order. You need to make a strong final decision one way or the other. Once again, I've seen it. I have pretty much seen it all. And, believe me, it causes too much stress for all concerned not to decide. Your life, as it is now, will be something she will never understand or accept."

"So I'm damned if I do and I'm damned anyway. Is this what you are telling me?"

"You got it in one. Have you ever been in love before?"

"I don't know. I think about her, obsess about her. I'm not sleeping. I'm drinking too much. I don't study. I don't pray. I can't eat. Anyway, she threw me out. She says I have to decide."

"And have you?"

"I don't know. I don't think so."

"Aah. This is first big love. It's an excruciating experience. What do you intend to do?"

"I have ended it. She threw me out."

"No, you haven't ended it. You are racked with guilt and confusion. You have come here looking for a solution rather than absolution."

"I want to decide. But I am too confused. This has cost me everything."

"Love usually does. If you love something, usually it involves great cost. Read the Gospels again, slowly. Think over what it cost Jesus."

"I think I am losing my faith. God means nothing to me. It's as though he has abandoned me. I don't even know what I am doing here. I pray and pray for guidance, to do the right thing, but I feel nothing."

"You need time. Take the time to sort out your feelings. You have to decide. You have to decide, Brother. Is this the life for you? Do you want this person more than religious life? More than this life? Why did you become a religious?"

"I don't know. I thought I did. But I don't know."

"If you allow this to continue, it will do incalculable damage. I strongly urge you to seek counselling, not for being in love, which is an entirely natural thing, but for what it has brought up, this issue with your vocation. Sometimes we precipitate these crises in order to unmask deeper issues, issues we cannot continue to live with. I strongly urge you to make a clear decision about what you intend to do, to minimise hurt for yourself and for the young lady concerned. You are a good man. God understands."

"How did this happen? Why did it happen?"

"Why does anything happen? Why do I have cancer?"

"You have cancer?"

"If you are looking for God to give you an explanation, stop looking. If you love God, you have to allow for the probability you will never understand why things happen as they do."

"Then perhaps I have made a mistake. This is so wrong. It does so much damage to my whole life. And yet it's the only thing. It's the-"

But Father Herbert O'Flaherty of the Order of the Calced Carmelites had decided that this was the end of the interview. He had dispensed his expert advice in a compassionate, detached manner, with Hemingway brevity and a Proustian elegance, that reminded me painfully of my thin and sharp-tongued now ex-friend. Perhaps Herbert feared that, if things were allowed to continue, maybe some vestige of friendship would develop between us, and there were so many others he needed to absolve before cancer took his life. I hoped he would survive his illness. I hoped he would live a long and happy life. I wanted to show my affection. Herbert's tone changed. I imagined I heard his tone change. He said:

"We'll see. You must decide. Indecision is the one thing this situation cannot sustain."

"I know, Father. Thank you."

"I wish you well. Is there anything else?"

"No, Father."

"I absolve you from all your sins in the name of the Father and of the Son and of the Holy Spirit, Amen. Goodbye," he smiled. And he closed the shutter and I heard him open the other one opposite.

Chapter Twenty

Alex and Des and Joe

So, Des went to Alex the afternoon after the six monthly meeting of the Central Council. Alex was proofreading.

"Alex…"

"Des? Come in."

"Are you okay?"

"Yes, I'm fine."

"What are you working on?"

"A book on prayer."

"That's your third book on prayer, isn't it?"

"What's your point?"

"No point. Just saying you write a lot about prayer, you know?"

"Okay then…Can I help you? Brother?"

Alex was worried about the manuscript he was working on. His publisher had called three times in the last week for final drafts. Alex was still unhappy with the text. He felt unable to go on. He felt that he was too distracted by his other responsibilities. He felt tormented by trivia, distracted by the many details of his many roles and responsibilities. This was not his best work. Deep down, he knew he could have done better. It was almost too late.

"I'm sorry to disturb you, Alex. We need to talk to Joe."

"Agreed. Not now, though. I have a full schedule. Anyway Joe has a headache. He didn't go to class today. He called in. I can't squeeze in a meeting with Joe until much later on. I have to fix this."

"Alex, I would like this done and dusted this evening. Really. This can't wait."

Alex smiled. "As you wish, Father."

"Okay, then." said Des.

"After seven o'clock?" Alex suggested.

"After seven o'clock, then."

"See you Des."

Joe wasn't well all that day. He woke up that morning with a headache and a sick stomach and stayed in his room for much of the day, unable to read or work. He spent the time mostly listening to music. When the Brethren were having their evening meal, he prayed alone. He tried not to vomit while reading the prayers from his breviary. He kept one eye closed as he prayed lying down on his bed. It didn't work. He closed the breviary and turned up the music and closed both his eyes. Then he went to bed to properly nurse his headache, changing into pyjamas. He was in terrible pain, one of those terrible headaches that were not quite psychological migraines, and not quite hangovers, but brought an all encompassing ache that took days to dissipate. It was fall out from working on the manuscript, a stress reaction. Or something, he thought. It was a slow pain that began in the cervical region of the backbone, which technically is not a headache, he told himself, but a backache. Then, it gathered itself to the back of the head. The pain was aggravated by interaction with people. There were so many conversations that impinged on his well hidden vulnerability, questions that required a demonstration of specific knowledge on his part, or recall of information. There were educated speculations or probing questions by visiting Brothers or clergy who had heard about this gifted individual. They wanted their fascinated imagination satisfied. Joe suffered discreet queries about his emotional life or sarcastic remarks. But most of all there were people, endless excessive crowds, people who came and went through the Monastery of the Seven Towers. Days, such as the days Joe had endured since he came back from Wicklow, left him with the overwhelming certainty that there was no safety in numbers. He was burnt out. Humans were predators. They didn't care. They simply took and left no payment. By six o' clock the pain had moved to his forehead, into the eyes. It had become unbearable. He felt his mind was slowly boiling. He felt he couldn't see, closed his eyes and tried to imagine life without this pain. Unable to eat lest he vomit, Joe took out his collection of painkillers. These were mostly provided by Rose, who knew herself an enabler, but knew preventing pain in her son a higher calling than obeying the law. Joe took two Vicodin ES 7.5-750 mg, narcotic analgesic, remembering caution as they may cause constipation, stomach upset, nausea, vomiting, light-headedness, dizziness, drowsiness, or flushing. If any of these effects persist or worsen, he told himself, contact your doctor or pharmacist promptly. Tell your general practitioner about side effects. Tell general practitioner of medical history, especially of liver or kidney conditions, history of alcohol use, heart problems, abdominal/stomach problems, breathing problems, seizure disorders, drug dependency, severe diarrhoea and of any drug allergies. Avoid alcoholic beverages. He took two pills and swallowed some gin. Now I have a supine state to achieve. A level of sweet release. Unconsciousness. Music. Yes, music. In order to increase certain side effects of drug, Joe put on some Wagner, and tried to sleep. Eventually after twenty or so minutes, as evening meal ended, some Brethren passed his tiny corner room, as usual mentioning the improper music that emanated from his room.

"That young Brother and Hitler would make a nice pair," said the First Brother to the Second Brother. And Joe didn't hear them clearly, not fully consciously.

"Ssh," the Second Brother said. "He'll hear you."

"I hope he does," said the First Brother. "I don't approve of that music. And I don't see why those in authority approve of that music. It's most un-Christ like."

"What about Parsifal?" The Second Brother asked as they turned to go further upstairs. And the first Brother, who knew nothing about Parsifal, except that it was a nice name retorted:

"What about Parsifal? It's the most blasphemous of them all, if you ask me. And terrible music, too. God, I had an uncle and all he used do was play Wagner. It's no wonder he left the Church. Anyway it was widely believed he was gay."

"Wagner wasn't gay. Anyway, does it matter?"

"I'm telling you. That's gay music."

"I see," said Second Brother, who strangely felt disappointed with the First Brother after years of friendship with the First Brother.

The Second Brother, whose name was Kevin Reynolds, the sacristan of the Church of the Seven Towers, had always liked Brother Joe Finn, who was by now sound asleep and dreaming. Joe Finn at the end of the interaction between the two Brothers was dreaming he was in Las Vegas working the slot machines. He puts in a coin and scores big. All kinds of bells and whistles go off at the huge golden slot machine he had put so much money into. Money and coinage of strange and unknown origin pour out of the golden slot machine and Joe doesn't have the pockets right then in his monks garb to properly collect everything he had won. It began to pile up on the floor and there, in the golden room in the golden hall by the golden slot machine in Las Vegas he was rich, rich beyond his wildest imaginings and he sees a little boy sitting opposite his horde looking sad. Joe reaches into the pile of money and gives some to the boy who says thanks and goes off to play the slot machines elsewhere. The pile of money is becoming unmanageable and Joe sees his parents standing near a door waving at him. He waves back and points to the pile of cash but they don't seem to notice. Security people arrive with special reinforced wheelbarrows to help him cash up on his legitimate winnings. And, just as the money is loaded onto the special reinforced wheelbarrows to go to the cashier's office to be changed into cash, everything changes and Joe is in the Library of the Seven Towers fighting for his life with the devil. The devil looks devilishly handsome. The devil is a beautiful man, a cross between Brad Pitt and Michelangelo's David. The devil is choking him. His beautiful perfect fingers are crushing his windpipe. Joe was fighting for his life, trying to catch his breath. He thinks about pleading for his life, but fights back instead. Joe pulls this devil's hands away from his throat, punches him, then holds the handsome devil down. Joe cries out "In the name of Christ I command you to come out of him," as Jesus exorcised the legion of demons and sent them into a herd of pigs that jumped off a cliff and then the fight was over and Joe had an orgasm and woke up. He took off his habit and went over to take a quick shower to wash away the stain. When he got back to his room, Des and Alex were standing at his door. A Brother had told them that Joe was taking a shower. Des smiled as Joe walked into his room.

"Do you mind if we come in for a moment? We wanted to discuss the manuscript that you submitted recently to the Council."

Joe didn't answer. He knew the news was bad. He had known the news would be bad anyway, but couldn't do anything about that. If he had written otherwise, he would have made a liar of himself. The fact that Joe didn't answer angered Alex greatly. He was more in favour of summoning that arrogant young Brother Finn to his office and giving him a lesson in humility. But this was not the way Des wanted to handle the situation.

"Please Brothers, have a seat. One of you will have to take the bed."

"Would you mind turning down that…music, Brother?"

Alex indicated the small stereo blaring beside Joe's small bed. There was little by way of clutter in the room, some books, mostly library books and some pages neatly placed one on top of the other in the corner of the room and on his table. A crucifix on the wall. A framed picture of Joe's parents, sitting with big colourful drinks before them at some night time beachside resort, smiling in each other's arms, hung on the other wall. Everything was spotlessly clean. Brother Joe was clean shaven holding some neatly folded, recently hand washed laundry in his hands. He placed them in a hand wash basin, tugged the folds of his snow white, heavy towelling ankle length shower robe bought for him by his Mother and waited for Alex to speak. Des usually looked to Alex to speak for him in situations like this.

"Though we, Brother Des and I and the Council, can only express our admiration, indeed fascination, with the quality of your work, the epic strokes with which you paint this portrait of the founder of our Order, not to mention the historical and cultural context that you place the founding of our great Order in, we have certain issues with the conclusions that you draw. We have detailed them here in this file. They relate particularly to your conclusions as to Giovanni Seipi's psychological state, particularly with reference to his alleged psychosis-"

Joe paged through the file as Alex spoke. He looked at Alex and held up his hand for silence.

"I had investigated the origins of the Order, and found our founder to be a deeply disturbed person who held a lifelong loathing of his criminally abusive parents, a young man who ran away from home and lived on the streets of Rome, a young man who sought refuge in a God he felt could never forgive him his sins. In the mind of Giovanni Seipi his biggest sin was to be born."

"Brother, that's highly suspect, deeply prejudicial." Alex's face reddened, and then he seemed to stop himself saying any more. Des looked on and decided not to comment.

"His second biggest sin was being beaten by his parents, or perhaps not being beaten enough."

"There is no hard evidence St. Giovanni was beaten like that." Alex waved his finger at Joe. Joe looked disdainfully at Alex's finger. Alex withdrew the digit.

"Save his own words, written down by his contemporaries," Joe smiled. "I, too, have written on the life of our Founder Brother. I, too, know what I am talking about."

Joe looked calmly at Alex and Des and said in a quiet voice, by way of reply to Alex's sense of outrage:

"Brothers, Saint Giovanni Seipi was a man who all his life beat himself with cords and sticks, not because Jesus was scourged, but because his parents beat him with cords and sticks. It's a pattern, the similarity is unmissable. He rolled in nettles and snow because he was left out in the snow as a boy for breaking a pot. It's not one single incident of personal purgation. It's when you take all the documented incidences together and compare them to his childhood experiences. It is in knowing the person, the broken fragile person, one meets their power. By clothing Giovanni Seipi in the robes of sanctity, one makes him inaccessible. He is no longer one of us. What was once portraiture has become propaganda, what was love is now sacrifice. What was once a young man looking for the truth like the rest of us is now another uniformed recruiting officer for the Church's teaching."

"Nonsense. You aren't a psychiatrist. Or a theologian. You haven't even got a primary degree. You can't say that!"

"As the executioner said, quod scripsi scripsi. I am nobody's intellectual meat puppet."

They shook their heads and looked at each other.

"The other problem we had was your questioning the miracles of Giovanni Seipi."

"Really, Alex, I thought it was obvious the miracles were bogus."

"We have contacted some of our finest Giovanni Seipi scholars and over all they take issue with you on this. If this book were published as it is, you would have a dog fight on your hands, the wrong kind of controversy."

"Not like now, where we have total unquestioning acceptance of the text."

"As you know we have many Giovanni Seipi scholars, established scholars. We spoke with them at length, and, though they disagree with you, we have asked and they are willing to work with you on this. You will be using some of the more exclusive Giovanni Seipi archives to tie up some of those questions you raise."

"I won't work with them."

"Why not, Joe?" Des asked. "We're trying to help you. You don't see that."

Joe looked at them, tears of rage just beginning in his eyes.

"I have read their work. Most of them are purveyors of garbage."

Des and Alex looked angrily at each other.

"Don't be childish, Joe," Des said.

They calmed themselves, and Alex continued;

"It is only with considerable revision that we would consider publication. I think personally this is a book you needed to get out of your system. Now that you have, you can move on. If you fix those problems, we won't withhold publication."

A long silence ensued. Joe listened to the music. Joe stood between Alex and Des, his back to the sink, as he hung his head, his arms folded, his brow knotted, and a look of fury obvious to all, except Joe who was busily trying to suppress the feeling of being suffocated, the crucifying lack of freedom, that there were so many forbidden thoughts, so many forbidden things, all unspoken, but implicit in everything he did, in this petty life that should be so great. No one spoke for a while and the music went on. Softly through the speakers, Seiglende sung to Seigmund 'let me press closer to you. Let me see clearly the light shining in your eyes, how your beauty stirs me with rapture. Let me try to remember these things about us we have forgotten. Let us be lovers. Let love save us.'

"I have no interest in winning your approval. And I will not rewrite the text in the way you want."

"Don't talk to Alex like that, Joe. This isn't about you. This is about what you've written. We have reached the terminal point of our patience with your insubordination. You think you are special, that there is a different code of obedience for you than anyone else. There isn't. Now either shape up or ship out!"

Des frowned. Joe looked at Des, a little shocked at his tone.

"I know you, Fathers and Brothers in the Order, have a problem. I know that. I also know that however bizarre it might sound to me more than to you, you want me to fix it for you. The problem is our Order has lost hope. We have lost hope because we cannot see a future for ourselves."

"Oh please, you are just a kid!"

"I'm young, that's not the same as being some fucking kid!"

"Mind your language Brother!"

"I think that's the general message of the evening. I have to mind my language."

"I don't know what little world you live in, Joe Finn, but this is delusional! The world doesn't revolve around you and you are looking at pretty serious consequences if you continue to disrespect your superiors."

"Des, have you ever considered the possibility there might be life on Mars?"

"There is no life on Mars," Alex snapped. Joe Finn smiled.

"Don't embarrass yourself, Joe, and don't make me do something I might regret," Des said as he looked down at the clean floor. Joe had never heard him so angry.

"I'm not embarrassed. I know you have to look good for your lieutenant, Brother Kingmaker here. You have to be the strong leader now I've let you down, not written what you wanted to read."

"Joe, that's arrogance. You would want to watch that."

Joe smiled. "Yes Father. I'm watching carefully."

Des stood up to leave. Joe stopped him. He raised his hand like a traffic cop, and looked coldly at him.

"Things could have been different. Politics did this. We should give up thinking we have the answer!"

"God is our answer," Alex said.

"That's what Giovanni Seipi said and how he lived. I said that, in the manuscript."

"Well, you could have said it a little more clearly, eh Finn?"

Des looked coldly at Joe. His remark cut Joe to the heart.

"Well, you've made your point."

"I think there's nothing more for the time being. Alex, will we leave this man in peace?"

"Yes, Des, I think we have heard just about everything we wanted to. Thank you for your time, Brother Joe. Do you have a copy of the manuscript?"

"No Alex," Joe said. "I gave you my only copy. I really am that stupid."

"Well, I'll leave this with you anyway," and he put down his copy on the bed. Alex indicated he was going and quietly padded out of the room. Joe watched as Alex held his head high and gently moved his arms in self conscious rhythm to his step, a kind of spiritual Jeeves, aristocratically tilting his large shiny head to one side as he walked. It was as though, Joe thought, that by his beard and his stance and his ponderous way of walking, he was making clear to all who met him of the loftiness of his position and the gravity of his perspective. As Alex waltzed away, Des hung by Joe's door, half watching Alex leave, feeling guilty. The music kept annoying him, though.

"What is that music you're playing, by the way? Some of the Brethren say it's blasphemous. You should use earphones. God, you should get some furniture into this place. Try some of the vacant rooms. Tell the guest master that I said its okay."

"Don't try to pretend we're friends after this."

"I'm not. I'm just asking about the music. I want to know."

"Why?"

"Indulge me."

"My Dad introduced it to me when I was in my teens, as far as I remember. He played it mainly over his headphones, actually. My mother didn't approve, which made it all the better to listen to. It's a story of how a young innocent fearless hero is used as an instrument given by the gods to restore a corrupt world order, or rather, to overturn a hopelessly lost corrupt world order, a world order lost by a God among lesser God's trying to fill the loveless void in their lives made by the pursuit of absolute power and world dominance. Because of all the corruption, this leader god is rendered powerless by all the pacts and agreements he made that got him into power in the first place. It makes him cranky and insecure. In a sense, his own ambition has destroyed him. He becomes a wanderer looking for a truly free agent that will break the cycle of control and manipulation. So, he allows this free fearless hero to be born. You see, this young hero has to be free. Otherwise, he would be subject to the cycle of control, dirty politics, and manipulation…"

"Joe, I don't mean to be rude, but I just wanted to know the name."

"It's Wagner, Father. He was Adolph Hitler's favourite composer, which is pretty ironic when you think of the message."

"I know that."

Des went to leave.

"I see, I see. Well I'll-."

"You know, of course, I am going to publish anyway."

"That may not happen, Joe. You might have problems…"

"And tell me, Brother Des, who will stop it?"

Des smiled.

"I want you to leave me alone."

"Huh? What are you talking about?"

"If this continues, if you try to make me be your intellectual mouthpiece, I will leave the Order."

"Brother, you are labouring under a delusion."

"I will leave, Des."

"Now you are repeating yourself. I thought you didn't do that."

"Some things are worth saying twice."

There followed a silence. Neither party knew what to say. Eventually Des mentioned the music still playing.

"Tell me, does the hero succeed? In the opera?"

"Yes, naturally the hero succeeds. You can't sell a failed hero."

"Wagner was clever."

"He knew you can't sell a work that says to the audience: Give your life to a hopeless cause. The hero does great things, slays the dragon and makes love to a Goddess. But heaven is destroyed and earth saved, even though he becomes a victim of the curse of all who wear the ring of power: Death."

"You are being just a little obvious, don't you think? Joe?"

"Maybe you just bring out the lampoonist in me."

"No, I don't, actually. I am disappointed, very disappointed."

"All your life…"

Des glowered at Joe. Joe looked coldly back at him.

"I'll pretend I didn't here that. I warn you, be careful, Brother. Now, I bid you goodnight," he snarled.

"Goodnight, Father."
And Des closed the door with a peremptory slam.

Chapter Twenty One

Frank

The Eucharistic Prayer was over. The choir sang: 'Be not afraid. I go before you always. Believe in me.' I don't know if Joe would like that as a hymn. I remember he used turn to me in the midst of morning or evening prayer and throw his eyes to heaven at the words of some of the hymns the Brethren were required to sing as part of the Divine Office. Sometimes, we chanted the psalms. Sometimes, we simply recited them. "What lyrics!" he would exclaim in a semi-audible whisper. Sometimes, I simply couldn't hold in the laughter. Once I left the choir in hysterics, unable to stop laughing. I remembered that day, as I watched the concelebrants take Communion at his funeral Mass. They ate Communion in bread form. Once it was forbidden to allow the bread to touch one's teeth. If you did, I remember, it was a venial sin. A venial sin is not like a mortal sin. It is only a slight stain on one's soul. One's soul becomes completely black, I remembered, if one sins mortally. It's like killing the soul, a mortal sin, strangling the pope or eating babies. It is a separation from God. Then the rule changed. It was no longer a sin to eat the bread of life using one's teeth. After all I figured, Jesus ate himself at the last supper, probably using his teeth. I remembered my First Communion. I wondered if they still had the sweet bread I ate for my very first Communion. I wondered if one could have that recipe. I remember taking my first Communion as a boy of six. I had a new brown suit on. The girl next to me kept pinching me. It might have been Geraldine. I was in love with her. And she kept pinching me as I was trying to pray to Jesus who was somehow inside me. Was he inside me or outside me? My problems haven't changed much, I thought, as Des, the chief celebrant, walked over to the chalice and drank the blood of Christ. Vampires, I thought. Then, I felt guilty. Cannibal vampires. The concelebrants, the dozens of priests in stunning vestments, aglow with the divine, creatures of the night, what sweet music they make, they who stood in a great arc of triumph around the huge glowing altar in the Church of the Seven Towers, more ancient than the Solar System, more ancient than the first atom, shining with the choirs of angels, glowing with the divine beauty, queued with reverence to drink the cup of life and then Des, with great sorrow, tears in his eyes, moved past the coffined Joe Finn, walked over to Rose and Gerry and gave them too to eat and drink of the flesh and blood of Christ. And the choir sang 'Blessed are the poor in spirit. Blessed the

Meek. Blessed those who hunger and thirst for righteousness. Blessed and come to me all you who need significance. I have it right here.' And the priests and the ministers of the Eucharist percolated throughout the Church looking for communicants and I went up to receive and Lisa squeezed my thigh as I passed her in the pew and I looked at her and she seemed confused and upset at me and I said,

"What harm can it do?" and she said,

"Who knows? You told me you don't believe - in this," and looked hurt and disappointed at me and I said,

"I want to remember how it all felt back then." She shrugged her shoulders and I went up to communicate. I walked up to the high altar, hoping that some of the old Brothers, the Brothers I remembered and had lived with, those who had not died or moved to other houses, would see me, or remember me and acknowledge me and give me the Eucharist. But a minister of the Eucharist, someone I did not know, was moving along the kneeling or standing line of communicants. She wore a knitted cardigan and a white blouse and a knee length skirt. Probably a nun in civilian disguise, I said to myself. She had a slightly breathless voice and snow white teeth. I wish I had teeth like that, I thought. She smiled and held out the bread and said to me "The Body of Christ" and I took it without saying the obligatory "Amen" and I ate of the Eucharist, and, though I did not believe and knew I could never believe, I was moved by the solemnity of it all and felt lonely and missed the old life and I looked around the Church and again saw faces I remembered and I thought to myself, the Church, the mystical body of Christ, was once again fed. I sat down beside my troubled wife and looked at her and smiled and she smiled and rubbed my thigh slowly and the choir sang on and the celebration of life and death and resurrection of Jesus, the celebration of the Trinitarian God moved towards its final phase.

Chapter Twenty Two

Frank

Bill called a few times for dinner and conversation in the weeks after
the funeral. He was most anxious to talk about Joe, I figured he thought
Joe represented some kind of unresolved issue for him. Maybe. Maybe
I thought Joe was a vehicle for Bill to connect with Lisa and I after our
imaginary fall from the grace of a God who lets the charnel house of
life go on. I was angry at the world at the time of Bill's calling. I was
reluctant to talk. But I made myself talk. After all, Bill was so kind, so
warm, so loving. I knew something was wrong.

"So," Lisa said. "Why did it take so long for Joe's work to find
recognition? I mean I hear something about it coming out in the near
future."

"Right," I said. "I think it should be out in the next year or so."

"I don't know for sure who did it, but I know, well I think they cut
off all avenues to him." Bill shifted a little in his armchair, and then
he took another sip of drink. He looked unsmilingly at us. Then he
remembered to smile.

"I don't understand. What do you mean they cut off all avenues to
him?" I asked.

"I mean that, after a year of searching, he was still no closer to
publication than the night Des and Alex gave him the judgment of the
Council on his work."

"So why didn't he rework it?" Lisa asked.

"He did."

"He did?"

"Sure he did. But he didn't re-submit."

"Why?"

"I think he was too proud. I think he became embittered. It prevented
him from submitting it again to the Central Council. And, day by day,
his bitterness deepened. He never finished his primary degree, refused
an offer to study in Rome, and went to work in a parish in one of the
poorest parts of Dublin. He dropped out, I suppose. And the Central
Council didn't ask him about the book again. As far as the Council
were concerned, they had given their answer. It was up to Brother
Joe to comply with their wishes and re-submit the manuscript before
they would question him on it again. Privately, though, they discussed
the matter amongst themselves. They speculated on what work he was
doing, if he had abandoned the project altogether, or become absorbed

in his other studies, or if he were working on something new. They had wanted him to take a degree first of all. They made discreet inquiries as to what he was doing. But, as no one could gain access to his room, no one knew. On the other hand, if he had taken the degree, they would have given him their full backing. Then, he would have been free to work on other projects. But Joe would not comply. Joe discontinued his studies, and continued to work on the manuscript in his room, typing and retyping, adding and subtracting bits and pieces of the rapidly growing tome, polishing sections, reading new research into Giovanni Seipi. And he tried to find a publisher for it."

"I was out of touch with Joe at this stage. He told me about the offer of higher degrees, if he took his primary. Mostly though, we weren't speaking after our big fight."

"He wrote to every publisher he thought would be interested in such a critical biography."

"How do you know?"

"They found so many countless rejection letters among his papers, all from the kind of publisher who, under normal circumstances, would be interested in a book like Joe's."

"It's just I imagined he'd be too arrogant for such a move, you know?"

"Well it seemed, month after month, letters arrived back from publishing houses declining interest in the text. Although he could never prove it, I'm sure he imagined this was Alex's or the Council's doing. You see quite a few people overheard that conversation in Joe's rooms that night. In reality, there is no such thing as privacy in a monastery like that. God knows those days are long gone. Nowadays we live in big houses or old courthouses or farms or small suburban communities."

Bill looked wistfully at his empty glass. I wondered what Joe had been thinking during that time. He would have covered every possibility. He used to tell me "if you want to win, no matter what game you play, you have to faithfully do everything to avoid losing, no matter how much ego it costs." He would have worried about the quality of his research, agonized about his style, read more and sent away for books and articles - 'Maybe it's my research'- or increased the number of footnotes on his text, widened the range of his bibliography, probably polished the style on the last few chapters, rendering it more readable.

"Apparently," Bill went on, "Joe wrote to some of the scholars who had written extensively on the subject. He wanted affirmation, I guess. He sent the text asking specific questions relating to some of the more controversial biographical details he had included. Some responded.

Some referred him to their published works. Then one day he received the following, postmarked Rome. Apparently he had sent the entire manuscript to this particular scholar. I have the letter."

"Can I see it?"

Bill handed it to me. I read it.

'Dear Brother Joseph,

Thank you for the opportunity to read your fine manuscript. It is densely packed with the most careful research and I greatly enjoyed reading it. Your arguments are cogent and compelling. Your style is lucid and beautifully evocative. You take the liberty (a most welcome liberty I might hasten to add) of quoting my poor researches into the life of our great founder. I direct you to *Giovanni Seipi Studies Number 15 Volume 3* for further research into Seipi's relations with his uncle Thomasso, if you care to read further on the subject. Overall, I think you have produced an interesting, but highly contentious, work and this is unfortunate. It is very much the book of a young man. I fear moreover your conclusions will ignite the type of controversy mainly damaging to the reputation of the author rather than that of your subject. You are too talented a scholar for this to happen. Giovanni Seipi is loved by millions and studied by thousands of scholars down through the ages. I beg you to reconsider this work. Put it aside for a while and see if these really are your conclusions about the life of our founder.

Yours in Christ,

Fr. Ricardo De Graza, OHF'

"I think he valued this guy's opinion above all others," I said. "We talked a lot about Graza's work. Joe thought he was brilliant. This would have hurt."

I imagined Joe dropping the letter on the floor of his room after reading it. It was handwritten with thick rich ink on beautiful yellowish vellum-like parchment, stamped with the Angelicum imprint in Rome. A soft nimble brilliant established hand had taken his pen and written this. I imagined Joe thinking of that hand, the hand of Fr. Ricardo De Graza OHF, taking his pen and some of that parchment from a nice neat pile of blank stamped parchment, and ending the life of Joe Finn. I imagined Joe trembling with heartbreak, shaking with sorrow and shock and despair. I understood, after looking over the letter, that this is what finally made him leave Ireland. Somehow they, whoever they were, had managed to close all exits to him. He had to get in line or get out. He knew nothing he ever wrote would find a publisher without their permission. Of course, he told himself. 'It's nothing. They wouldn't do that. Paranoia generates enemies where none exist.'

"So, Bill, how did you get this?"

"I can't tell you. But I knew you would be interested in it."

"Why?"

"I know Joe's life fascinates you, and I know some day you'll put all of this down in a slim volume." I grinned at Bill as I filled his glass again. "You're a funny guy, Bill," I said.

"So who is this person?" Lisa asked. "You guys are like two ex-boy scouts discussing secret handshakes, or something." Bill laughed.

"In some ways, well, you're right. Fr. Ricardo De Graza was an international authority on the Giovanni Seipi. Not only that, De Graza was a scripture scholar and a well known theologian."

"So Joe would have been greatly intimidated by the letter," Lisa said.

"I suppose so. Eventually, he put the manuscript aside."

"The whole thing was probably driving him mad," I said and Bill nodded and emptied his wine glass, "and he knew deep within that he couldn't write what he wanted. He had to write what they wanted."

"Right," Lisa said.

A literary butler, I thought. Joe would have to write tender, carefully thought out, meticulously researched, compellingly well wrought words to lull the good, the great, and the faithful into a false sense of security.

"So, a few weeks later he stopped researching and writing altogether and began working exclusively in the parish where he now lived. Rumour had it he was frequently drunk and taking prescribed medication. I think he kind of gave up. His chess was quite well known. He is the only Brother I ever heard of who took out his chess board and played a few games with the Brethren, even letting them win now and again. Otherwise he did crosswords, or drank, or watched movies late into the night. The Brothers didn't bother him much. Except for Mother and Dad, few called for him, not even the parishioners he helped."

Bill smiled sadly. "And he went foreign."

"That's quite a sad story Bill," Lisa said. "Is it true?" It was very late. Bill didn't answer. Both of us were exhausted and troubled by Bill's stories and, significantly enough, his visit, so unexpected despite our extending an invitation to him on the spur of the moment at Joe's funeral. Both of us had work tomorrow. Both of us had worked hard all day. All this was too much and Bill was only warming up after a long absence from our lives. He gave the impression of a man settling down for a night-long session of discussion and debate. Soon he would ask me about life outside the Order, our marriage, talk about his own promotion to the Central Council, his decision to take up training as a psychotherapist, and so many other vital details that make up the matrix of our lives. I wanted to go to bed. I was not made for night time discussions. It was close to one in the morning.

"I just thought you might be interested," Bill said.

"You said that."

"Why don't you keep the letter? It's not the original or anything. I came across it. I can't tell you how. I scanned a copy. I thought it might be of interest to you."

"Very thoughtful of you. It is." I said.

"Would you like tea or coffee, Bill? I think we are fresh out of wine." Lisa stood up and put the kettle on. Bill smiled.

"It's great to see you both. It really has been too long."

"I think so," I said. "I think so."

Chapter Twenty Three

Lisa

We eventually got Bill to leave about two o' clock that morning. As I lay in bed afterwards that night, too tired and upset to make love, I figured Joe's long struggle with his book was going on during the time Frank and I were apart.

After Frank and I broke up, that terrible night in my apartment, I began to see things I never saw before. I saw how alone I was, how alone people were. I thought, 'I have been living in a dream. There is nothing special about being unhappy, so why feel sorry for myself?'

We need to make friends because we are alone. We become what they, other people, need us to be because we cannot be alone with our misery. I thought about this and knew thinking had nothing to do with fixing my life. The answer is silence. The answer is no answer. I was just the same as all the rest. I was one of the lost. I had no one.

And so, after I lost the only thing truly worth living for, love, I rejoined the human race. I became friendly once more. I spontaneously joined in with casual conversations. I understood how painful being alone could be. I realised how arrogant and aloof I had been. Before meeting and falling in love with Frank, I expected to meet someone warm, innocuous, not too brave, and not too smart. These were my expectations built from life experience. I had no career and no gifts. I was a nice dull girl who would meet some equally unchallenging spouse with few expectations, who would make a happy, well adjusted, average partner. He and I, my future imaginary partner and me, would be sane and happy, because we accepted reality as it was. So, I became modern. Frank was history, part of my addiction to acquiring emotionally unavailable partners and friends. I had to become real. I had to declare myself powerless over my addiction and seek a higher power. I began to work the program. I decided that self worth and self image were the same. I became open minded and friendly. I stopped smoking and drank less. I dyed my hair and went to the gym. I ate more vegetables and stopped drinking myself to sleep. Cancer, after all, could kill me instead of time. I moisturized my skin with expensive product and ran three miles a day. I began to look better. I wanted to be cured of this death I felt. I called up those old girl friends I lost touch with and went out to really great parties, where interesting sensitive and educated men, with prospects in the service and financial industries made it clear, by their witty and warm demeanours, that they were interested in a sexual relationship with a view to long term commitment. After all, I had a great body, a good mind and an ivory smile. I didn't threaten anyone, as I worked as a librarian. All of these men seemed fine to me. I engaged in countless sexual encounters with these people, night after night. I dated some. Some of them were married or in permanent relationships. Some fell in love with me. Some of them had children or were divorced. Some were divorced with children. I should have felt more guilt, but I didn't feel guilt. I didn't want anything except the feeling, that sensation of two people touching. I wanted to escape the prison of skin. I wanted to escape my tiny life for the time I was with that one other person. It largely worked. The vegetative calm of sex and work helped. My job got better. It didn't matter that it was largely pointless and filled with disturbed, depressed people, disappointed megalomaniacs. I didn't care about their agenda. Their petty inane insanities didn't bother me. I even got a promotion and a raise. I began to save for a mortgage. I was getting older, the weight of expectation weighing down from within and without, friends settling down, having to smile at tedious dullards married to old friends, evenings spent sipping wine, eating salmon or cheese or bad Chinese food and talking about old times. This was the time I spent after Frank left me. "Well, Lisa, whatever happened to that young monk you were dating?" they would ask me. "I mean it all seemed so serious for so long, eh?"

As nothing was serious in these people's minds, or, as friendship served as a passport to unwarranted intimacy, nothing was treated as serious or too sensitive to mention. I needed new friends, I thought. Then I changed my mind. Who really cares? I thought. And I would swallow my hypersensitivity and grief and loss and smile and say something innocuous. "Oh, that? It ended so long ago. So long. Ago." And then I would ask them about their wedding plans or what they were going to call their first born. Fachtna, Eamonn, Richard, Fiachra. Liam. And if it's a girl, Grainne. Apparently they were still arguing about the girl's names. I forget the names of the couples now. I don't see them much. Time doesn't stop. They stopped.

Then, two years after I stopped seeing Frank, I stepped out of the library one Tuesday to get lunch. I walked down Rathmines Road to buy a baguette and a mixed salad and a mineral water and sit in the sun and eat when Joe Finn passed by. I was sure he saw me. He walked past me without looking me in the eye, with that mixture of arrogance and shyness only those with a clear sense of their own superiority possess in such liberal quantities.

"Joe?" I said. I spoke loudly enough for him not to be able to ignore.

"Yes?" he said. Joe turned and looked at me embarrassedly, then smiled a thin, mean spirited smile, a smile that said I dislike you, but I am going to pretend otherwise for the sake of some empty propriety.

"Lisa, how are you?"

He put out his hand to shake mine, so instead I threw my arms around him and hugged his thin body. His face looked older, his eyes sad and troubled and tired. We stood and looked at each other for a moment, each not knowing what to say.

"Well this is awkward, isn't it Joe?"

"I, well…"

"I couldn't just let you go by without greeting you. How the hell are you? How's Frank?"

"I…" Joe began some excuse.

I felt this urgent need to explain myself to him. I wanted to tell him how Frank and I broke up, how somehow he seemed to be a part of that break-up. I wanted to open myself completely to him and receive his full understanding, that understanding brings forgiveness and, above all, I wanted forgiveness from somewhere. But I looked at him. I saw him for the first time as who he was, warrened within some obfuscation of his own making. He was someone distracted by his own dreams and imaginings and thoughts. I thought he looked ill. I wanted to advise him about diet and exercise. I wanted to nurse him better, cradle his gifts and set him free. I wanted to hold onto him, wring from him his understanding and maybe a little forgiveness. So I launched into him, there and then on Rathmines Road, in the sun with the passers by passing by, with my salad and baguette being slowly cooked in the ultra violet heat.

"Look, let's be clear, Joe."

"Oh? Clear? Go on." Joe winced a little, as if signalling some need contrary to his words.

"I know you hate my guts."

"Don't put words in my mouth. I have enough people doing that."

"I'm saying it as I see it."

"Congratulations, it's good to voice one's prejudices. Then one can work on them."

"I know you think somehow I broke you and Frank up, that I nearly spoiled Frank's vocation, that in your mind I am some kind of scarlet woman."

"Oh please, Lisa. I have places I need to be."

"No, no. But you're wrong. You just don't understand. Despite all the obstacles, Frank and I had an understanding. We were drawn to each other."

"That's nice poetry, Lisa."

"I wish you could see as I see. That Frank is unhappy."

"Look Frank – he was happier before he met you."

"I think he has always been unhappy. Meeting me just made that all the clearer to him."

"How convenient for you. Paint your heroic portrait all you like."

"I'm not painting anything…!"

"It won't change anything. What you don't know is what its like to be a religious Brother, a monk."

"Maybe not, but I…"

Joe began waving his finger angrily at me.

"You will never get the spiritual bond, the pursuit of the spiritual life, spiritual perfection even, the immense privilege of a calling to follow God in this particular way. You can call me whatever."

I thought – the religious doth protest too much.

"All this…sound bite…advertising. I have had dinner in your refectory. I have seen what goes on, to an extent…."

"I don't care…no matter what, you were on the outside and you were never sympathetic. But Frank has this calling. Being with you has damaged him, perhaps forever. And I think it has damaged you too."

"I just wish you could have taken the time to get to know me. I'm sorry you feel like that."

"Frank is a good Brother in our Order."

"So you have said in so many ways. I think your life is unnatural and damages people."

"God helps us. You need to believe…"

"I believe people choose their illusions, Joe. Nobody wants to be disillusioned."

"This is reality, and, from what I hear, Frank is doing great work. He is going to be ordained in a year, maybe two."

"Do you see him much?"

"I moved out to a parish."

"In other words you fell out with him. Tell me, do you have any friends?"

"He and I had a disagreement. Over you, actually."

"Wow."

"He thought I betrayed him to the authorities. I was very angry he would accuse me like that. He pushed me around, yelled at me in public. It was an ugly scene…"

"Did you betray him?"

"You weren't exactly discreet now, were you?"

"Discretion is the better part of cowardice."

Joe grinned and sadly shook his head.

"I'm sorry to have hurt you, Joe. I really am. I think you could have made a fascinating friend."

"Don't appeal to my vanity, Clarice."

Then, he seemed to be struggling for something to say to me. I waited for a moment, then he smiled a little, wincing in the sunlight he put his hand up to shield his eyes and said:

"I am going away." He stretched his fingers out as if reaching for the intangible, and then he withdrew them into a tight fist. He didn't seem to notice this involuntary action. I wondered at the neurological implications of it.

"Where?"

"Probably to Los Angeles. We have a small community there. I can probably work in peace there, hopefully write something."

"Write what?"

"I dunno. I always wanted to write something. I might like to try fiction. They want me to take further degrees. I am not sure it is what I want to do. I don't mind college."

"Frank said you did, Joe."

"Frank said I did what?"

"He said you hated college. That you thought it was a place that ossifies the mind."

"Frank idealized me. He caricatured me. It came from his insecurities. He's wrong."

"He specifically said that to me. A couple of times. Anyway you played his insecurities. You didn't support him."

"I don't remember it like that. Anyway I think he may be right. Who wants to fill their heads with junk?"

"Well, Joe. It's easy for you to talk like that. The rest of us have to read things, get them into our heads, learn somehow. We don't have the comfort zone of your snobbery."

"Ever tried reading, Lisa?" Joe grinned at me. I smiled. Now he was toying with me, trying to make me angry.

"Well Joe, I'd like to read something you wrote, when you're not being an ass. Have you drafts of anything?"

"Yes, but it's not ready. I am just not happy with it. I might be able to work better over there."

"They must be really pissed at you."

"I don't know about that. They said yes six months ago. It'll probably be another six months before I get to go."

"Maybe we might get in touch before then."

"Frank and I don't see each other much now."

I smiled and nodded. I could see I had failed to change his mind on anything. He still blamed me for everything, but, of course, though he blamed me for everything, he forgave me for everything. After all, I thought, I had apologised. I had acknowledged my guilt. I should, I suppose, have loathed his righteous condemnation, his coldness. But I never could. I saw it as the shield of a man who was uncomfortable with his own uncertainties, who did not really know how to deal with people. I remember watching him slowly disappearing into the sunlit lunchtime crowds, looking so thin and nervous, avoiding brushing against people, not looking right or left, wanting to escape back into the safety of the monastery until he could escape yet again somewhere else, this time Los Angeles. Though I imagined I saw him afterwards, in the midst of crowds, in bars and restaurants, in retrospect, I never did. I only heard he went to Los Angeles after Frank and I got back together.

I look back on that moment watching him disappear into the crowds, as particularly heartbreaking, especially as I picture it alongside seeing him in the midst of the crowded church in that small coffin. I keep thinking about that time as something monumental, something that changed everything. I know that all that time has gone and all we have is what we remember. The crowds walk up now to commiserate with the Finns, as the undertakers discreetly position themselves beside the coffin. Then, the undertakers carefully turn Joe's coffin around so that his feet travel first down the main aisle past the mourners, as Rose and Gerry, both in black, their faces stained with tears, file solemnly past. Behind them walk people who I assume to be relatives and sundry school friends, and then come the Concelebrants, in brilliant whites and browns and stained glass reds and greens, solemnly filing past, their heads bowed, deeply troubled most of them, followed by dozens and dozens of the Brothers, many of whom I recognise from the time they employed me to work for them. Frank begins to weep uncontrollably. I put my arms around him, unable to really imagine the degree of loss this terrible day signifies to him. Then the clergy and the Brethren of the Order of the Holy Field, as they went down the main aisle of the great old gothic Church of the Seven Towers, the choir sang 'be not afraid I go before you always', rather badly as I recall, as the bulk of the congregation filed down the church after the brethren, and made their way outside to the open air. The mourning car and the hearse drove to Glasnevin cemetery where they buried him. I always imagined Joe was someone who would want cremation rather than burial. I imagine cremation as so much more dramatic, and drama was something Joe loved, something he lived for and created when it wasn't there. I remember Frank talking about all those dreadful operas he used put up with when visiting Joe in his little attic room. Joe surrounded himself with fearless mighty heroes, rings of fire and vengeful mystic Goddesses. Fire, rather than earth, should consume him. Yes, that's it. Fire should embrace him in the end.

I remember now as though it remains in the continuous present. I keep thinking over it all, that moment in the church, everything Bill had said, my meeting with Joe that day outside the library. Then I turned over and kissed Frank, who murmured something unintelligible and seemed to smile. He had already fallen asleep. I wondered how long it would be before I fell asleep.

Chapter Twenty Four

Frank

When I really knew, when the bomb dropped, it was hell. I remember there were few days I did not think of her and the thought of not seeing her again was beyond anything I had ever endured. Time stretched out before me like a dead measurer, a marking off of pointless empty heart beats. I went on living, less than dead and, as I died, I slowly re-inserted myself into religious life, numbly following the rituals without feeling anything for them. After a few months, they became all I had. I had given away everything I had to stay in the OHF. After all, I had done my duty, done the will of God and ended my liaison. There was nothing more to do, except take my love for Lisa, all the memories of her, and offer it to God. I sat alone in the church at night. And, in the dark, I prayed and wept and waited for the love of God to come and fill the void. I looked out there in the dark of the Church of the Seven Towers and saw the tabernacle light and the vague shadows of other Brothers who, like me, preferred being in the big church, instead of the more intimate, more comfortable choir, and I sat there, with those anonymous others, and whispered my desperation to God. Where are you? How could you do this to me, make me choose between my love for you and my love for another human being? How did I become this fucking cliché?

I sat there in the dark and the sacristy light went on and cast a half light along the polished sanctuary steps and lit up the stiff white marble saints, with sad, dead saint's eyes, with their impossibly well tended hair and beards and Mary, Mother of Jesus, with her kind, meek, reticent eyes and nun-like clothes. I stood up, moving to the edge of the middle aisle, walking along the transept to the far aisle, to make a quiet exit. I went into the sacristy. Brother Kevin, the sacristan, was laying out the priests' vestments for the following morning's six thirty Mass. He nodded to me as I passed into the sacristy.

"You are the last one out. Gathering brownie points from the Lord, I see."

"Yes, sorry to keep you."

"Spending a lot of time alone out there these weeks. Don't you like the choir?"

"Too public for me. Everyone watches who prays there. Spiritual exhibitionism," I said, half joking, mostly in earnest. Kevin scratched his chin. He rubbed his moist oily forehead. Then he coughed asthmatically. He looked ill, the vague self punishing suffering of the penitent visible in the sad desperation in his eyes.

"I agree," he said. "Tell me, how are you, Frank?"

His voice registered real concern. Kevin eyed me with more than a passing interest. Kevin was someone who rarely said much, ever. He certainly was never one to ask you how you were. He had the self absorption of the mystic, the robust masculinity of the hardened monk, the intimidatingly wizened features of the seemingly wise. Joe used say he was "pathologically silent" and used particularly enjoy button holing him during meals to discuss priestly vestments and their relative aesthetic merits and monetary values. It disturbed many of the younger Brothers to be seated near Kevin at dinner or during recreational periods, excepting Joe of course. I remember Joe once asked him why he didn't argue with anyone.

"What do you mean?"

"Everyone else seems to argue about things."

"That's good."

"What do you mean 'that's good?'"

Kevin impatiently put down his paper. It seemed he was going to explode with temper at being pressed so often for opinions he didn't want to proffer, but he controlled himself and answered. Joe seemed to enjoy the danger of having his feelings hurt, perhaps for days, and waited for Kevin to reply.

"It's a good change. In the old days it was much worse, if you didn't like a Brother you suppressed the feeling and got on with it. After all, you might have another thirty years living with him. Now at least we can talk it over, or argue it out. It's messier, but better."

"That's interesting. Thanks for that."

"Right." And Kevin went back to his paper.

I thought Kevin looked particularly ghastly that evening I walked into the sacristy, after my little moment of atheism. I cannot remember a time he had ever spoken to me before that night, but of course he had. I had never realised Kevin was not shy at all, merely silent. No wonder he intimidated others so much.

"Okay, Kevin. You?"

"I have a cold. I am going to bed after this. I don't feel at all well."

"I'll finish here," I said. "Go to bed."

"No. I'll finish. It's practically done." He folded a vestment expertly, took a long white cord the priest wrapped around his waist, put it across the white vestment, and smiled.

"I hear your friend is leaving."

"Who?"

"Brother Joe."

"He's not my friend. He has no friends. He? Leaving the OHF?"

"No. I hear he is going to Los Angeles. I hear they are pushing him to go."

"Really?"

"Really. Goodnight now. And keep your opinions to yourself. You know how things get repeated around here."

"Is that an opinion?"

He ignored me and locked the church door, after checking for one last time the church was empty. Then, he stood at the sacristy door, waiting for me to leave. Then, he switched off all the lights as we walked the dark corridor that linked the Church of the Seven Towers with the Monastery of the Seven Towers. Somewhere in the distance, I heard music playing. Brother Kevin turned towards the kitchen. I went upstairs, suddenly not interested in sitting in front of the television for the time intervening between then and bed time. I was now standing on the narrow return between two stairwells. It was after nine o'clock. All the Brethren gathered in the common room to watch the nine o'clock news. It was as inflexible a ritual as morning Mass and evening vespers. Silence reigned in the common room during news time. The television news trumpeted its usual infotainment. Brothers emerged from all quarters of the monastery. Newspapers were put down and conversations put on pause. And I went down to the monastery phone booth and closed the little door behind me. I rang the Brethren in the Parish of the Holy Faith.

"Hullo, Hullo? Yes? Could I speak to Brother Joe? This is …"

"Frank, I know. Well, hello there, Frank."

It was Joe. His voice was dried out, a little softer and more inaudible than before. It was the voice of a smoker, or a drinker without the drawl.

"Hi Joe. I hear you are heading off. Out of the country."

"Where did you hear that?"

"Kevin told me. He has a cold. Gone to bed. I think he's sick you know."

"Who's Kevin?"

"The Sacristan. You know Kevin. You used talk to him during dinner about vestments."

"Oh Kevin. Right. Is he sick?"

"Definitely unwell. So are you going foreign?"

"Probably."

"Where?"

"Los Angeles."

"Freakshow. You gotta be insane to go there."

"It is an environment that supports freaks. New world. A new order from nothing."

"I don't like it, Joe. Are you sure you are doing the right thing?"

"The freaks shall inherit the earth. I go to my salvation. What are you doing?"

"Ringing you, you freak. What do you think I'm doing?"

"I see"

"So?"

"So what?"

"What's parish life like?"

"Pointless. Tedious."

"Aren't you doing good works?"

"Always with the propaganda. I drink too much and play a lot of chess."

"You are a chess kitten. Anyway, I don't believe you do nothing. It's not like you."

"I am a chess kitten. But I enjoy the game. Besides, I don't care what you don't believe."

"Soooo"

"Want to meet for a drink? There's a lunar eclipse tonight."

"Okay."

"Right then"

"Good. Why not? I just wanted to say… about before, I'm…"

"Forget it, you lunatic. You can't help it if you have your little bouts of psychotic behaviour now and again. Tonight's the night. We have the lunar eclipse, a few bevies. What more is there to worry about? How about Madigans, Middle Abbey Street, about ten o'clock?"

"Maybe a little later…"

"How later? The place will be closed."

"I have to shower and change. But I'll be there."

"Fine."

I went to go find Bill to borrow money from him.

Chapter Twenty Five

Alex

Alex was sitting in the mourning car with Gerry and Rose.
'O God be merciful to me a sinner,' Alex prayed.
Alex's otherwise calm, slim, handsome face registered tiny facial tics
of tension and irritation, as he sat uncomfortably with Des and Gerry
and Rose, his perfectly tailored outfit framing his beautiful Tolstoyan
beard, his beautiful slim hands sitting on his slim lap, as he listened to
Rose's soft-voiced, tearful conversation about what a good boy Joe had
been, how brave and fearless about his childhood and other matters of
general babbling insignificance, how he used love to draw and write,
even then, and how good he was at sport, winning medals and all, how
his academic gifts were obvious to all and how his school recommended
he be tested and how they brought in a psychologist and tested him
and even then they were surprised at the results. Alex had seen the
boy's scores. Everyone who wanted to join the Order of the Holy Field
was tested and assessed. But Joe's scores were intimidating. Alex had
demurred when he seen them. He had pointed out the difficulties
attendant to someone like that adapting to the life. But Des wouldn't
hear of it. No, not now, not then, he thought. Such a stubborn man.
Looking for a son. Frustrated fatherhood, Alex thought. He liked the
mourning car. The mourning car was a spacious six seater Daimler
Benz, driving slowly behind the hearse towards Glasnevin Cemetery.

"O God be merciful to me a sinner,' Alex prayed, remembering Franny
and Zooey and fearing he would never say anything original again.
Then, he thought about the car, hating and loving and enjoying his own
angst and seeking a distraction from this self-created tension. They
must have done so many modifications on this automobile to make it
this spacious, he thought. I couldn't imagine it being readily available
at some multinational Undertaker's Supplier. This is so difficult. So
boring. The Finns seem so resilient. So strong. Almost too strong. Yes,
they are holding it in. Must be holding it in. They smile that sad smile
at me every so often. As though trying to convince me they know young
Brother Joe is in Heaven. Gone to Heaven. Monkey. O God be merciful
to me a sinner. What am I to tell them? What can I say? Passing the
old school he went to. Doing the rounds of the city. Will we ever get
there? This is Kafkaesque. Alma Mater after Mater Misericordie. Such
a good school. Great reputation. They wanted to pass Joe's school. A

roundabout trip to Glasnevin dead centre. I remember Synge Street, my own alma mater. I remember it well. George Bernard Shaw. John Millington Synge. All the sycamores, with their leaves adrift on the autumn and the young Joe walking home. Maybe not. He lived more than a mile away, maybe two. Shortest distance between two points. Maybe Rose collected him from Mater Misery. I had to walk or get the bus. She probably drove over in that big car of theirs. I imagine her waiting, the engine running and her praying for her Joe to step out of class. Joe Finn. 'O God be merciful to me a sinner.' I celebrated Mass in Harrington Street a few times. Love that church. Big congregations. Beautiful altar. Very gothic. Film maker's paradise. Atmospheric. Vampires. O God be merciful to me a sinner. Poor Joe. Long goodbyes to poor Joe. What happened to him? The manuscripts. That book he wrote. Rose talks so much. It's too much. Now she's talking about the poems Joe wrote. I have to nod and smile. About the road. Trees with fickle leaves. His verse. I took his manuscripts and disposed of them. God the something or other. No, that's wrong. Try again. "Giovanni Seipi at Home", that's the name. Full of grudges, that book. No it's a manuscript, not a book. I got rid of all of them. No more grudges. No more manuscript. Such a waste of talent. All that bile poured onto the page. He could have done so much more by pursuing a less neurotic agenda. I took care of the problem. I took the manuscripts back from the Council. Not good to have material like that in general distribution. Shredded them myself, then recycled them. kept one in a locked closet. Insurance. Like the suicide tablet astronauts take with them. For all the reasons one cannot foresee. O God be merciful to me a sinner. Terrible day. Such a tragic loss. So long. I feel for Gerry and Rose. Good people. I saw a great future for him, a distinguished life within the Order. In that, Des was correct. But he did not want evolution. He wanted revolution. If he had his way, shoppers in Eason's or Barnes and Noble would be buying "Giovanni Seipi at Home". Extraordinary.

Chapter Twenty Six

Frank

Joe sat uneasily on a wrought iron seat down the back of Madigans, in a sweater and an old pair of jeans and runners. He seemed oblivious to me as I sat down opposite him. He was drinking Stout, and had a pint ready for me. I had money, despite the fact that Bill wasn't around. I had gone into Bill's room, rifled through his drawers and found money, then wrote him a note. Dear Bill. Extenuating circumstances necessitating theft. Best, Frank. Bill would be angry. He would thump me for it but I would take the thumps and being shouted at and being called a shite, which is something of a technical term meaning one is a disappointing friend, a poor quality human being who has a tendency to abuse the advantages of friendship. I had stolen from him before, and he always forgave me. It was an emergency. I hoped I had cash enough for whatever Joe had planned for the evening. Going out for a night with Joe Finn was always something of a voyage into the unknown. Joe looked at me briefly, smiled, went over to a nearby cigarette machine and began feeding money into it. Then he sat down.

"Well, then," he said, as though preparing himself for a board meeting. "You are probably wondering why I called you here this evening." I grinned. Then he then took out an extremely sharp pen knife.

"Where did you get that? It looks pretty expensive. And, I imagine, illegal. As these hostelries are normallement video camera ridden shall we secrete the lethal weapon?"

"Your paranoia is well founded, Frankin Ryan, OHF. In these phobic times, it is the empowered individual who is the enemy of the state. That being the case, I sometimes need it for impromptu surgery, lock picking, and threatening bishops. Just in case we have any trouble tonight."

"I promise to behave."

Joe grinned.

"Very funny," he said.

"No, how much was it?" I said.

He didn't answer, as he took a cigarette and, digging the tobacco out of the paper cylinder, he cut up little bits of hash ten spot he took from a small pouch.

"Ah, I see we shall be adding possession of a prohibited substance to our list of charges for the evening. I hope you have a good lawyer on speed dial."

"No, but mummy does."

"Fucking snob," I grinned.

He laughed, muttering something about inverted snobbery being the curse of the lower classes. I laughed and slapped him. He mixed the hash with the tobacco, and with a rare dexterity, put the enhanced tobacco back into the cigarette. He should have been a surgeon, I thought. He lit the newly enhanced cigarette.

"You do realise they have security cameras here. And you can get arrested for what you are doing"

"That's the thing I like most about Frank Ryan. He knows how to have fun. Oscar Wilde liked his cigarettes dipped in laudanum. I like to grow my tumours with a certain sense of euphoria," he remarked. "I started smoking four months ago. So, by the time I am forty, the metabolic activation will have well bonded with my DNA. There will be genomic instability; genetic material normally inactive will suddenly become active, expressing itself as a cell phenotype. Then comes carcinogenesis, structural alterations in certain locales throughout my body, daughter cells with inherited genomic instability growing and multiplying. My little children of the night will begin proliferating, prodigiously cloning themselves, getting malignant and delinquent, devouring surrounding tissue, a type of internal ethnic cleansing, nothing except cancer allowed to live. Then, one day, I cough blood, or feel a certain unknown pain, or know something is terribly wrong. That day, I'll say to myself, it's either cancer or I'm turning green like the Hulk."

"You need to see someone about that little problem of yours. That tendency to talk. Using words…weird inexcusably technical words".

He grinned. "Only kidding. No, seriously. Drug use is the new battle ground for democracy. Drugs are demonized while taxes on alcohol and cigarettes rocket because the authorities need a grip on our private lives, how we think and feel and most of all how we behave. How is it that so many make so much money with drugs? Because the authorities let them," he said.

"Yeah right," I said, "That gives new meaning to the words delusional thinking. You know I can imagine you living in a bunker with reinforced walls and doors and a security surveillance system, just to be able to sleep at night."

Joe grinned sheepishly, already just a little stoned. He took a long drag out of his hash cigarette, and offered it to me. I declined, but a very attractive girl beside us smiled and raised her eyebrows at him. He gave her the cigarette. "Keep it; it's a gift from the Order of the Holy Field." She looked at him strangely, and then laughed. I don't know if she understood the significance of his cynicism.

"Do you find her attractive, Frank? Do you want to have sex with her?"

"As a matter of fact I do. Will you fix me up?"

"Naw, I don't pimp for my friends."

"So now we're friends, are we? I thought I had sinned against the Father and the Son and the Holy Joe."

"Sure we are. By the way, Lisa sends her love…I met her, you see. She looked well."

"That's nice. I am glad for her. Did you want to have sex with her…?"

"Of course not." Joe looked away suddenly, as if embarrassed by my question.

I took a long drink from the pint he had bought me and looked around at the busy bar.

"You want another one? I brought lots of money. I decided it was a little late to go out for dinner somewhere."

But I wasn't listening. Rather, I heard his voice remotely as I looked around the bar, remembering I didn't come to these places so often since Lisa and I broke up, and, even then, I hadn't gone out too much for fear of discovery. I was taking in all the people and the voices and their faces and the way they held their bodies, not sure what I was looking for, but hoping, out there in these people, who knew nothing of either Joe's life or my life, that some signature of a solution might appear.

"Frank? Do you want another?" He took a passing bar person by the arm and ordered another round.

"By the way, about Lisa. I want you to know I didn't betray you, Frank."

"Don't, please, Joe"

"I didn't betray you."

"I really don't care, Joe."

"I can't agree."

"I really don't give a damn whether you did or not."

"I didn't. It's important you know."

"Life has changed. We have moved on. Well, I hope…"

I started mechanically shaking my head, and caught the eye of the hash smoking girl. She had chestnut hair and cute carefully cut fringes and creamy skin and wore one of those mini dresses that excited me too much. I was embarrassed by my excitement. I wondered how Lisa and I had gotten together in the first place. I was so shy generally, despite appearing almost overconfident to most. The girl smiled at me and turned to her friends, now having teased me a little, proceeded to tease me with her indifference.

"I think the proto-deacon doth protest too much. How does it feel to be ordained to the priesthood you no longer believe in?"

"I believe. I have faith issues, and I am receiving help."

"And you were talking to me about delusional thinking! Eh?"

"I'm sorry?"

"Look, these people are members of the psyche core."

"The what? What are you on?"

"They are the equivalent of professional interrogators or mind control experts."

"Joe, you're crazy. Something has you fucked up."

"I'm not. A bit disturbed maybe. I'm sane though."

"No, really. You're wasted. You're eyes are great dark holes. Like kittens eyes, when waiting for saucers of milk. I can see them now."

He paused for a moment. I grinned at his absurdity, and then, provoked as usual, I responded to him.

"I admit I'm fucked up. Good metaphor, Ryan"

"No, Joe. These are good people, therapists, trying to help people with issues."

"These people are professional brainwashers, disguised as therapists and spiritual counsellors."

He was talking rapidly, sweating, his hands, slim long-fingernailed hands, trembling. He went on:

"Their job is to make you keep rewriting your own personal self interpretation until it's in line with the deposit of faith."

"Big Brother will forever fuck you up, eh?"

"And I thought I had the monopoly on the dramatic twist and there you are, going all eloquent and literary on me. Yes, something like that. Big Brother. Frater superior."

"You seem to have a lot of opinions tonight, Joe."

"Have you regained your faith? Eh Frank?"

"Fuck you." I stood up to leave.

"Now you have lost Lisa, you have found Jesus?"

I stopped and turned around and putting my face close to him, I spat back the following words.

"Faith is a gift. Such descriptions are moot."

He grinned drunkenly, drunkenly stonedly.

"What good is faith if you have to believe, if you go to hell if you don't believe, if every thought, if expressed, is used against you, if every moment they watch what you say or do? Sit down, sit down. I'm sorry. Sorry, man."

I sat down.

"It's not like that. That's the drugs talking."

"It's not the drugs talking. I swear. I fucking swear. I have become a good citizen, a true party member. You fall in line, one incapable of unlawfulness, without criticism or debate."

"Oh, shut up Joe! You are talking bullshit."

"You have buried your heart along with your time with Lisa. You know you don't believe. You live inside the ideology. Voluntary self suppression for the purposes of-"

"You're one to talk."

"You know you know…"

I grabbed him by the wrist and squeezed. After I break his arm, I thought, I'll beat him up. I can't beat him up here, what with the security cameras and all. But later. Later, I'll do him. Just to send him a message. I knew I did not look strong. I knew I was not a big man. Suddenly his face whitened. He saw how murderously angry I felt.

"I don't want to hear another word from you about her. Lisa is not open for discussion. Anyway, at least I'm not escaping across the Atlantic Ocean. You would have gone without a word."

"Let go."

"Fuck you."

"They want me to be someone I am not. Let go. Let go, or I'll find a use for the knife you liked so much, you fucking fascist."

I let go. He rubbed his bruising wrist.

"Sorry about that, Joe. I saw red."

"Me too."

We drank in silence for a while.

"I tried to write something for them and they hated it."

"You mean the stuff you never showed me?"

"The same. I was afraid you wouldn't like it."

"Didn't you write it for yourself?"

"No one writes for themselves. They write because of vanity and insecurity and the desperate need for attention. That's a literary fantasy propagated by Nobel laureates and publishers."

"Who cares what they think? Fuck them. You have plenty books in you."

"I don't know about that."

"Back in a sec."

"Where are you going?"

"To phone the police. It's my duty as to report you to the authorities."

"What?"

I went up to the bar and waited to be served. The girl with the fringe walked past me on the way to the toilet. I resisted talking to her. Then I feared offending her, hurting her feelings. Suddenly everyone in the world was as sensitive as I was. I was being ordained in six months. No woman would ever look at me again. I was going to be a deacon in six months. I was truly fucked.

"What'll it be, sport?"

One of the bar men stood in front of me. He had an oily face and a chin dappled with the cratered after effects of acne. He was tired, sweating, impatient. I was obviously wasting his time, waiting patiently to order a drink.

"Two Guinness. Or Murphy's if you have it. Thanks, sorry." I looked around. The girl had gone. There was only the emptiness after her.

Joe was smoking another hash cigarette. Maybe the girl would try to get that one off him too. Joe didn't care much about things. He would give money, clothing, books, raincoats, towels, anything, away. His room was mostly empty, despite the fact that his parents regularly sent money and gifts. What an idiot, I thought. What a waste of talent.

"Guinness? Thank you." The tired impatient barman handed me my change and I went back to Joe.

"So?"

"So what?"

"What is this, some kind of Beckett moment? Tell me about the thing, your book with the putting of words together and what not."

Joe took the drink and drank half a pint of Guinness. I wondered how someone so slight could hold such a quantity of liquid.

"Thirsty work, you know. So, here's the thing. Alex, God be good to him, came to me about a year ago and gently suggested I go for ordination and take a doctorate in the Angelicum in Rome and that a seat in one of our Major Universities might be the best route for someone like myself."

"How distinguished," I said. "He does that. He offers you the world so he might own you."

"I thought you liked Alex."

"I don't hate him, like you do. What did you say?"

"I replied I had considered the possibility of being an academic, but that I had joined the Order of the Holy Field to serve the Lord in the Holy Field."

"It's scary you can fit so many clichés in one small sentence."

"I used that exact language as a way of especially annoying him, as he so likes to patronise and condescend. I said that I know I am bound under the vows of obedience to obey, but I strongly preferred not to pursue a professional academic career, and, if necessary, I might volunteer to go on the missions to avoid such a fate."

"I'd say that our holy Brother Alex was greatly cheered by your words."

"You can just imagine how pissed he was, how angry. Alex had called me in."

"Into his offices?"

"Right, and Alex stood there and his normally calm, warm, moist demeanour suddenly assumed a clear, but unmistakably artic, aspect. His voice lowered and, in a half Hannibal Lecter whisper, he said that, perhaps a trip to the missions might well be the best fate for such a Brother as myself. You know that filing cabinet of his, in his office?"

"Most Council members have a filing cabinet. They're for files."

"Sooo anyway, I saw he was going to organise it that either I went on the missions, or I went to the Angelicum in Rome for four years, doing some awful Doctorate in some ludicrous angels dancing on pinheads theology and spend the next thirty years wasting my life teaching rubbish to dullards, smoking crack on the side and growing one of those aforementioned tumours."

"Too much Thus Spoke Zaranthustra for me. Lighten up, man"

As ever, he ignored what he didn't want to hear.

"Des will be out of a job come next June. So, I knew I was in trouble. I had to figure some way out of it. I thought and looked around. Nothing. And I was at the point of giving up when one night I was sitting up watching a movie by myself. I was pretty drunk and stoned. I struggled to get up out of my chair when the movie ended and, asI reached down between the cushions, I pulled up one of those Provincial Newsletters. I paged through and there it said that they were looking for Brothers to go to guess where?"

"Los Angeles, perhaps?"

"Los Angeles. So I applied and they said yes."

"Of course they said yes. Alex fixed it. You pissed him off and he fixed it. He made some calls…"

"Exactly. I counted on his vindictiveness. No is the default answer. Always no. Even if it's the right thing to say yes, they always say no. They want you to say yes to them, not vice versa."

"So, what happened then?"

"I checked around. It seems in the United States I am out of their way, well out of their way."

"Out of Alex's way."

"Exactamundo. I have, have crossed more than Alex. I have crossed myself out, I guess. Let us say, I am great distance from the concerns of the Irish Province of the Order of the Holy Field. I will be on loan to the Western U. S. Province of the OHF, directly reporting to Rome."

"How unusual."

"I have full permission to write there, and I can attend the college of my choice. The hope is I will settle there and, all things being equal, I just might do that. It's my only chance. Over here, I will simply die. Living here is killing me. Modern life has its own peculiar busy emptiness. It's rubbish. I am no longer having fun, Frank, to say the very least."

Joe looked down on his half finished third pint of porter. He looked away and winced when I mentioned how I would miss him. It was after twelve o' clock at night. He pointed with his thumb to the bar man who was shouting "Time people, time. Have ye no homes to go to?"

"This place is closing or haven't you noticed? They'll be putting on the thumbscrews if we don't get out of here. I have to go take a piss."

He got up and struggled down to the gents. I followed him, swallowing the last of my drink, and depositing our glasses at the bar. The barmaid there nodded in appreciation.

As we stood together at the urinals, Joe seemed alarmingly unsteady on his feet.

"I try to ignore obnoxious bar people who throw you out at closing time," I said.

"Yeah, I don't like it either."

"Joe?"

"Huh?"

"Did you take anything else besides the hash, with the porter? Joe? You seem - wobbly on your feet."

"I'm okay. Thanks, thanks Frank. I've been under a lot of stress. So, where to now?"

"We should check out the eclipse. Are you okay with that? Eh Joe? When does it happen?"

"So, it's just turned April the fourteenth. It's what, 12.30 am. At 2:19 am it should be in full mode. If there aren't too many clouds from now on we finally get to see the dark side of the moon."

He zipped up his trousers and staggered from side to side. I caught him. He grinned.

"People will begin to say we were in love."

I smiled.

"Maybe we might go somewhere, and just sit for a while. What did you take? Come on, I'm not going to report you."

"A little Vicodin to lift the general mood. I have, as I said, been under pressure."

"Vicodin. That stuff is addictive."

"Affirmative. I should report these unpleasant side effects: loss of coordination, confusion, irregular heartbeat, irregular breathing, dizziness, anxiety or tremors. I should report this, but I can't."

"Because someone gave you these drugs."

"Right. Let's go sit somewhere. I shall have to stop taking them."

"It's worrying. You could get cancer. Your liver or kidneys."

"Go into rehab mode. Get a therapist. Those dreadful people."

"There's nothing fashionable or bohemian or revolutionary about what you're doing. All it brings is misery or madness or death. I have relatives with such problems."

"You're right, of course. I should stop drinking smoking taking drugs. That is part of the plan for Los Angeles. I am away from the forces of destruction, eh?"

We were outside the bar now, crossing O'Connell Street Bridge. Joe steadied on his feet. Above, the earth was beginning to block the light from the sun. Its orbit and the orbit of the moon began to align so that the moon was gradually becoming unable to reflect the silvery light of the sun. Joe was talking incessantly about it. It seemed that the cocktail of drugs flowing through his bloodstream and changing his brain chemistry were making him garrulous. Saying how the length of the moon's shadow varies from three hundred and sixty seven thousand and three hundred and seventy nine thousand kilometres, and that the moon is between three hundred and fifty seven thousand and four hundred and ten thousand kilometres from the earth, and I said I didn't care and that he should shut up and, eventually, thankfully, he did. We sat in a late night coffee shop, looking out and seeing the moon occasionally peeping out between the clouds and the rapidly rising rooftops.

"The entire city skyline is littered with high rise cranes, lit up like Christmas lights," I said.

"Do you like that?" Joe said. His eyes were lazily moving right to left. Then his eyelids were closing, then opening. I was alarmed by his demeanour, but I tried to appear calm.

"What? Do I like what?"

"The way the city is, all lit up?"

"I don't know. I like the business. Busy ness. Business of being busy. But no one talks to you."

"I didn't know you were so lonely," Joe said.

"I'm not lonely," I said.

"Do you want to walk, my atheist friend? Lisa would want you to walk, to savour the moment."

"I thought we agreed not to mention her. Shall we go? Do you feel a bit better?"

"A bit. A bit better. I'm glad we met."

"So am I," I said.

We walked about and watched the skies. By one o' clock the moon was half in darkness, its silvery light being eaten away by the encroaching earth. All that was left on the dark side was a rapidly growing grey brown disc. It was occasionally occluded by cloud and Joe and I watched the darkness grow and the streetlights becoming more intense and colder in the passionless light they threw on the passers by. Despite everything, the city continued its endless St. Vitas' Dance. Even in the middle of the night, apartments were being built. Elsewhere, we witnessed other high rise construction going on. The surreal glow of arc lights betrayed the endless labours. Somewhere in the city, especially the centre of the city, buildings were stretching out, growing atop the impromptu graves of other, older buildings, replacing in quick, unpredictable gestures the old signs of less profitable, smokier, secret structures. Vestiges of slower life forms, of less cosmopolitan, less opulent times, were in the process of disappearing. The new buildings seemed strangely warmer and less forbidding than in the ordinary light of day.

"My parents are terribly excited by my going to Los Angeles, you know. Every so often they put more money for me in an account they started for me when I joined the Order, despite the fact I have a vow of poverty. I do use it every so often. They give out to me if I don't break my vow of poverty at least once a month. It's a problem, so I go out to dinner with someone, usually Des, who likes fancy restaurants. It makes him feel like a bishop, or a tribal chief. Do you like fancy restaurants?"

"No. I get self conscious. I have poor co-ordination, so I tend to spill expensive foods, usually over someone else. Once I spilled a whole bottle of Chateau Neuf over a psychiatrist friend of Bill. It was the worst moment of my life."

"Red or white wine?"

"Red, naturally."

"Dear God, remind me never ever to dine with you."

I laughed.

"It's probably a matter of self confidence."

"Do you need money?"

"No, thank you. My Lord, look at the moon."

We looked at the moon. Two thirds of the disc was in shadow, two great craters like eyeless sockets looking down from the dark side, clouds slowly drifting past as we stood on South Great Georges Street.

"You know something, Frank - they will never forgive you for leaving. You regard yourself as a pedestrian member of a little regarded Order, and you luxuriate in your own insignificance. But in the end you will remember us; you will remember the little things, the little things that constitute us. You remember because you know who you really are and are in flight from that. You are very forgiving, Frank. I always liked that about you. It will take you places."

"I have no idea what you are talking about. I fear you've messed up our time together with all your drug taking. It's very hurtful."

"I'm sorry, Frank."

"Okay, don't worry about it."

"Are you hungry?"

"Not really. I'm kind of tired."

"Me too. I might go home now and make a sandwich. We really must do this again soon. A few weeks, perhaps?"

"Why not?"

"I think we have seen as much as we will of the moon. The penumbral eclipse covers about two thirds of the moon's surface from Dublin. Thankfully we didn't get too much cloud. It's what, about twenty to three. And I'm cold."

"No. Not a lot of cloud."

"And no rain."

"No rain. Though it is cold."

"Yes, it's cold all right."

So we walked down to the taxi rank and Joe insisted on paying my fare. We said our goodbyes and I left him with one of those ironic half smiles on his face. I didn't know what the smile meant. I wanted to call him up the following day and ask him what he meant by that smile, but I didn't. I kept thinking about what he said to me, about my lack of faith, about ordination, and about Lisa.

He flew out to Los Angeles a few months after our night of penumbral lunar eclipsed drinking and laughing and arguing, quietly disappearing from my life in the same manner as he had quietly appeared. I did not feel the loss. I don't know why. Perhaps I was unaware how depressed I was. Perhaps it was because he softened the blow by writing. I destroyed the letters. I wish I had them now, something I could read through rather than recording from a poor memory of what he had written. Joe wrote to me and, for a while, I did not respond to his letters. Mostly because he did not invite me to his farewell parties. Maybe he thought he was being kind to me after what I told him about my fears of restaurant occasions. I don't know. He could be rather literal about things. Gerry and Rose, so he wrote, confronted him that night about his decision to go to the United States. Rose said she hadn't been sleeping for fear of what might happen to him. Joe, she said, was not good at taking care of himself. Anyhow, they said, what was he doing? It all seemed so precipitous. It all seemed as though he were running away. Joe's parents were filled with misgivings about his life plans, his great new departure. "Why do you need to go away to write?" they asked. "Why can't you stay here, or go less far away from Ireland?" they asked.

Joe made excuses. It was a great opportunity. The difference in cultures would fire his imagination. It was a welcome change from dreary Ireland. Ireland is not dreary, they said. It's a great country. They had health concerns too, about Joe. They were less than certain that Joe could properly look after himself. But, one way or another, he had decided. And no one could stop him.

I looked at them, Gerry and Rose, and remembered Joe's letters. I looked at them getting out of the mourning car and walking with such dignity to the graveside on this beautiful, clear blue skied, stiflingly hot June day, with the trees so gorgeously verdant, the air hot with love filled possibilities. Perhaps their heartbreak is a matter of lifelong privacy, a matter between God and those who love and mourn, those left behind after love's short moments, those bound by time, life ending moment by moment. The coffin was placed over the grave, a small plastic carpet of fake green grass beneath the beneath to shield the void, beneath the dark down where Joe would eventually decompose and dissolve. And the prayers began with Des praying over Joe's coffin, his face a picture of suffering, his eyes closed as he seemed to remember all the prayers by heart, his memory not failing him at this crucial moment, all the Brothers crowding around, the Finns front and centre with their cries of devastation softly audible above the voice of the priest consigning the Brother, their son, to his last place on earth.

'And he will rise on the last day when time will end and a great trumpet will call out and, in the end, as the last moments of the atomic clock tick out, a great apocalypse shall unfold and at last, after countless millennia of horror and torment and beauty and love and hate and war, there shall be only love and justice and all this pain will be over and the beauty of the world will no longer will make us sad, because it will never end. It will be the beauty of God.'

I know in my heart that was not what Des said. I know it was not liturgically correct. But it is what I heard, and I wonder what others heard. Then, Des stopped speaking. The silence, like a membrane suspended between the oval shaped crowds, broke, and the weeping, with the gradual lowering of Joe Finn's small slim remains into the ground, washed away the horror and the absurdity of his death, his random slaughter by some random passing person carrier. Rose cried out in anguish for the other great love of her life besides God and her husband. Gerry clung onto her lest she throw herself on top of her son as he finally left them forever. Then, as Joe hit bottom, the cables were pulled away and gradually each of us took a little soil and tossed it on top of the beautiful coffin, topped as it was with roses and lilies cast by tearful mourners as the coffin went down. Goodbye, we said. And it seemed we had let him go, but I knew I hadn't. It was only afterwards I fully realised this. I realised that I had stood there at the graveside and refused to accept his departure, refused to accept that all I had left were these memories, that all my compassion for Rose and Gerry, my indelible images of Des and Alex with such a deep sense of irrevocable loss on their faces, my mind recording the tear faced Brethren and relatives, was simply a way of not feeling. My refusal to indulge myself, my lack of self absorption at the loss of a loved one, one so deeply a part of my life and soul, a friendship that I could never, with all the self actualization or well-crafted therapeutic skills, recreate because it was a friendship forged by the magic of chance, a love that had somehow made me, brought me out from the darkness of faith into the Eden of doubt, forced me to face my love for Lisa and my lack of a vocation. Joe Finn was one of the great loves of my life. I could never replace him. And at that moment, I could not face that awful truth. So, instead of feeling, I watched.

Chapter Twenty Seven

Gerry

After we buried our beautiful boy, we were taken home. I couldn't drive that day. My hands shook. My stomach ached. When we got home, we craved isolation. We wanted to be left alone. But they wouldn't leave us alone. For much of the day, people milled quietly about our house, talking and consoling and watching us to see us through this critical time. Neighbours called to pay their respects. Relatives I hadn't seen in years dropped in to express their sorrow. Old wounds were healed, I think. Overall, everyone kept an eye on us. I didn't know what they expected of us. Both Rose and I felt our lives were over. We couldn't have any more children; we had made no secret of that. The therapists made it clear that it was healthier for us to be open about such things. But Joe was different. Nothing or no one could replace Joe in our lives. We knew that. Joe was unique. And everyone was so kind that day. I could claim I remember everyone or everything we met or spoke to that day. Joe would say that if I were put under hypnosis I would have total recall. I remember one of his letters about that, about eyesight. I remember he said we don't know what we see, that our minds tell us what we see, that they are finding a computer chip to record a lifetime's experience, downloadable into other minds, that he was reading about it in Los Angeles, but that we all have different patterns of recognition, something that makes us unique. I remembered all these things as we sat there drinking coffee and whiskey, not that any of it made sense to me, not that any of the disconnected memories I had would explain why he went out that day to get the papers and died crossing the road, why he had lived to that exact moment and not a second more, if there was a plan to these things or not, and I would smile every so often and wonder what Joe would have to say about that absurd little gathering in our house that day. I remember particularly that no one knew what to say, except Alex, who seemed to have an affinity for dealing with tragedy. The rest of us stuck with casual talk, simple things, comments about the lawn or the state of the house, or the amount of pollution in the air. But I remember Alex's professional concerns, his not so spontaneous kindnesses, and his well rehearsed compassion. He helped a lot, I think. I think Des found him a bit excruciating. But he was trying his best and, overall, I think the time was made easier by the kindness of friends and relatives. Our every need was taken care of. Busy people busied themselves in the kitchen making it so very spotless, making food and tidying and seeing to our needs and we sat in the back garden and sipped whiskey and wine and coffee and talked quietly about inconsequentials and cried every so often and occasionally I looked up to his room window on the first floor where it looked out to the garden, getting a good view of the trees and the pitch and putt course out back and all the golf balls he would find in the back garden, coming in with a few more to put in the bucket he kept by the back door and the sheer sight of it like a knife in my heart and I knew. "Look Daddy", he would say, "look, we have thirty-six balls here. Thirty-six." And he would hold the bucket of golf balls up for me. He would be collecting them for me. He knew I liked pitch and putt. I remembered these little things, not his exam scores or his abilities. I remembered the pictures he drew me or the golf balls he collected for me and I just knew there was no getting over this time. Rose and I knew the truth of it. A part of us, a part of our lives had simply dissolved, fallen into a six foot hole in Glasnevin Cemetery, with nothing to show for it but memories. After they left, our friends and relatives and members of the Order of the Holy Field, we sat in the house and did nothing.

"Well," I said. "We should go to bed. It's two in the morning."

"I don't want to." Rose said.

"My love, we should go to bed. Just to lie down. Just to give sleep a chance. We can't just sit here. Not here like this in the dark."

I don't think we were in the dark. I just said in the dark for effect. It worked. Rose stood up and we went upstairs to the bedroom. I helped her dress for bed and folded her clothes carefully, which was important to her. Then I got into my pyjamas myself and I put on a little music in the bedroom. I can't remember what music it was. Glenn Gould, perhaps. Maybe I put on the radio and it magically seemed to be the right music, like when I was a boy listening to the sound of the shipping forecast seemed to be so calming so reassuring and made me ready to sleep: Lundy, Fastnet, Irish sea, Rockall, Malin, Hebrides, Bailey. I had no idea what the words meant, but together the words were like poetry, like music. Then I stopped remembering when I was a boy. I remember I drew the blinds and got into bed with Rose. We held each other. Then we cried and somehow fell asleep.

Chapter Twenty Eight

Frank

First, I began to have tiny doubts about my faith. Like splinters in one's mind, that hurt so bad, but were too small to isolate. They crept in unawares. I suppressed them, using my considerable talents at self censorship. Then, after an indeterminate time, the whole notion of a creed, any creed, including non creed creeds, seemed too much to accept, which I again denied to myself. It was then I became afraid. I had panic attacks and insomnia, uncertain aches and pains. Those tiny splinters again. Because I was deeply uncertain, I began to seek total certainty. I read voraciously on the one true faith that led to salvation. I prayed for guidance. I meditated for hours on the Gospels. I became a model citizen of the city of God. You see, Ego, I told myself, I have given up my life of sin and turned to Jesus. My own personal Jesus. But I knew the truth. I knew it was all a sham. Jesus had gone. I had killed Jesus. Took Jesus down a back alley and executed him. One in the head, two in the sacred heart. Doubt and lust and thought feeding the hate. I checked my six then the corpse. No wallet no id no signs of life. Give him three days, I thought. He'll be back. But right there, no chance at resuscitation. It's dead, Frank. Instead of faith and hope and charity, I felt nothing except the impulses of duty. I was a dedicated man. I had my uniform. I was part of something bigger. I was the trooper defending the flag of a fallen nation. Something was gone. Such a monumental centrepiece of my personal belief system had long gone. I was high and dry. I was alone and lost and filled with self pity. I needed desperately to get laid.

I liken what happened to waking up one day and realizing one has been for a long time unwell, or realizing one has mistaken illusion for truth, or being stoned for true emotion. It's like mistaking a dream for real life. Unless one realises one has been dreaming it all feels so very real, something worth dying for. It began as a depression. I was depressed for weeks and months without knowing the cause. I talked to therapists about Joe and Lisa. I opened my soul to spiritual directors. I went on retreat, changed my diet. I tried anti-depressants. I practised yoga. I took up jogging. I gave up meat and alcohol. Nothing really helped. I knew I was really in trouble when I started helping to give retreats, spiritual direction, and preaching at Mass. I needed to belong, desperately needed to be just the same as all the rest. When one works so hard at being one of them, one is in truth no-one.

So, I went through days and weeks and months wheezing asthmatically for the first time in my life, sucking in inhalers, resting, itching and getting flu, knowing somewhere inside that this beautiful life laid on for me to interiorise, with all its virtuoso potentialities for goodness, its prayers and study and good works, the hours spent pursuing God in all her many elusive guises, was a lie. It was all a lie. The matrix had me. I was pursuing ghosts, the ones who haunt and torment you in dreams or distracted moments. I feared greatly that the Brethren likewise were also pursuing chimeras, some kind of grotesque amalgam of their own deepest needs for salvation and happiness, for we cause ourselves and others so much pain in the pursuit of happiness. Then I lambasted myself for my arrogance. How could such an ancient institution be founded on a lie? Didn't it produce saints? Weren't the walls of our monasteries dappled with their portraits, these people who had lived lives of supernatural virtue? We had libraries of books about their lives, a ten most wanted list of lives of supernatural virtue. I had helped shelve such libraries. And each day weren't new miracles offered to Rome for its ruthlessly scientific scrutiny? The life of a saint was the Church in microcosm, its unofficial history of love which was sacrifice. It was the history of virtue held up to all of us in the Order of the Holy Field as an example to be followed. Each new saint we acquired was a validation of our way of life, a reason to go on and make others do likewise in the Field of the Lord. It proved that perfection was possible. By a process of comparison, my tiny life against the ancient and mighty Order of the Holy Field, or even greater, the Church, I was a nothing. I was a speck of dust disappearing down the corridors of their history, forgotten before I was ever thought of.

Perhaps it was that very sense of my own insignificance in this great system that made me act as my time for ordination approached. I had no proof I was in the wrong line of work. I could never prove anything. I could never really defend my deepening doubts. I could never counter my growing unease with myself. I felt that the life I was living was an act of infidelity. I feared history was being rewritten each day, in some nameless spin doctoral ministry. I sensed good did not win, that we were unfree, and that taxation was ubiquitous. I could prove nothing. I knew I wanted out. I knew reality was beyond the tangible, that the love of God seemed incompatible with human life on earth. It was in the books I was reading, the Brethren I spoke to, the hours of meditation

I suspended myself within. It was in the air I breathed. Something was wrong with the world, and with me.

Looking back, I know I was no different to the others around me. I sensed they too saw something wrong with their world. I felt like the kind, intelligent, responsible, hardworking householder, one with a loving spouse, a house, and children who come down to breakfast each day before trotting off to school and look you in the eye and you see your own self betrayal in their gaze.

But no one except Joe had the courage to say something like this. No one except Joe looked me in the eye and told me I was a liar and a fraud. Now he was gone from my life. And here I still was. I was a sham. I had taken a vow of poverty and become an elitist member of the Order of the Holy Field, which afforded me endless privileges. I was chaste, yet filled with endless sexual longings I had frequently satisfied. I was obedient to systems obsessed with power and its accumulation. I was alone in a community, a common life in an ancient monastery surrounded by monks I had nothing in common with. My friends had gone. Something had to give. So I went to see Lisa.

Generally, I had repressed my need for Lisa. It was an effort requiring enormous energy and bringing on strange stomach disorders, headaches and the aforementioned feeling of general lethargy that required medication. Even up to the moment before I decided to go see Lisa, the idea of it was the most unlikely thing in the universe for me. I hadn't seen her for two years, months before summer exams in my second year in college. I had drifted since then, going through life trying to find the love of God. Alex had put such a spell on me. Alex knew how to control people, I decided. He certainly knew how to control me. Maybe I was predisposed towards such control. He activated the necessary triggers, the necessary repressions. Up to the moment before I decided to see Lisa, the thought of ever seeing her again filled me with such dread and remorse and desire and loneliness and confusion that I had to stop thinking about her just to get by from day to day. Then, my ordination approached and I was filled with misgivings, sleepless nights, excessive drinking, depression, a general sense of dread of unknown origin. Before ordination came my final exams. I studied eight hours a day for weeks. I had to succeed. It was vitally important to my self-esteem that I do well. The lingering experience of living in close proximity to the kind of casual brilliance evident in Joe Finn did much to sharpen my academic ambitions. Joe distrusted academia. But I had to prove to myself that I was no slouch. I had to prove I was a worthy contender for the company of Joe Finn. Such was my pettiness and insecurity and sibling rivalry.

How I went to see Lisa was intimately tied in with my final exams. I felt I had failed with her. I felt Alex had made me fail. I knew somewhere within I was a dead man without her. And yet, I knew I was dead anyway. Lisa, along with Joe, had merely pointed out my post-mortem status. I finished my degree on a Tuesday afternoon in mid May. I was to get a first. Obviously I didn't know that back then. I left University College Dublin without meeting my fellow students for post-exam drinks to finalise summer's hopeful arrangements for parties and get-togethers. I walked out of the last exam hall in a trance-like state, suddenly obsessed with seeing Lisa again. I have no specific memory of how this obsession took hold. I think at some point during that final exam I saw the light. I gave up on being the person God might love. And, feeling the great relief of such an impossible burden's removal, I felt calm for the first time in years.

As soon as the exams were over, as soon as I left the great hall with the hundreds of desks strewn with papers and desperate students, I had to be with her. I cycled into the city centre and went to Lisa's apartment and sat outside on her steps for the afternoon, drinking water to keep myself hydrated, with a lingering miserable anticipation of the few days of exhaustion headaches and irritability to follow, that inevitable phase of recovery from the trauma of major exams. At six o' clock I saw her, wearing hipster jeans and a t-shirt that said 'Debbie is a crack whore.' Who's Debbie? I thought. Her perfectly fitted t-shirt probably signified a type of wit and irony not available to men, I thought. She had cut her hair and wore flat leather sandals. Politically incorrect shoes too. She looked shocked to see me. She tried to hide her utter shock and disbelief. But I knew.

"You cut your hair," I said. She didn't answer. She stared hard at me and went to angrily push past me on the stairs. Suddenly, I was an obstacle she could transcend by dint of will. I couldn't let her pass. I wanted her anger. I stopped her. At first I stood in front of her. I told her I was wrong. I was wrong and she was right. I told her Joe told me I was wrong and she was right. I said I accepted that Joe was right. She told me to get out of the way. I didn't. I said I wasn't going anywhere.

I held her by the shoulders. She said she was going to call the police. I said she should do that after I had my say. She tried to pull away. I held on to her. She punched me in the jaw. I didn't move. Then she hit me again, on the shoulder. I didn't move. Then she slapped me on the face. I let her, tears coming from my eyes. Then she stopped. Her eyes filled once more with tears and grief. I tried to manfully ignore the pain and imagined the bruises she left on me. I imagined how much it would hurt the following day, which it did for more than a week. How we ended upstairs making love on her sofa, I don't actually remember, but we made love for most of the evening, despite her phone ringing several times. Then we showered and went for a long quiet drink. That day was the happiest of my life, the day my life changed forever, one of the few moments of absolute certainty I have ever experienced. I remember her taking a set of keys out and opening the door. I followed. Now I keep thinking of the stairwell struggle and the people passing us and seeing us fighting. I remember my mounting paranoia at our lover's fight. I wanted it all safe and sound behind closed doors, or in some open space where no one could see us. I think of the insane way we reconciled. I think of all the possible misinterpretations of the theatre of disaster enacted that day between Lisa and me. She was hitting me, crying and hitting me. Thankfully, no police came. There were no arrests and questioning. The press was not informed. But we went upstairs to her apartment. I told her I had betrayed her by going back to the Order of the Holy Field. She said she had moved on. She looked fitter, happier. She had cut her hair and found promotion acceptable in her upwardly mobile career as a librarian. She was seeing a new man. He was, I discovered later, a dentist, thirty two years old, with a house and a gorgeous car and was buying a house down the country where she and he would go for long weekends, fishing and driving and looking at the perfectly acceptable romantic scenery. His parents were wealthy and loving, polite, and, of course, they liked Lisa, and she liked them. So, things were good for Lisa. She had achieved the cliché, I thought. Good for her. Another year and marriage would be on the cards. An acceptable passage of time and Seán would propose to her during a Shannon cruise, or on an autumn evening in that lovely country house he was buying. And whatever the physical circumstances of his proposing, I know Lisa would have accepted, knowing full well that meeting a man like Seán, more human than most men, a man with his circumstances, were unlikely to recur, considering her socio-economically challenged status, knowing equally full well that romantic love is either a temporary state or an illusion, knowing too that life is short and the pursuit of happiness destroys its object. And then, there was the Frank factor. After all, I, Frank, had left her. And I had very nearly ruined her life. For myself, I imagined Seán proposing to Lisa down the country on a cold winter's evening, rather than one of those awful cruises I originally imagined. The fire would be beginning to catch in the grate and a steak meal would be sitting before them, perfectly cooked and ready to eat, and Seán would ask her to be his wife and she would smile and say yes and they would kiss, and then finish their dinner lest it get cold.

But I screwed up her chances for a step up that remorseless social ladder, with its cold beauty and endless demands and artic aspect. I stopped that possible future. That beautiful romantic proposal never happened, because Lisa and I got back together soon after that absurd violence filled evening. I began to call on her. We would go out for a drink or a bite to eat and end up back to her apartment and a few months afterwards she broke up with Seán. Six months later Seán married a beautiful haematologist from Brazil. Lisa and I laughed a lot about such a meeting of medical minds and bodies. We were even invited and went to the wedding. They were a beautiful couple. Seán seemed to be a very decent person. I had never met him or even seen him before that day. Lisa was careful that way.

Chapter Twenty Nine

Frank

I was sitting in my father's car on a Sunday afternoon outside the former monastic site of Glendalough, now turned into a tourist spot filled with walking tours, safe footpaths and strategically placed seats and bed and breakfast houses and bars, and a well known hermitage for those of a more contemplative mindset. I was there at my mother's suggestion. Knowing I hadn't spoken to Dad in months, she proposed he and I spend the afternoon driving around. I had resisted the idea initially, wondering if it were possible to put off telling them about my troubles in the OHF. But Dad knew. Because of his detached gaze on a world he had long grown disgusted with, he rarely missed anything that might confirm his lack of enthusiasm. He wanted me to say something about what was happening for me. So I didn't. We small talked as we drove out of Dublin through heavy traffic south to Dun Laoghaire, then along the coast to Wicklow, turning off towards the woods, Roundwood, where we stopped to picnic in the pine forests, drinking hot sweet tea and munching Mother's salad sandwiches and watching the squirrels and swallows and finches and tourists and easily distinguishable regular visitors coming and going, having food, walking around. Then, we drove to Glendalough, to visit, for the hundredth time, the ancient lakeside monastic community founded by Kevin, first driving to Laragh then turning west towards Glendalough with the Glendasan River barely visible to our right. It would be probably full of people, I said. We took a walk around the ruins, then along the river to the lakes.

"I hear you are having trouble. Big trouble," he said.

"How do you know?"

"I hear things. You didn't seem too keen to talk. What's happening?"

"I haven't said anything to my superiors, but I am having faith problems."

"What's her name?"

"What do you mean?

"I mean, is there a girl involved?"

"If you really want to know, then let me explain."

"Okay, then. Go ahead. I'm listening."

I couldn't think of anything to say. All my inner rehearsals seemed to drain away from my mind.

"Well? What have you heard?" I began.

"People talk. You know that. Your mother was talking to some of the parishioners. By the way your sister is pregnant. It's a girl."

"Again?"

"Yes."

"Don't they know how that happens?"

"Now that's not nice."

"Is this what you are afraid of? A child out of wedlock?"

Dad didn't answer. He looked at me with a clinical smile. He was waiting for me to get to my next point. If I had no point, or my point was of insufficient interest, then the smile would narrow somewhat. I was worried at what I would say, worried if I went on too long, or was dull or stupid, then I would lose him. All I ever did was lose him, I thought. I was telegrammatic, a sure sign of my fear and inner trembling.

"All I'm saying is I have issues with the faith."

"The faith? Is there such a thing?"

"I started studying theology. It doesn't bear up well to a lot of rational scrutiny."

"What issues?"

My father's voice had dropped an octave.

"I don't see why you have to talk to me like that, Dad."

"Like what?"

"It's like you don't believe me."

"Sure I believe you. I just don't understand."

"What don't you understand? I just answered you. Didn't you hear me? I have faith problems. I didn't know I did. It wasn't something I knew would happen to me, but it did." I said.

"What's wrong with the faith?" he snapped.

"I don't know, Dad. I thought it was me. How do you examine something outside anything you can sense?"

"I think things can be explained in terms of what we really need deep down. That makes sense, to me anyway."

"And yet, before, everything seemed to make some kind of sense. Now I feel very lost. Faith in God doesn't answer my questions anymore."

"I have found there's always some bit of skirt at the back of a spoiled priest's philosophizing."

"Don't be too cynical about this, Dad."

"I'm not being cynical."

"Are too."

"Not a chance, my boy. Don't go there."

"I think you feel as negatively about my choices as you do about your own. All the anger you are hiding behind your mechanical sensitivities doesn't blind me to how much you cannot help disapproving of me, precisely because you know you and I are so alike."

My father grinned and shook his head.

"You've been practising your speech, haven't you?"

I smiled.

"A little. Give me a break, this isn't easy."

"Relax. I haven't seen you in a long time. I missed you. I miss our talks. When you went into the monastery, I felt I had lost you. And now, all this stuff about faith issues and my mechanical sensitivities, what is this, recovery stuff? Have you been to therapy or something?"

Clearly I had been. Clearly I had unconsciously wanted to say all these half truths for a long time.

"No, I haven't."

He clearly didn't believe me.

"You should give your sister a call. She has been asking after you."

"I'll do that. I'm thinking of taking a little time to myself. You know, go away somewhere?"

"Like where? Where would you go?"

"I don't know. Maybe travel around Europe. For a year maybe. Take a break from studies."

"You are good at studies. These are dangerous times. It's not safe to go travelling. The police pick up people like you. You have been off the grid for too long."

"How many degrees does one need to take before one gets a crack at life?"

"You tell me. You're the expert. You have too many degrees."

"These professors just want you to become like them, think like them. Take degrees like they take, drink wine and hang around campus and revive the corpses of long dead ideas. It's depressing. It's not life. I don't want to end up like them."

"Who says you will? Maybe you should devote your energies to some other discipline. Write something else. Do something that gives you life. Be happy."

"I don't know what else to write."

"Give it time."

"You know, I think I inherited this atheism from somewhere."

"Faith is not like a disease. By the way, your mother will be distraught."

"I know. I dreaded telling her. I mean I tried, unsuccessfully. By the way, I'm not exactly doing the flamenco over this."

We walked for a long time. Then he said,

"I have to ask you this. Tell me, why did you join in the first place?"

"Everything seemed so empty, so pointless."

"Yes. That's adolescent. And that's not a reason."

"I know. I was so much younger then."

I didn't know what to say. My mind went blank. Dad rescued the situation.

"But I know how depressed you were. We were all worried for you. I think everyone goes through that kind of crisis at one time or another."

"Then I discovered prayer and faith and it took over. Suddenly, life was filled with possibilities, and I wanted to devote my life to God and Jesus and all the things which gave my life a point. You know deep down I could never work out what it meant to have a vocation, or how one knew God was calling you."

"Maybe you need to look at that."

"You know, every year there are thousands upon thousands of marriages."

"I like weddings. Your mother loves going to weddings."

"Right, but how do all those people know they are marrying the right person?"

"I don't know. I guess check the divorce figures."

"Exactly. So, what's the big deal with my deciding this life is not for me?"

"That's a bit simplistic. Every break up is traumatic. It's very upsetting. And your mother will be distraught. So will your sisters, and your little brother. The family has changed since you entered the monastery. Things have gotten better."

"I tried to explain things to Mother. It didn't seem to register. It reminded me."

"Look, I just think you should be a lot more embarrassed than you are."

"Why?"

I looked at the two lakes, still as glass, the mountains on each side, and all the exotic beauty at the doorstep of the metropolis. I looked at the old monastery walls, over a millennium old, some of it. I looked at the church, the huge round tower. Dad had seen all this before, or, at least, I looked at him and, as we spoke, I decided he was a tired old man, exhausted and cynical by overexposure to the disappointments of living. Moreover, my dad didn't like the obvious being pointed out to him. But to me, I had never seen, never really looked into these artefacts, seen and then realised I had inadvertently pursued parts of myself in the Monastery of the Seven Towers, things older in myself that I had inherited from dozens of generations before me.

"People come here to keep the faith alive," I said "A faith not in a dogma or a religion, faith in who they are. In history, the opposite of propaganda. Or mere tourism."

"No. It's a tourist spot, mostly now. In most people's minds this is a tourist spot," Dad said.

"It's ancient Ireland. It's a part of us that has survived invasion and oppression."

"That's a bit old hat, isn't it, Frankie, I mean Frank?"

"Well, I think it's a little bit of heaven. I do, really."

"The kingdom of heaven is within you."

"It's kind of difficult to live one's life by something unseen, unheard, unfelt, something written about but never experienced."

"I think God, I mean you need faith. Well, Frank, I mean it's actually a very sad thing you have lost your faith."

"My faith has been my life. Or I thought it was. Now it's over. That's sad. I have a new life."

"Whatever you do."

"What?"

"I mean I wish you well, Son."

"Thank you."

"So, how do you feel?"

"How do you think I feel?"

"I don't know. That's why I'm asking."

"I don't know how I feel."

"Okay then. I guess all that therapy, well I mean to say - "

"I feel like shit. I feel guilty."

"I think you should reconsider this decision"

"I haven't decided."

"Are you sure about that?"

"I'm trying to convince you I haven't made this step lightly."

"I know, I know. I'm sorry."

"And I know now I've been wasting my time."

"Look Frankie, I mean Frank. Frank," he corrected himself. "Sorry. I mean to say, you should be a lot more embarrassed than you are, a lot more embarrassed. I mean it's natural to be embarrassed. I know your mother will be distraught."

"Mother has always been distraught, Dad. If you had taken a look at her distress fifteen years ago, maybe she might not be as troubled as she is."

"That's a rather hurtful thing to say to your father."

"I'm sorry. I'm sorry, but you aren't exactly being sensitive either."

"Did you talk to your mother?"

"I tried explaining."

"And?"

"She didn't seem to understand."

"That's rather strange, don't you think?"

"She kept talking about you, Dad. About what a good man you are. About how proud she is of you. Is she okay?"

"Great, fine."

"You know, I called in to see her and just as I was going to go back to the Monastery of the Seven Towers. She suggested this day out. As though on some level she understood what I was saying to her."

Dad smiled his eerie hundred megawatt smile. His sharp blue eyes seemed to assume their most formidable gaze. I wondered if I would inevitably become him, a clever man with no real outlet for his abilities, in a marriage that had long ended without either party prepared to admit the truth. I felt my stomach knot. I wanted to get out of the car and walk back rather than spend another moment with him. I took a breath. And then I exhaled.

"You okay. Where did you go to just there?"

"Nowhere. I think we'd better go. It's late."

He said:

"I'm glad we did this, Son. And I want us, I mean I want us to -"

Dad smiled at me. I nodded to him and smiled. I couldn't help it.

"I'll probably be leaving in the next weeks or months. I have to talk about this to my superiors. I'm not sure how they'll take it."

"What will you do for money?"

"I'll get a job."

"What kind of job?"

"Let's get out of here. I have an appointment, Dad."

Dad liked to ask impossible questions to irritate his interlocutor. I thought of it as akin to an old interrogation technique. The car hadn't moved.

"Let's go home, Dad. Drop me off at the monastery, okay?"

Dad started the car. He put on some music. Then he turned it down. It was music I didn't like much, playing at a barely audible volume.

"How will you tell the rest of the family?" he asked.

"I imagine they will be kept very well informed anyway, in a more comprehensive manner than I could ever accomplish," I carefully answered with as casual air as I could muster. And, from that saying, we drove mostly in silence to the monastery.

Chapter Thirty

Des

Lunchtime at the Monastery of the Seven Towers is not fun. For me, it's business. Nothing personal, you see. It's invariably a time for deal making, meeting arranging, and those tiny critical conversations that change everything. Bishops and priests from other parishes stop by to eat and meet, and, inevitably, let something slip about diocesan politics they later, equally inevitably, regret. Also, I get to hear things from some lickspittle from our community wishing to ingratiate himself. I harbour something of a dislike for such people. But I need them. In my business, toadies can save one's life. I keep a few on call. I thank God for such disappointing Brothers. There are other, better, moments too. Brothers wish to discuss change. Other Brothers with something on their mind unconsciously sit beside or near you, because they want to talk about something they can no longer live with, in complete confidence of course. So many people confide in me. They confide in me they are gay, or have children, or are sleeping with their therapists or other brothers or their brothers' wives, or live secretly with the memory of dead loves or lost children or alcoholic desolation. I am not surprised, nor am I particularly moved to judge them. If they have broken a law, I refer them to the police. They tell me things one cannot keep secret, things I confide in trusted friends. But part of the job is the acting. I have made peace with the responsibility of acting as if I were that person, that person you can trust, that image of the moral leader. Maybe I am that person. I fear I am not and it makes living in my skin a less than happy thing. But I am good at what I do. I know that. I visit the Brothers on the missions; I arrange for the allocation of funds and ensure we have enough money to do the usual - housing, education, transport, healthcare, personal and legal costs, repair and maintenance, and ever diminishing retirement funds. Funding the ever increasing age of our Brethren is becoming a huge issue within the Order. We have to find new sources of revenue. More of the Brothers need to have careers to cater for those among us who are too old or have a contemplative vocation. We have accountants, lawyers, architects, doctors, and cooks. In many ways, I help to run a small tribe, a civilization and a culture within a wider culture, a society within a society. At least, this is what the group psychologists and the sociologists tell me. It makes sense, but it reduces the truth of who we are, a spiritual community. I tell them we are so much more, but they think as they do because of their lack of history, or rather, because their minds cannot understand what only faith can inform. I fear many of the Brothers will think as they do. I fear for the future and pray for vocations. So, I turn up for lunch, maybe more out of fear than love, out of a fear I might lose power or lose face. I make myself available for such moments which might help the Brothers, though I believe it important not to appear either too available or too unapproachable. This is in order to strike that delicate balance between the office I hold and the person of the office holder.

So here, during lunch, I deal with pressing problems. I organise meetings and take coffee after dinner by myself in the refectory, as the young students wipe down the tables and clean the floors and take the flat food trays and leave them scrubbed to dry in the back kitchen. I chat to them, those bright young things, with souls like diamonds. The innocent conversations I have with those young men are the highlight of my day. They are the bright hope for the future. Their youth and optimism gives life to our dreary, memory-laden Monastery of the Seven Towers. They teach us about the times we are living in, despite their youth. I listen to them. They are not yet ordained. They usually do not stay long in the Order. They are here for a few years, learning about our life in all its ancientness, talking to me about their studies or asking me about Giovanni Seipi, as though I were an expert, or laughing about the little things, the things that make these times happy and worthwhile. I spend my time drinking coffee and listening and waiting and talking to them, hoping that when they leave they will take good things with them, or if they stay they will make good monks. Occasionally, a particularly sad case comes my way. For instance, last week a young monk approached, Brother Frank. He had decided to leave the Order. Apparently a young woman is involved, someone he met in the library. I can see he is a good man and that is what makes this such an awful business. The relationship has been going on for some time. I hear a year or so. And she has completely turned his head, changed his mind about things. Alex's intervention stopped it for a while, but I believe he is in love, and that is something too powerful to legislate against. Apparently, too, he has lost his faith. That usually lasts a few years, until he has children, or loses a parent or gets ill. Then the faith returns. We cannot live without God. As I say, very sad. I spoke with him for a good while. I told him I feared for his future happiness. I also told him I believed that he has a vocation to the Order of the Holy Field, and, having discussed the situation with Alex, I know he agrees with me on this. He is only months away from ordination to the deaconate. So, I sent him to Alex for further counsel and said we would make a decision later on in the month on his case. He didn't argue with me, but I saw the defiance in his eyes, something I remembered I continually saw in the eyes of his friend, Joe Finn. Once I saw that look in young Frank's eyes, I knew he would surely leave us. It saddened me. He would have made a good Brother, perhaps gone far in our Order, given the right direction and a willingness to get over whatever father issues are holding him back. Besides that little impromptu encounter during coffee that particular afternoon, I remember I had two meetings with our accountants, and one with our legal team regarding a Brother who has been accused of paedophilia. I think he will be convicted. In fact, I think it just he be convicted. He has had something of a reputation for quite some time now.

Chapter Thirty One

Lisa

As the months passed after I broke up with Frank, my new life of happiness and fulfilment and healthy living and trips to the gym and parties twice a week and dating and drinks and meets with the girls began to fragment. I woke up with inexplicable aches and pains in indeterminate parts, phantom aches, my legs and arms stiff and unresponsive, my fingers not working properly. I looked fine. My body fit and toned, my skin relatively clear, my eyes equally clear, neither pained nor bloodshot. But, with the aches and pains, came depression, dissolution into reclusive behaviour, and an unfashionable reading of French novelists who describe the loneliness, the boredom and the meaninglessness, but offer no solution. Nevertheless, they were something of a comfort. And I knew why I was reading their words. I was filling up the void, playing the game of living. All this tension and depression was caused by the strain of acting, the strain of being constantly on stage to me, and to other people. I was the person pretending to be over Frank. I was the independent woman who was past her great love. I was Lisa. I was pretending I had friends I loved. I was the person pretending I had a full life when, in reality, I got by from day to day. And the girls would call me up every Friday, wanting to meet and I would make my excuses some weeks. Other weeks, despite my deep misgivings, I would say yes. One week when I said yes I met Seán and, by accident or design, we sat near one another and our conversation quickly went beyond professional banter or the calm well practised conversation of the experienced social personality and we saw the connection and I went home with him to his absolutely fabulous and yet very understated place, filled with paintings he occasionally bought, and a view of the Phoenix Park, and we made love between beautiful sheets I saw only in soap operas, and I thought I was living in a dream, and I looked into his eyes and knew he was a wonderful man and something spoke inside me, something deeply cynical and cold and calculating. I knew I had two choices as he dressed for surgery the following morning at eight o'clock. I was sipping coffee and eating oatmeal bread and reading the morning paper and listening to Mahler playing from his stereo, for he was music obsessive, and I, feeling insecure at my own perceived failure to acquire money and covetous of someone else's, said to myself 'I can marry this man, for I know he will ask me. I sense it. I feel it. I can spend my life with someone decent and kind and sensitive, and have children with him, or I can be alone and spend my life in loneliness and become the bitter alcoholic spinster, who shelves books and resents the younger, happier library assistants who have the youth I once had and lost.'

It was my lowest point. I felt desperation. I had lost Frank. A life without love was unbearable. I felt it shouldn't be an 'either or' situation, either loneliness or company. Very often both co-exist. Life isn't an 'either or' situation. But then, as I was thinking this, Seán came over to me, as I was sitting there reading the paper and taking coffee on this beautiful teak breakfast table thinking terrible things and listening to music, and he leaned over and kissed me. It was by his kiss I betrayed him. I knew by his kiss my chances of meeting another like him were slim to none. It was all down to degrees of compromise. So, I decided to compromise the least.

I had no real basis for my calculations. I had deep intuitions, voices inside me calling out in the lonely spaces I was drifting through those weeks and months. I liked Seán. I even had the beginnings of love for him. He was a loving person. He was warm and sensitive and never hurt anyone. He was strong and self confident. He was a successful dentist with his own practices. He took great care of his beautiful, well muscled body. I thought to myself, 'he would make a wonderful father.' Why wasn't he married? The market usually snapped up successful alpha males. They usually found their corresponding alpha females.

But Seán wasn't in the game for power and trophy mates. He wanted love, and love is the ultimate trophy, the ultimate victory. It seemed the more I got to know him the better a partner he would make. I was looking for something wrong with him. I thought for a long while he was gay, but he wasn't. Rather, Seán had had one other long term relationship before me. It had broken up badly about six months before we met, when he discovered his fiancée was unfaithful with the girlfriend of his best friend. I told him about Frank. He told me about Laura. We listened to each other and I felt such guilt at my calculations. I was strategising relationships and alliances like a member of the court of Louis the Fifteenth. Perhaps, I consoled myself, perhaps he too was performing his own secret computations of the heart. Who truly knows? Would I be spending my life on stage again? Would I be exchanging the theatre of the confident single woman for the theatre of the happily married woman? Do we have to lie to be with another? Is there such a thing as compatibility? Would I be found out? Would I discover myself as I gave birth or conceived a child? Would my children see through me?

But I was, in a way, happy. Seán and I spent all our spare time together. I would come home after work to his waiting for me, having cooked a meal and secured tickets for some show and we would eat and make love and laugh and slowly I began to appreciate the complexity of Seán, the depths of him. Unlike me, he seemed never on stage. Perhaps this was why he so loved music, the theatre, opera, cinema, ballet. His life was more fully expressed. He had less to hide. We went to see everything, sometimes flying over to London to watch the Royal Opera performing or to theatre one simply didn't get to see in Dublin. He loved it all and we laughed and cried and talked and made plans and shared our personal biographies and I met his parents and he endured mine and never stinted to pay for most things, despite my loud objections or even the odd argument. At this stage, I had a considerable sum saved, practically the down payment for a house. I began to look for houses and Seán had friends in the real estate business and he organised meetings and together we saw the best places and he wanted me to have a place of my own as he had a place of his own and soon he told me he would own a house in the country and we were going to go down there soon as soon as the builders had finished working on the place.

But there was no trip down the country to the house when it was finished. When it was about three quarters finished, he showed me pictures. It had been a farmhouse once, stationed on three acres of land, a fetching south facing aspect, close proximity to all amenities, including shopping and a hospital within driving distance, a perfect investment opportunity for all those in the market. I loved brochures. Seán kept them all. Now it was a three bedroom dwelling house. It was going to be beautiful. I never saw it in real life. This was because, one evening in May, I went back to my place to change and shower and get ready to go out later on and I met Frank outside my apartment. I was in the process of buying my own place. I had begun to pack my stuff into boxes, feeling the anxiety lessen, the sense of life's futility, the possibility of a life suddenly emerging when before I was waiting. I was also engaged to married. Now, there before me, was Frank. Frank was the person who had caused me such heartbreak. I hated him.

"Hello Lisa."

"You can't do this, Frank. You can't do this. I'm engaged."

"I don't care."

"You don't care? You fucking egomaniac!"

"Lisa. Please!"

"Look! Leave! Leave right now! You can't come here like this. Tell me things I want to hear and leave me in carnage. Leave here now or I'll call the police. I'll tell them things. I'll tell them whatever will keep you away. Your reputation will be in tatters. Are we clear?"

"I came here to tell you what you wanted to hear."

"No!"

"Look! I came here to tell you that you were right. You were right and I was wrong. I was being a liar to myself in the Order of the Holy Field. It was all a lie. It was all a lie and I am sorry. Please forgive me. Please."

I went to walk past him and he held onto me. I wanted to scream. I wanted to scream something like 'take your hands off me' or something suitably incriminating. Waiting for me at my apartment was the most stupid thing he could possibly have done. But he held onto me. I started hitting him as hard as I could and he took the blows, kept saying how sorry he was, that I had been right all along and that he had been brainwashed or subject to mind control, that Joe Finn had changed all that and that he no longer listened to things he needed to believe in to get by and, in the end, I let him in. He kissed me. I kissed him back and we took off all our clothes and there on the floor of my apartment in the midst of half packed boxes we made love for hours.

"I have a boyfriend. I am engaged to my boyfriend. I am now a liar and a cheat and I am a slut and I hate myself."

"What's his name?"

"Seán. He's nice. We might end up together. I have a good life now."

"I'm sorry, Lisa. I am not here to ruin things for you. This was a terrible, wonderful, wonderful, mistake. I wanted, so wanted, to see you. I finished my exams today. I finished my exams and I kept thinking about you. I so needed to see you. I needed to make amends. I didn't expect this. I didn't have any big plans. I'm sorry for hurting you. I'm sorry, Lisa. I wanted to see you because I love you."

"You should go. Please leave."

"Come for a drink with me. Please. We need to fix this. Just one drink. You can shower and see Seán afterwards. We'll go our separate ways after that. I am sorry. Please forgive me. Please forgive me."

"No. That's a bad idea. Forgiveness is a bad idea."

"Okay. It's a bad idea. You're right. Bad idea."

So we went for that one drink, that drink that sealed my fate and my forgiveness of Frank and I called Seán, or Seán called me, I don't remember. And I lied to Seán, then just as I had lied to him all along, just by being with him and plotting to marry him, as I knew, in the end, he would marry me and I made excuses about meeting the girls and drinking late and I saw him later on that night and slept with him. And, slowly after that, Frank and I saw each other secretly while he was still in the Order of the Holy Field and I saw Seán as we moved ever more inexorably towards marriage and eventually it became clear that I had to choose. I chose Frank. I wasn't in love with Seán. I think he was too nice a man for me. It didn't seem real. Sometimes I wonder what is real.

Chapter Thirty Two

Frank

Joe Finn was buried. I imagined him there, in absolute stillness and silence beneath the surface, as we were leaving the graveyard to go our separate ways. Bill came up to me as we moved away from the graveside down the gravel walk, conversations stirring all around, and hugged us both warmly. We had all been crying.

"How ya doin? Eh? Missed ya. How's life? I haven't been in touch, I know. I gotch yer messages. I know I should've returned them. Look, there's a do in the Finn's house. Do you know where they live?"

"Look, Bill. I don't think I could handle people now. Bill, I, I mean. God, I keep crying."

"Don't worry about it. I know. I know."

"Thanks," I snivelled. "I certainly couldn't handle some of the other Brethren. Alex or Des particularly. Want to go somewhere for a quiet drink?"

"I can't. I'm driving a few of the Brothers. I'm trying to cut down, you know."

"Oh right."

Then Bill looked conspiratorially at us and said:

"Des got re-elected. Twice! He pushed Alex out. And the others! "

Bill just couldn't resist a good gossip, even at a graveside.

"Wow, that's a surprise."

Bill smiled salaciously. Lawyers love gossip, I mused. He continued;

"Alex's star is beginning to fade. Des is becoming the kind of leader we really need. There are big changes. Sorry, so great to see you, Lisa. Sorry to talk shop."

"Not at all, Bill. Good to see you too. We must get together for that drink. Why don't you drop by? Give us a call before hand, though. We're working odd hours."

"Ya betcha. Givvus a hug, you two. Talk to you soon."

And Bill was gone. He got into a car. Des looked over at us through the car window, smiled a little and nodded. I nodded back. I saw Alex too in the crowds, glad handling people, smiling and moving towards his car. Bill was driving him too. Some of the others I had known were there. They seemed older, though it had only been a few years. We were no longer a part of each other's lives now. The car drove off and we took a taxi home.

Chapter Thirty Three

Frank and Joe

Hermitage of the Little Flower
Convent of St. Joseph,
Mc Curtin Street,
Limerick.

October 4ᵀᴴ 20–
Dear Joe,

Thanks for your letter a month or so ago. Sorry I haven't written sooner. I have been getting ready for exams and I tried to write you a few times and just didn't know what to say. I feel much better now. You seem to be doing well over there. That's good. But then you always do well, don't you?

So, I went to see Lisa after my exams were over. I got a first, by the way. I know you despise examinations of all kind and I know you think I am too ambitious for my own good, but I am really happy about my result. So, be happy for me. I have something else to tell you too. Lisa and I are back together. I am leaving the Order of the Holy Field. I don't know how you might feel about that, but I think you need to know - from me. I hope we can sort out our differences and I'm sorry I accused you of betraying me way back when. It still bothers my conscience, as though my conscience was some kind of cantankerous pet that needs regular grooming. Until some kind of resolution about religious life is reached, Lisa and I still see each other in secret. But I know there are people watching me. I also went to see Des and Alex and the rumour mill is running full tilt this weather about my impending disaster. Alex begged me to reconsider and sent me down here to Limerick to a hermitage, all expenses paid, so that I might have time to reconsider my decision. So, I have spent the last week listening to Samuel Beckett short stories on tape, lent to me by this spiritual director, 'Call me Bernard' who reeks of gin and an oily obsequiousness, just detectable under his aftershave, when he calls to see me in this dreadful hermitage. I go out in the evenings, under the radar, for a quiet drink and sit in a pub with a single pint of Guinness, with the locals looking at me as though I just beamed in from the Mothership. Then I call Lisa at about eleven o' clock and slip back to the hermitage and go to sleep. It's unnaturally silent here as I drop off asleep with the words from 'Dante and the Lobster' in my ears. I am almost frightened to let sleep come, as it inevitably does here. Then Bernard arrives the following morning about ten o' clock. He has just left now. He looks so young to be a drunk. He sits on a chair and looks at me smiling with those bloodshot eyes and waiting for me to talk about my prayer life, or the circumstances that led me to come here to reconsider my vocation. I have no intention of telling him anything. I have no intention of telling him how I lost my faith, how I fell in love, how I have no real plans for the future except to live with Lisa and try to find some kind of work that will not leave me suicidally bored. I am looking for something that has no connection with religion or working with ill people, as so many ex-religious seem to gravitate towards nursing or therapy as an outlet for their guilt at having left the Church and religious life and let their parents down. I have tried to sell this priest 'call me Bernard' the story that I want to be alone, that I am uncomfortable with sharing my feelings and other such decoys, but nothing seems to be working. I am not angry with him, as he thinks, nor am I angry with the Order, or the Church, no more than usual. I was angry, I suppose, with both within a year of joining the Order of the Holy Field. That isn't what led me to go. He doesn't seem to be breaking off his charm assault. He seems to be committed to the thoroughly dishonest business of making friends with me. I want to say to him 'look Bernard, you need help, not me.' But I can't. It would be hurtful. This small hermitage they gave me a week or so ago is fully fitted with a bath, a shower, a small kitchen, a bedroom, and a room dedicated to the adoration of the Blessed Sacrament, or, as you liked to refer to it, the Holy Hedgehog, the monstrance being in a hedgehog shape. You really loved to shock, didn't you? Anyway, it's all over here. This extended last minute period of brainwashing will end on Friday. On the other side of the wall, the wall separating the convent from the hermitage, the Sisters of the Sepulchre continue their twenty five hour a day adoration of the bread of life. I have spent an hour or two in here in this oratory, where I am writing my angry letters. I bring with me Freud's *Interpretation of Dreams,* the Bible, and a copy of Beckett's trilogy of novels in one less than slim volume. It makes for imaginative sitting. I imagine them, the nuns and Jesus in the Bread, looking at me through the glass panel with a single milky glaucoma gaze, from the other side of the oratory, the side facing their church, as I hear them chant during the day, as though they have heard of all monstrous acts I have committed, praying there on the other side of the altar through a sin proof screen, wondering what I am doing, whether I am praying, and how long it will be before I finally leave. I wish I could leave now. So, all I do these days is wait. Alex has made no bones about the fact I am making a very bad decision, one that I will regret for the rest of my life. That scares me. Write soon about the consequences of yours. I miss you, Joe. I miss our conversations. I wonder often what you are doing. I fear the mediocrity of what will happen now, tedious days spent working in some futile money amassing form of employment to generate income for the banks in mortgage payments or more bad food filled with hidden carcinogenic elements, televisions or awful selfish children, or holidays in the sun and a house in the country, which seems to be all the rage now the economy is doing so well. We will read of ordinary, decent, loving people dying in other countries and secretly thank God that the bullets hit those other people. I fear falling victim to the middle class illusion, that our lives somehow will be happier if we are insulated from insecurity by social position and money. I fear a lot of things. Most of those fears come from conversations with you. Before we met, blissful unthinking ignorance made my days long and happy and my nights insomnia free. You cannot escape yourself. I hope you haven't gone to Los Angeles to escape yourself, to escape your gifts. Your mind is like a phone constantly ringing off the hook. Of course it's going to torment you. Imagine what it's like for other people. You have to answer it. You have to listen to the caller. If you hang up and pretend it was some crank call, like some oppressive inner parental figure, the calls will only become all the more insistent. I fear greatly for your well being if such a thing were to happen. I think we discussed this once before. I'll finish now, Joe. I must go for a walk in the garden before dinner. They have the most beautiful roses and gardenias here.

Best,

Frank.

I heard nothing from Joe for months after I mailed that letter to him. Then, just before Christmas, after I had left the Order of the Holy Field, when Lisa and I had settled down somewhat, having heard nothing from the Order of the Holy Field, a letter from Joe arrived one day. It had been forwarded from the Monastery of the Seven Towers. I hadn't given them my address. Maybe Bill had done the forwarding. I had rung him one day, just to catch up. He had been a little distant with me over the phone, so I hadn't rung back. Whatever the reason, the letter arrived.

Monastery of the Mother of All Mercies
West Thirty Second Street,
Los Angeles, California.
December 15ᵀᴴ 20–

Dear Frank,
Happy Christmas! I will not be returning for Christmas this year. I intend to put down roots here and the only way I can do that is to stay. I have applied for, and will probably get, a green card, as the Brothers have rather elaborate political connections that will enable them to get most, if not all, of my immigration requirements. Who knows? I might even become a citizen of the United States, if they'll have me. I will probably have to publish something successful first, though. How trying.

I am unsurprised you are leaving, Frank. Maybe you have gone by now. I imagine you poring over books and making notes and plotting some text or other. Is that impression correct? I always sensed you did not believe in the Church. Unlike you, I inherited my faith from my parents. I could not live without it. I think you are trying to rationalize leaving the Order of the Holy Field so that it sits well in your conscience. It never will. If you looked into your life, or saw yourself as I do, you would see it as natural that you would leave. Being a born sceptic, you were so desperate to belong, so tormented by all the confusions and contradictions of the faith. It is simply unnatural for you to accept something like the Catholic faith. It is too irrational for you, too inconsistent, too filled with guilt ridden controls, too parental, too ancient, and too filled with errors. At heart, you are a romantic, someone who longs for friendship and, at the same time, sees the futility of friendship because we are trapped by the confines of our bodies that wear out and die, by words that fail to carry real meaning, by thoughts we rarely fully explain or hardly understand. Anyway, my opinions of you do not matter. Whether or not I believe you cannot live with this faith, or this life, or this death that will come, or whether you need the faith of another, someone you believe truly loves you, to make it bearable, is irrelevant. What matters is what you desire, what you want now. I think that's what upset me most when you two met in the library that day, to see you two so drawn to each other, finding another in another body who desired as you desired, and the exclusion I felt, the sense of being abandoned for another. I struggled with these feelings and dealt badly with them by abandoning you. I am sorry for that, for how I judged you, by not being the friend you needed. I often think of the night we spent looking at that eclipse. It is one of the happiest memories I retain, though I must apologise for my lack of sobriety that night. I was, as they say over here, in a very bad place. My therapist (yes, a therapist!) has suggested I am in denial of whole regions of my emotional life, that I have been anaesthetizing feelings with drugs and alcohol and living in my mind rather than in my body. Normally I would react with some kind of sarcasm, something about the obviousness of such an observation, perhaps reveal some kind of vulnerability in someone suggesting this. But one of the reasons why I acted so badly when you and Lisa first became acquainted is how hurt and abandoned I felt seeing you together. I had lost you to her and I couldn't cope with that. Living over here has given me the space to admit that. There are few areas of alternative culture unexplored in Los Angeles. I am trying to benefit from such perspectives.

In other words, it is wonderful here, Frank. I am sleeping eight to ten hours a night. I eat regularly, mostly vegetables. No more fast food. I work mostly with the sick and the poor, which is very difficult and painful for me, but I keep going. I have become a religious cliché, but it is something which gives me life now, not as a political act, as something personal, intimate. This is what I always wanted, and away from the unreasonable and futile demands of academia. In the mornings, I rise at six for meditation. Then, after breakfast, I spend a few hours writing. I am working on nothing major, not like before when the pressure was so intense I could think of little else except writing. I am toying with a novel, perhaps, or a book of essays. Nothing coherent is taking shape during this time. My body and mind are finally healing after years of physical and psychological self abuse. I have no bitterness against the authorities. I rather believe I put myself in the way of trouble, as a way of seeking attention and affirmation.

Oh, and another thing - I am clean for about six months now. 'Clean,' is the term used over here for not abusing drugs. Fr. Barnes, my director, confronted me way back about my drinking and drug taking. He found my stash. I was enraged that he went searching in my room behind my back. I told him to go fuck himself. I called him every name under the sun I could think of. He didn't flinch. He looked at me coldly and said this had to stop, that I had to give this up. He went on to say that, if I didn't stop, I would be sent back to Ireland, which is the spiritual equivalent of shaving my head and rejoining the SS. It was unthinkable. Going back to Ireland was the one unbearable thing. Anyway, I knew I was sick, mentally and emotionally and spiritually. My liver was shot.

I had shakes, felt as though I had a permanent flu, wasn't getting out of bed, missing duties. Things were bad. I was fucked up. But, anyway, back to the intervention. After a long period of screaming, I looked at Fr. Barnes and smiled. He didn't smile back. He looks a little like Edward G. Robinson. He looked at me and said I had to stop what I was doing, that I was going to die or go mad. He sent me to meetings and counselling. I went. Slowly, I began to change, something that didn't happen in Dublin, as the size of the community made my drinking and drug taking easier to hide. No one notices you are missing so much in a community of fifty. After a month or two, I began to feel the effects, reduced headaches and stomach problems and paranoia. Then, I went away for therapy for a few weeks and came back more alive than I have ever felt. I began to pray again, Frank. I began to feel something other than depression or pain. My mind was no longer an instrument of self torture.

My parents call once a week, sounding tearful, but happy I am doing better here. They, naturally, were very shocked to hear of my using drugs and alcohol. They knew all along. I know that. They sound sad. But I know they're happy I am doing so much better over here than in Ireland, though it's hard to believe someone like me could be happy here in this huge terrifying city, with all its superficiality and violence and tension and poverty and immense wealth. I feel at home here. This area first settled nine millennia ago. Of an evening, I go for a walk by myself, just to soak up the life. In the morning, I go out to get the papers. I try to live a regular life, try to not lose track of the day or the night. I try to not get lost in ideas that used make me so sick or so frazzled. There is so much death and life and money and power and violence and love and peace here, so many different ethnic groups and industries and tribes and power bases.

The monastery, if it could be called such, is eighty years old, an old brick building with a small church attached on the corner of West and Twenty Third. It is in South Central Los Angeles, a mixed neighbourhood, mostly Hispanic with some African American. Everyone drives. Everything here is automobile-based and I have to take driving lessons twice a week to be any use to the Brothers. Here Kevin, Brad, Casey and myself work as best we can for the people who come to us. There aren't many vocations, as you might imagine - one postulant at the moment. I have to give him lessons in Scripture and Church history. I throw in a little philosophy and psychology when I can, just to keep him thinking. He is very (how shall I put it?) enthusiastic. It's quite funny, though I keep my mirth private. This young man, Joshua, is so very willing to do literally anything that I sometimes try to wear out his enthusiasm, by giving him ridiculous jobs, just to make him angry. It never works. Perhaps he is 'on' to me. Or perhaps I shall wake up one morning with a horse's head in my bed, and only then shall I begin to treat Joshua with respect. It's unlikely I will stop. I'm having too much fun at present. Will keep you apprised.

Best to you and Lisa,

Joe.

And that was the last we heard from Joe. I had no contacts within the Order any more. I presumed that he came home, but I lost touch, even though I wrote a few times. I even called the number a few times for his monastery in Los Angeles, but he never came to the phone. I presumed he wanted to put down roots, so he said in his letter. So, gradually, he drifted from our awareness, except for the occasional reminisce.

Lisa and I married the following Spring. We had no honeymoon as we had no money. The service was brief. In a registry office, with two witnesses we literally pulled off the street between ten and twenty past one morning in April. Looking back now, we married for all the wrong reasons. We married for security, for the comfort zone of institutionalising and legitimising something we feared was wrong, but of course wasn't wrong, so we told ourselves. We married to put a legal and moral distance between ourselves and our families. We married for tax reasons. We married to escape our own histories. We married out of a fear of losing each other. We married for the simple reason to be able to say 'we're married' at social gatherings, to neighbours, or in lawyers offices. Despite this socially engineered madness, this recipe for divorce, we seemed to draw closer to each other, a type of mutual empathy bordering on telepathy slowly evolving from our proximity to each other. It seemed that, despite all the resistance to our union, the strangeness and the risk implicit in such an unlikely relationship and the enormous failure rate in such relationships within the culture of ex-religious, we seemed to have a life together. We had survived, maybe even thrived. We were in love.

Lisa continued working as a library assistant until I was made permanent in the bank. Then the unbelievable happened as it inevitably happens. I was promoted and actually brought in a good deal of money. I received in house training, was given more responsibly than power and my sick days increased and I began the slow decline that led my leaving the job under a cloud. So Lisa changed careers midstream, took up working with animals, and eventually qualified as a veterinary nurse. It was when she neared her final exams, that day I slept in the garden drunk, we got the call from Bill that Joe had died in the States. Afterwards, after the mourning and the loss, at different times, we took the burden of being the main earner from each other. I did it when I discovered I had a natural affinity with computers, something pointed out during those awful few years in the bank when they trained me in the rudiments of programming. Eventually, I even finished a degree in information technology. Lisa was earning well by being a qualified veterinary nurse. I escaped the bank and became self employed fixing computers. It wasn't long before I was in constant demand. I could charge whatever I liked depending on the size of the job and the relative degree of the emergency. I was discreet if the problem was embarrassing or highly controversial. I asked no questions and was naturally paid well for my discretion. I made it clear I would have no truck with pornographers, crooks, or perverts, and, for the most part, I rarely had the displeasure of working for them. When I did, I never informed on them. I guessed, if I did, something terrible would happen to us. We paid our mortgage quickly and I hardly noticed how I completely lost touch with the Order of the Holy Field. It was as though I had never been a member, as though the years I had spent with them had been erased from the collective memory of the Brethren. If I saw one of them, someone I knew or had known or lived with, on O'Connell Street or Grafton Street, or coming out of a café or restaurant, they would pretend they didn't see me. It was as though I simply wasn't there. Bill never called, and, though I rang and left messages for him, he never returned my calls. I even wrote him a few letters. Embarrassingly enough, I never received a response.

Strange to say the only meaningful contact I had with the Order of the Holy Field after I left all those years ago, were the conversations we had after Bill rang me to tell me of the death of Finn. I guess I shore up all I have lost with these memories I capture and recall now and then when not distracted by the twin devils of obligation and habit.

Chapter Thirty Four

Joe

Monastery of the Mother of All Mercies
West Thirty Second Street,
Los Angeles, California.
December 15TH 20–

Dear Mother,
Happy Christmas!
Thank you for the enormous parcel you sent. Though I don't eat caviar, some of the Brethren were absolutely delighted with it. In fact, I think my popularity raised several notches as a result of my leaving the jars in the fridge for anyone who wanted it. A little party ensued. I don't eat much meat at all. They call me a demi-vegetarian here and I endure many jokes as a result. They say being a demi-vegetarian is something like being a little bit pregnant. Apparently you can be a little bit pregnant. Isn't that strange?

I wanted to say thanks too for the music you sent me. I left most of it behind in with you and Dad, after my holidays before I left to come here. It was really sweet and thoughtful of you to spend so much sending such a large parcel to me, and yes, I'd love it if you came over for a week and had a little holiday over here. It's a really great place and there's so much to see. It's such a different world with very different attitudes to things.

A lot of the music you sent I haven't listened to in a long time. The reason why is mostly to do with the recovery programme I'm on at the moment. I guess it's been about six months since I've touched alcohol or drugs. Strange as it might sound, I have found so many links between the music of Wagner and the kind of rage I felt at the world and against myself, the same rage and disappointment is there at the heart of that music, such that I have practically stopped listening to it altogether. This is about the emptiness I feel inside a lot of the time, a yearning I feel, a longing for the kind of world that I know now only Jesus can give me, a longing for acceptance and a loathing of the casual carnage we call everyday life. Though I believed in God, I really think I didn't. I hadn't really surrendered myself to the love of God. I longed for love and beauty and truth and this music seemed to temporarily satisfy that longing. I really wasn't dealing with my feelings at all. I was getting high and/or getting drunk and listening to Wagner describe the creation and destruction of the world and the death of God and sinking deeper and deeper into helplessness and apathy and despair. Not exactly a life of faith and hope and love, don't you think?

So, a lot of what I was experiencing had to do with my addictions and a long, long time of not dealing with my feelings. Once those blocks were removed, I rediscovered the joy and love of God in my life and have found a happiness I never considered possible. Sounds kinda corny, I know. But it's how I feel these days. That is not to say I have a kind of dull vegetative euphoria and womb like comfort zone of the convert to a kind of cult mindset. I have, as they say here, my good days and I have my bad days, and, in order to fully recover from my many years as an addict, I need to embrace each of those extremes of emotion that becomes possible once one stops anaesthetizing oneself. So, part of my recovery involves my letting go of one of the great loves of my life, my love of the music of Richard Wagner.

Another great love that I have to let go of is what accompanies this letter. This is a manuscript I have been working on for the past number of years, long before I ever requested permission to come over here. Its genesis was quite troubled and there were certain difficulties with obtaining adequate permission to publish because of the views expressed by me therein. I have obsessively rewritten and extended the entire text so many times in the light of new research that it has become an all consuming obsession. As you can tell from the title, the book deals with the life of our Holy Founder, Giovanni Seipi, and I feel a lot of the highly contentious conclusions I have come up with these last few years forms a projection of my own rage and disappointment with the Order of the Holy Field, rather than an accurate picture of the man. The book, if you like, is a projection of my own self hatred. I want to get past all of that. I don't want to destroy what I have done. I have discussed this in group and with my therapist and superiors here. The opinion seems to be unanimous: that I should give it to you and Dad for safekeeping. I need to embrace the negativity I feel so strongly and felt for all the time I wrote about Giovanni Seipi, but not cling to it as though it were my identity. Yours is the last copy, I have, aside from the earlier inferior versions with Des and Alex. They were under the mistaken impression I was giving them a final version, when I explicitly told them what I was giving them to read was a work in progress. I have tried to destroy this manuscript, but I know that despite, and because of, its many flaws this is everything that I am and I cannot destroy it. I have burned my notes and given away the few drafts I had of this manuscript, but I cannot burn this or throw it away. It would be a kind of suicide. But, if I leave the manuscript anywhere I can look at it, I will begin working on it again and I will return to my old obsessive compulsive ways. So, I give you this as a gift, a token of my love and deep appreciation of everything you and Dad have done for me. I love you both so much I am crying as I write this. I cry too much, I know. I should laugh more. It is time for me to let go and I let go of my life and times of my beloved Giovanni with a lot of pain and a sense of loss I cannot describe to you. It's a death, really. In a lot of ways, working on that text, trying relentlessly to know everything about my subject so much so he became alive to me, a living breathing being, trying to prove how right I was, mostly to myself, was the meaning of my life. It's time to give up that kind of life, for it is vanity and a struggle that will never end if I do not give up and realise some day I will die. I saw a great movie last week. I keep thinking about it. It's very violent, but brilliant. Not like me at all to like that kind of movie. It's called *Fight Club*. One of the Brothers here was a professional boxer. Bob. Got it on Disk. Said his brother saw it and thought it was really cool. It's cool.

So I wish you both the very best for Christmas. Give my love to all the relatives and hugs and kisses to you both.

Joe.

Chapter Thirty Five

Alex

Rose Finn called me up this morning about eight o'clock, wanting to meet me. I normally don't take calls before ten o'clock in the morning. But my caller identification indicated the call was coming from the Finn home, so I took it. She sounded extremely distressed over the phone, crying and so on, so I arranged she arrive that afternoon. We met downstairs in one of the consulting rooms. She was wearing a beautiful powder blue suit, carrying a matching handbag and a large brown paper envelope that she put on the table between us. I never remembered her wearing anything like it. It's as though she had gotten a makeover. We were talking for only a few minutes when she got straight to the point.

"Father Alex, I wish to make my confession."

"I am unsure I am the person to be making a confession to Rose."

"Excuse me, Father, but I think you are."

"You do?"

"Yes I do."

"Why do you think so?"

"It's a strong feeling. Almost like God was speaking to my heart."

"We can talk about that for a while if you like."

"I think you know everything there is to know about me, Father. I'd like to make my confession."

"Well, I don't think it's a great idea, but if you want to, I cannot refuse to hear your confession."

"Look, I don't want you to hear my confession if you don't want to."

"I know that, Rose."

"That's good, Father. I feel relieved."

"Okay, then. Please feel free, if you wish, that is…"

Rose looked at me for a long time. She smiled and blessed herself.

"I, more than anything, wish to confess myself to you, Father Alex."

"Very well. May the Lord be in your heart and in your mind so you may be worthy to make a good confession."

"It has been three weeks since my last confession. I wish to confess I think I killed my son, Father. I think I drove him from me by my possessiveness, by my excessive religiosity, by my desire to mould him into the kind of son a mother like me would want. I didn't know. I didn't know at the time I was doing it."

Rose was clearly plagued with guilt. When a person feels like this, more than anything they need to ventilate their sense of guilt and receive words of comfort so they know they are still loved by God. The idea that Rose killed her son was of course preposterous.

"It's all right. It's all right, Rose. Just tell me what you want to say. Let it out. Say what is in your heart. Don't worry about how unreasonable it might sound. God understands."

I wanted to give her every opportunity to say everything, no matter how absurd. At first, I thought it might just be guilt. But now I thought it was something more than a sense of guilt. I wasn't quite sure what she was saying. It just seemed important not to stop her here, not to ask too many questions that might make her unconsciously edit herself. She had something to say. Let her say it. She was crying freely now. It didn't seem to stop her. She went on:

"I have been very depressed."

"I understand."

"It made me think a lot about myself."

"I see."

"I think I wanted Joe all for myself. I think the faith was a way of binding me to him forever. It was a way of keeping Joe, not only from his father, but it was a way of keeping Joe from the world, from having his own life, a life separate from me. I wanted him to love me exclusively, and the faith was a way of doing this. We knew the faith. The faith was our life. And the world was, after all, an evil place. And we left the world to find Jesus, and Gerry was busy, always working. So there was just Joe and me. With Jesus, Joe found me too. Together we had this intimacy based on our love of God. And within that love, that cocoon of love we were inseparable, because it was the love of God, an eternal love, a love that would never die. And Gerry didn't understand. Now don't misunderstand me, Father Alex. My Gerry is a wonderful man, a wonderful father. Gerry loved, worshipped his son. His love was a more selfless love, less manipulative love."

"Yes, but . . . "

"But it was always a question of religion that divided us. Gerry did not believe as we did. Not that we fought over it or anything like that. We fought, naturally, like every couple argues and debates and works through their differences. But religion divided us, though we loved each other and stayed together. And, of course Gerry had his own life, a separate life that involved the world of work and business, the world that provided so handsomely for us. In fact I don't think many people realise how much money we have at this relatively young stage of our lives. I'm in good health, Father. We could both retire and never have to worry about money ever again. Not many people know that. We don't live ostentatiously. We had a separate fund set up for Joe in case he changed his mind and left the Order of the Holy Field. I didn't realise the existence of this cocoon. It's hard to believe that now. You see, I didn't look to myself. I was too busy looking for God to do that. I didn't believe that self awareness was necessary for self advancement. I thought it was a form of narcissism, self-love, the opposite of love of God. My bereavement counsellor helped me past that. You see, I was an only child too, Father. My mother drank. My father wasn't there a lot of the time. God was my only friend inside that cocoon. You could say I had distant unloving parents. I know that now. The most important thing for me was not to repeat the terrible childhood I had endured. I was devastated when I found out I couldn't have any more children. I thought of adopting, but Gerry didn't want that. We were afraid it might negatively impact on Joe, especially as we became quickly aware how unlike his classmates he was. So, from the earliest days, Father, I know I imbued my child with a strict sense of moral values. I had him reading Scripture from the earliest time he could read. And, as you well know, because of his gifts he wanted to know everything…then to a special school, somewhere that might see to his needs."

"I know. Go on."

"I directed him to certain books. Books I had read. He developed his first crisis of faith, which we helped him through, by the time he was fourteen. Then he began to have therapy, then spiritual direction. I became frightened for his well being. Joe seemed to be desperate for the truth, not some kind of temporal scientific truth. He wanted to understand the world, the nature of God's presence in the world. He prayed a lot. Naturally, we couldn't stop him praying as much as he was praying, nor was there anything we could do about the deep search he seemed to be on. His nerves suffered. We put him on tranquillisers. He became dependent on them. Then, all we could do was support him in any way we could. All I could do was pray with him and for him and hope at the end of it all there would be an answer. He tells everyone he never sat an exam, Father. But it's not true. He passed his exams, went to college at sixteen, and by eighteen he had a first class honours degree. They wanted him to do a masters or a doctorate."

"I don't know if we have that on record."

"He was always hiding the truth about himself. No one knew Joe. Joe played everyone off everyone else."

"You didn't challenge him on that? That he lied to us?"

"He didn't want to be treated like a freak."

"I see."

"He asked us not to tell when he wanted to join the Order of the Holy Field. I mean, we didn't know what to do, and he seemed to know everything about the Order. He was reading books about Giovanni Seipi before he joined. And Gerry and I had never expected this. If you were to ask me was there any difference in our relationship, was he cold or distant with us, did we feel he was trying to escape from the strange family he had grown up in, I would have said no. But looking back, the Order of the Holy Field had everything he needed to escape Gerry and me. Joe was pretty unemployable, too nervous, too oversensitive, just too difficult. He wouldn't have lasted in an office environment for long. He needed somewhere. And the Order of the Holy Field, it had a family structure. It was dedicated towards the perfection of the soul, enlightenment and sanctity, and it had a strong intellectual bias. In other words, by imbuing my son as strongly as I did with religious doctrine, I drove him to this life, a life where his gifts could never ever achieve full flower, no more than at home could he ever be fully himself. He was always running, our Joe, always searching, always looking for something he could never find here on earth."

"We tried hard to encourage him, Rose. But what do you think he was looking for?"

Rose had stopped crying by now. When I asked her this, tears once more came to her eyes. I felt terrible I had upset her once more. I let her cry and then gently encourage her to talk. "Rose?"

"Happiness. Friendship."

"He seemed happy, at least to me. And he certainly had friends."

"Did he?"

"Sorry, did I use the plural? He had one friend. Frank."

"Frank. I see. I don't think I met Frank. No, I may have, maybe he came to dinner, once."

"Good. Frank was a nice chap. I think he is engaged to be married, or is married now…."

"Really? That's nice. Frank, yes?"

"I see…Was there anything…else, Rose?"

"Anything else? Anything else….There was something else I wanted to mention, just in passing, Father. I just can't think of it. Give me a second. Let me see….oh yes! Did Joe write anything?"

"I don't understand."

"What do you mean you don't understand?"

"Joe, I believe, was always writing. I believe you received a trunk load of his writings. Joe had published before he even came to us."

"Yes, yes. I know…They were notes, drafts of manuscripts, fragments.… I have put them away. I was looking for something more specific. I was wondering if you had earlier drafts of a completed manuscript. To the best of my knowledge it is called "For the Love of God the Father – Giovanni Seipi at Home". I believe my son was interested in publishing something on the life of the founder of the Order of the Holy Field."

"I shall certainly check my files, Rose. I do recall something about that. I will have to see if I have anything on it."

I clasped my hands and tried to assume the attitude of an information giving friend, one who understood the other person's problems and wanted to really help. But I wished she would leave. I did not wish to discuss Joe Finn's impenetrable text that had caused so much controversy. It was so overwritten, and, now that the boy was dead, it would be hailed as something exceptional, simply because the boy was dead. This did not honour his memory. Rose seemed to sense this and segued back to the subject of Frank.

"So tell me something about Joe's friend. Were they close?"

"Frank was a Brother here for several years. He and Joe were very close. Unfortunately Frank left. But Joe did find friendship here in the Order of the Holy Field. And I believe he was happy. Given time, too, his gifts would have found an outlet. We are only human, Rose. And we are full of faults. I would be the first to admit our many faults. The Order of the Holy Field would, in time, have adjusted to having someone with such gifts as those that Joe brought to our midst. You gave Joe the most precious gift you have."

"Oh please, what nonsense!"

"You gave him the gift of a deep and abiding faith in the one true God. I cannot understand how you could ever think that might not be a good thing."

"It brought him only torment. It drove him away. It drove him from me. I understand my son, Father. It was only after I lost him that I understood how much I understood him. I knew how much damage I had done to him. I knew after he went to Los Angeles that something was terribly wrong. I tried to get it from him. Naturally, we provided for him in case anything went wrong, but he would have none of it."

"He went to Los Angeles for his own reasons. I am not aware of any-"

"Why are you being so defensive, Father?"

"Well, I'm not. I really don't think I am."

"Really?"

"I am worried about you. I feel a bit helpless, but I don't believe I have anything to defend."

"Pardon me for saying so, Father, but I do think you are being very defensive."

"No, no, no."

"No one is being accused of anything here, except me that is."

"Excuse me!"

"I think, secretly, you feel as guilty as I do. I do think you had something to do with sending him there."

I took a deep breath, calmed myself, and tried to reason with her.

"Rose, I think you had huge issues with your son long before he went to Los Angeles. I think you should consider addressing those issues so that you can get on with your life in the way Joe would want you to. As for me, the only thing I feel with regards to the death of your son is a profound sorrow at the loss of a fine Brother, and the certainty he is with God. If you wish, I can provide you with the names of several superb people who can help both you and Gerry through this time, people fully au fait with the strong faith dimensions you have to your life. I urge you strongly to think about this. It is not something that will go away without a lot of work."

"In other words, this is my problem, nothing to do with faith or the Church or the way the faith is taught." Then she paused and looked coldly at me. I wasn't falling for such an obvious trap.

"I didn't say that, Rose."

Rose decided to continue regardless.

"I see. There is something else, Father," she said. It was then she opened the large brown paper envelope that had sat on the table between us for the duration of our dialogue. It was a manuscript.

"What is it?"

"I have this manuscript, Father."

She took out the manuscript. It was Joe's manuscript. It was considerably bigger than the one I finally remembered I had, perhaps twice the size, with footnotes and an index.

"May I see?"

"Sure, go ahead, Father."

I turned the pages and read some of the text. The language flowed beautifully. I knew immediately he had really done it. He had reworked the entire text, extended and elaborated his original themes, found his own voice. Joe had matured. Though it still retained the original title, a title I always disliked. I read it out.

"For the Love of God the Father – Giovanni Seipi at Home"

"Yes, Father. A very long title, but my son never took shortcuts. He pursued his goals to the end, even after death."

I found myself putting my hand possessively on the manuscript. I took it off again.

"This is fascinating, Rose. I do believe there might be another version of this somewhere in my files. I hope I can come across them."

"I took the liberty of showing this manuscript to a few publishers. They were really interested. A book like this, giving such a different view of Giovanni Seipi, a hugely popular saint like that who inspired millions upon millions, whose sayings one can read in most churches or even books of poetry and music and devotional books of so many religions, sells big, so I am told. I'm surprised it hasn't found a publisher before this."

"You are?"

"I think so. I have letters from publishers calling this a truly original work, something that I and Gerry will form a little company to publish, something eccentric yet beautifully executed. It will make a fortune and Gerry and I are going to donate the money to Joe's original school, the school that helped him so much."

"I see. That's...great."

"So, I would like absolution, Father."

"Certainly."

"I want everything said here under the seal of confession. So this is never repeated."

"Of course."

Then she said something that shocked me.

"May God forgive me, but I do not trust you. I always had the sense that you and Joe never got along. Now I understand why. And, by the way,"

"Yes, Rose?"

"I have my own therapist. You forget that having a gifted child in any family is an enormous strain both financially and emotionally. One naturally needs a lot of therapeutic support, though I believe I will use such help differently than before. I will, I think, listen to what they have to say now."

I looked imperiously at Rose. I was outraged. I now understood from which side of the gene pool Joe's abrasive manner had emerged. She had never spoken to me like that before. Before, Rose played the role of the distracted, spiritually-obsessed mother of her clever son. It seemed she had emerged from this loss as a different person. I held my dignity as best I could and proceeded to absolve her.

"I absolve you in the name of the Father and the Son and the Holy Spirit, amen"

"Thank you, Father."

"Rose."

"Yes, Father?"

I took Rose's hand and held it and looked into her eyes, tears welling up in my own. I remember my voice shook a little as I spoke:

"I am truly sorry, Rose. I am truly sorry that this has to end like this. I am very fond of you, and of Gerry. I know you might not want to speak to me again, or that when we do meet, we might merely exchange pleasantries. But I must tell you, this is not what I want. I want us to remain friends."

Rose took her hand away from my gentle grasp. She took my face in her hands and drew me close to her.

"Alex, I have made terrible, terrible mistakes in my life. I was given a wonderful gifted child and I made terrible mistakes, selfish mistakes I will take with me to the grave. I will, I hope, somehow, by God's grace and love, find the strength to bear my cross. But you do not understand error, Father. I think you hate error and you avoid it. You need control, at all costs, especially human cost. I too am sorry, sorry for feeling this way, sorry for judging you. I wish you well. Goodbye, Father."

She kissed me on the lips and she left with her parcel and her handbag.

Chapter Thirty Six

Rose

"Monastery of the Seven Towers? How may I direct your call?"
"Can I speak to Father Des?"
"One moment please. I think you might get him in the sacristy."
"Sacristy here."
"Can I speak to Father Des?"
"He's celebrating Mass. Can I take a message?"
"This is Rose Finn here."
"I recognise the voice."
"Who am I speaking to?"
"This is Kevin. Will I get Des to call you?"
"No, no. It's just…"
"Yes?"
"Did you know my son?"
"I did, Mrs Finn."
"Did you know a Frank?"
"I did, Mrs Finn."
"What's his surname?"
"Ryan."
"Do you have his address?"
"It's in the phone book. I'll get it."
He gave me the address and phone number.
"Thanks Kevin."
"No problem."
"Look. I . . . "
"I know. I'm sorry."
"Don't tell Des."
"I won't. Take care now."
I hung up and rang Frank's number.
"Can I speak to Frank Ryan, please?"
"This is Lisa here, can I say who's calling?"
"Rose Finn."
"I'll get him."
"Hello?"
"Hello Frank, this is Rose. Rose Finn."
He said nothing. I think he was really shocked.
"I, I just wanted to make contact with you. I think it's a great shame that you and I never met, especially after all that's happened."

"I agree. Joe had this terrible habit of compartmentalising his life."

"I was wondering if you would like to meet for a drink, perhaps some dinner?"

"Okay."

"Good."

"I don't mean to be rude, but is there -?"

"What do you need to know?"

"I don't want to be rude, but is there something."

"Joe's manuscript has come into my possession."

"I see. He never showed me his work."

"He was probably intimidated."

"I doubt that."

"I want you write an introduction to my son's book."

"But I don't write."

"We can talk about that, if you want. We should meet. What do you say, eh? Frank?

Chapter Thirty Seven

Epilogue

Eight years after Joe's funeral, I found myself looking at what was once the Monastery of the Seven Towers. The entire structure, including the church, had been gutted and renovated and turned into luxury apartments, called, imaginatively enough, Seven Towers Apartments.

From the high, carefully repointed apartment wall facing me, a mounted, gaunt, copper statue of a saint, with an oval copper halo around a tonsured head, dressed in the ancient robes of the Order of the Holy Field - the ones worn before the conventional black and white adopted after the OHF renewed itself post Second Vatican Council - gazed with infinite tenderness on passers by in suits and open necked shirts, on joggers and delivery people, on the members of the upwardly mobile community who now lived in or around the Seven Towers, an area once poor and largely forgotten, except by the monks. I do not know what happened to all the people who lived by the monastery. I remember their faces, their playing children who flocked around, their cars and loud conversation. They seemed to be all gone, along with their houses. Presumably they sold the homes at a profit and moved elsewhere. I looked at the metal saint, wondering if it was a rendering of Giovanni Seipi, or some other saint from the Order. I remember there were few descriptions of Giovanni Seipi, aside from unreliable hagiography. The statue had one hand hidden underneath the folds of secret cowls, the other held aloft in a sign of universal greeting.
"I used live here," I inappropriately told passers by.
"That's nice," one answered. The rest ignored me and walked on or kept talking to one another, holding latte or cappuccino cups with safety spill proof lids on them, carrying laptop computer shoulder slung bags or in open shirts with identity badges clipped to their belts, or hanging around their necks with special safety clasps that prevented strangulation or serious injury should it become snared up in the likes of a car door or in the hands of a mugger.

I saw iron gates with an automatic locking mechanism and a key pad entry and an intimidating camera over the small carefully delineated car park. Before, the gate and the door were, for the most, part open all the time. I walked around the building. Beside what was once the Church of the Seven Towers, a small chapel had been built, the Chapel of St. Giovanni Seipi. I went into the walk-in chapel, largely to have some quiet time and process all the changes I had seen. I also was consumed with curiosity. I had to see the new little chapel. I wondered if any of the Brothers lived nearby. It would be unusual for the Brethren to just up stakes and move to the suburbs and leave no presence in a quarter of the city they had been associated with for centuries. I saw no indication of living quarters, either outside the chapel, or inside. I sat there for a while. I saw a confessional light on. I saw the name of the priest. Father Benjamin Barnes. Never heard of him. I went into the confessional.

"May the good Lord be in your heart and in your mind, that you may be able to give him a good confession. Hi there, I'm Ben."

The priest spoke in a marked United States accent with hints of a southern Irish intonation in his vowels, probably Cork or Tipperary.

"I don't know what to say."

"Say whatever you like, whatever comes to mind."

"I came here, today, for particular reason. I used to be a member of the OHF a long time ago. I got married and I found myself in this part of the city for the first time in a, I don't know in how long, and I saw the entire place has gone. I guess I'm a bit shocked. The Monastery of the Seven Towers has been here for centuries. It's shocking."

"I heard they tried to slap a preservation order on it," Ben said. "But the Brothers got around it. Friends in high places…I think it's a pity."

"They can do that. If they have to they can influence…Was it Alex? Was it Father Alex who got the preservation order revoked?"

"I don't know. I don't think so. I doubt it. Alex had been ill for some time. Father Alex died two years past, poor man. I love his books."

"What did he…?"

"Cancer. I was in the States at the time. Didn't get home for the funeral."

"Wow, I'm sorry to hear that. I have been out of touch, well not completely out of touch. I did not know. Otherwise I would have gone. Yes, I would have definitely gone. Probably the biggest funeral since Joe."

I wondered why Bill did not tell me about Alex's death. I was somewhat wounded at being excluded from such knowledge. Bill had told me of Joe's death, but not of the death of Alex. Nor had I read or heard of the end of the Monastery of The Seven Towers. It was as if I was being put in my place by fate, excluded from certain intimacies, and reminded that I was by my own choice no longer part of the Brotherhood. Perhaps

I was over reacting. I was too sensitive, I told myself. Ben, on the other hand, seemed suddenly interested.

"Did you know Joe Finn?"

"Yes. Were you at the funeral?"

Ben seemed to brighten up, while at the same time trying to maintain the distance necessary from someone like me who might want to talk. I was already regretting my presence in the confessional. Behind me in the small cramped confessional I noticed a bench, presumably for someone who did not wish or could not kneel. I sat up on it, feeling relief in my knees. I had always hated kneeling, even when it was obligatory or seen as a kind of virtuous act.

"I was, as matter of fact. I concelebrated Mass that day. It was a long time ago now, though, I guess."

I was remembering the funeral, images of the coffin, the congregation, and the long walk to the graveside. I didn't remember him. The fact that I didn't remember him hurt me. I remembered Joe, the source of that hurt.

"Joe was a friend of mine, for a time…"

"I was in the same community as him in Los Angeles. He was a great guy. We were very sad, you know…a great guy, so smart, you know?"

"I know."

"I didn't know he was a writer. Did you read his book?"

"I did, Father."

"Ben."

"Ben, sorry. Old habit."

"I think his book is coming out in the U.S. next year."

"Really?"

I knew that. But I didn't tell him. I didn't want him to know.

"Yeah, I heard that from, I dunno who. I had a few problems with his book, I have to say. Funny to think someone like Joe would hold those views. When I lived with him in Los Angeles, he came across as a very conservative guy. Actually, I am going back there to Los Angeles next week. I'm just filling in for the usual guy on duty during lunch hour."

He leaned closer to the grille, as if preparing himself for a long and interesting conversation, one I was increasingly uncomfortable with. I looked through the dark matrix of the grille and saw a bearded ruddy smiling face near mine. The Brothers preferred the old fashioned confessional with the kneeler and the darkened closet and your barely visible interlocutor behind a grille to the open room where confessor and penitent had each other in plain sight across a table and could recognise them afterwards in the street, especially if they had something shocking to say. Then I got a distinct whiff of whiskey from Ben's breath. It was enough. This was all too cosy. I did not do cosy.

"Well, Ben, I'd better let you get back to the real penitents."

"Okay then. Thanks for stopping by."

"It was nice to meet you and nice to meet someone from Joe's last community. Take care."

"You too. May I ask your name?"

"Frank. My name's Frank."

"Okay then. Good to meet you. Take care, Frank."

"You too, Ben."

And I went home. (Dublin 11 October 2005)